KEY CHANGE

Books by Children's Theatre Company
Published by the University of Minnesota Press

Igniting Wonder: Plays for Preschoolers
Peter Brosius and Elissa Adams, Editors

The Face of America: Plays for Young People
Peter Brosius and Elissa Adams, Editors

Key Change: New Musicals for Young Audiences
Peter Brosius and Elissa Adams, Editors

Fierce and True: Plays for Teen Audiences
Peter Brosius and Elissa Adams, Editors

KEY CHANGE

NEW MUSICALS FOR YOUNG AUDIENCES

CHILDREN'S THEATRE COMPANY

PETER BROSIUS AND ELISSA ADAMS, EDITORS
PREFACE BY JEANINE TESORI

UNIVERSITY OF MINNESOTA PRESS
MINNEAPOLIS
LONDON

Listen to song samples of these musicals at
http://www.childrenstheatre.org/anthologies

Published by the University of Minnesota Press
111 Third Avenue South, Suite 290
Minneapolis, MN 55401-2520
http://www.upress.umn.edu

Library of Congress Cataloging-in-Publication Data
Title: Key change : new musicals for young audiences /
Children's Theatre Company ; Peter Brosius and Elissa Adams, editors ;
preface by Jeanine Tesori.
Description: Minneapolis : University of Minnesota Press, [2016]
Identifiers: LCCN 2015044267 | ISBN 978-0-8166-9809-7 (hc) |
ISBN 978-0-8166-9810-3 (pb)
Subjects: LCSH: Musicals—Juvenile—Librettos. | LCGFT: Librettos.
Classification: LCC ML48 .K49 2016 | DDC 782.1/40268—dc23
LC record available at http://lccn.loc.gov/2015044267

Printed in the United States of America on acid-free paper

The University of Minnesota is an equal-opportunity educator and employer.

22 21 20 19 18 17 16   10 9 8 7 6 5 4 3 2 1

CONTENTS

vii PREFACE
Jeanine Tesori

ix INTRODUCTION
Elissa Adams

1 Tale of a West Texas Marsupial Girl
Lisa D'Amour
Music by Sxip Shirey

79 Madeline and the Gypsies
Barry Kornhauser
Based on the book by Ludwig Bemelmans
Music by Michael Koerner

143 Buccaneers!
Liz Duffy Adams
Music by Ellen Maddow

205 A Year with Frog and Toad
Willie Reale
Based on the books by Arnold Lobel
Music by Robert Reale

262 CONTRIBUTORS

Jeanine Tesori

hen I was in fifth grade, I was the musical director for *The Sound of Music* at our local elementary school. Those were the days when I would memorize a score, including the cues, to save myself from turning pages during the performances. During one music rehearsal, I asked our director (also known as the sixth-grade math teacher) to please stop singing with the nuns because she was out of tune. I was drunk with power.

That was the same year I played Ismene in an all-girl production of *Antigone*. We wore costumes made of bedsheets, and mine had a faint pattern of Batman and Robin on it. I wouldn't be involved again with theatre for another nine years, but when I returned, it thrilled me just as it had back then. I felt at home. I felt part of something. I felt equally grounded and airborne.

For me, the great joy is this: theatre happens entirely in the present. It reminds us to keenly witness the ephemeral moment before we mourn its passing. It brings a group together—an audience, be it one or ten or ten thousand—and instantly creates a community, a community that will never gather again in the same way, as no two audiences are ever alike.

I don't know where I would be had I not been introduced to the theatre at the tender age of eleven. I try to keep that eleven-year-old's enthusiasm and wonder intact, even at my present age of fifty-three. Though I can no longer memorize scores and cues to save laborious page turns, I have since learned to write scores for others to try.

I applaud Children's Theatre Company's support of artists like me who have found their voice and their sense of home in the theatre. I hope the musicals in this collection will find their way into the hearts and minds of young people and be greeted with the same enthusiasm and wonder I still recall in my eleven-year-old self.

INTRODUCTION

Elissa Adams

Musicals can cast such potent spells. Most of us have experienced those transcendent moments when a character moves from language into song, taking our hearts with them. We have felt the swell of energy as a cast of actors begins to sing and dance, lifting us practically out of our seats. As Jeanine Tesori, the Tony-nominated composer of *Shrek the Musical*, *Thoroughly Modern Millie*, and *Caroline or Change*, recalls so eloquently in her preface to this anthology, musicals can get under our skin and change our lives.

Throughout its fifty-year history, Children's Theatre Company has celebrated the power of musicals season after season, producing well-known and well-loved shows like *Annie, The Wizard of Oz, Shrek the Musical, Peter Pan,* and *Once on This Island.* But CTC is also committed to creating brand-new musicals, commissioning and developing music theatre pieces designed to expand and enliven the canon of American musicals. It is these new musicals, and our collaborations with the remarkable artists who created them, that we celebrate in this anthology.

Tale of a West Texas Marsupial Girl, Lisa D'Amour's contemporary myth about a young woman harnessing the danger and

possibility of the pouch she was born with, was originally written as a one-act play for adults. But, like many great myths, it felt
like it spoke to people of all ages. Through a partnership program
between CTC and New Dramatists, a renowned playwright organization based in New York, the opportunity arose for D'Amour to
write a play specifically for young audiences. I suggested she consider turning *Tale of a West Texas Marsupial Girl* into a full-length
play. Initially, there was no thought of it being a musical, but as
D'Amour continued to write, the pouch became not just a physical
characteristic but the portal to Marsupial Girl's inner voice. With
that voice came the need for music. D'Amour knew of an extraordinary musician/performer named Sxip Shirey who uses unexpected
objects to create instruments and sound—tubes and pipes that
amplify and manipulate his voice, combs pulled across corrugated
tin, all with the propulsion and intensity of a carnival barker. Not
only did Shirey and D'Amour together give voice to Marsupial
Girl's pouch, they created a full-scale musical that is at once a classic outsider tale and a grunge-rock musical rooted deep in West
Texas soil.

　　CTC has a rich history of adapting Ludwig Bemelmans's
books about Madeline, the little girl who, much to the dismay of
her teacher, Miss Clavel, has a difficult time staying in line. Past
CTC adaptations included *Madeline* and *Madeline's Rescue.* But
CTC artistic director Peter Brosius was interested in creating a
new adaptation of one of the books. Inspired by Circus Juventas,
an extraordinary circus-training school in St. Paul, Minnesota,
he decided that *Madeline and the Gypsies* would provide a great
opportunity to revisit the delightful characters in Madeline's world
and to bring a circus alive onstage. Playwright Barry Kornhauser
and composer Michael Koerner were invited to turn the book
into a musical. Koerner dove into the world of French cabaret,
English music hall, and European circus music, while Kornhauser
embraced the inherent musicality in Bemelmans's rhyming language to expand the book and create lyrics. The result is an infec-

tiously fun world where music and song are constantly in the air as Madeline's adventures with the gypsies and the circus eventually lead her back home to Miss Clavel.

Another wonderful adventure story brought to musical life is *Buccaneers!* In this neo-Victorian musical, playwright Liz Duffy Adams and composer Ellen Maddow center on Enid Arabella, a poverty-stricken lass whose parents decide to send her away. When instead she is captured by pirates, Enid Arabella defeats a pirate king and becomes the leader of the crew of captive children. Like *Tale of a West Texas Marsupial Girl, Buccaneers!* grew out of CTC's partnership with New Dramatists. At once a thrilling, seafaring adventure and a meditation on the qualities that make a great leader, the musical sparkles with Adams's extraordinarily rich and intelligent language and Maddow's rollicking, world music–infused take on traditional sea shanties.

A Year with Frog and Toad, based on Arnold Lobel's beloved stories about bumptious Toad and his elegant friend Frog, premiered at CTC before transferring to the New Victory Theatre in New York and then to Broadway, where it was nominated for three Tony awards. Our journey with *A Year with Frog and Toad* began when we placed a call to Adrianne Lobel about acquiring the underlying rights to her father's books. We were longtime fans of Arnold Lobel's books and felt strongly that Frog and Toad, with their vaudevillian rapport and remarkable friendship, belonged onstage. Adrianne Lobel (who is not only Arnold Lobel's daughter but one of American theatre's great scenic designers) told us that she, too, believed Frog and Toad should be on the stage. She was, in fact, in process with a musical about Frog and Toad that she had commissioned from the composer/librettist team Willie and Robert Reale. The script and score were nearing completion, and Lobel and the Reales were looking for the right home for a first production—was CTC interested? Listening to the song demos and reading the script, it was apparent that they had captured the tenderness as well as the humor of Arnold Lobel's characters. CTC was honored to mount the first production of *A Year with Frog and Toad*. We couldn't be more thrilled that it has taken its place in the canon of beloved American musicals and is produced so frequently around the country and the world.

Each of the musicals in this collection is the blueprint for a distinctive, delightful theatrical experience. I hope you will read them, listen to their scores, and produce them in your own theatres and communities. May these new musicals join the great musicals of the past in casting potent spells!

KEY CHANGE

Tale of a West Texas Marsupial Girl

Lisa D'Amour

Music and story consultation by Sxip Shirey

Directed by Whit MacLaughlin

The world premiere of *Tale of a West Texas Marsupial Girl* opened on January 19, 2007, at Children's Theatre Company, Minneapolis, Minnesota.

CREATIVE TEAM
Scenic design by Donald Eastman
Costume design by Richard St. Clair
Lighting design by Matt Frey
Sound design by Victor Zupanc
Dramaturgy by Elissa Adams
Stage management by Erin Tatge
Assistant stage management by Danae Schniepp
Assistant direction by Shannon C. Harman

ORIGINAL CAST

MARSUPIAL GIRL	Anna Reichert
MOTHER	Autumn Ness
SUE	Nadia Hulett
LIBBY	Jessie Shelton
PEARL	Teresa Marie Doran
DR. POUCH	Luverne Seifert
FRED LUDBERGER, DOCTOR 1, ACTRESS 3	Gerald Drake
INA SHAW, WOMAN 1, ACTRESS 1	Leigha Horton
LACEY RUBBERTREE, WOMAN 2, ACTRESS 2	Marvette Knight

MRS. PENNYWHISTLE, WOMAN 3	Kelsie Jepsen
ENSEMBLE	Eva "Chava" Curland
	Casey Smart
	Susanna Stahlmann
	Ashford J. Thomas

CAST OF CHARACTERS

OLD MAN (DR. POUCH)	MRS. PENNYWHISTLE
MARSUPIAL GIRL	ACTRESS 1
WOMAN 1	ACTRESS 2
WOMAN 2	ACTRESS 3
WOMAN 3	ACTOR 1
DOCTOR 1	GROCER
DOCTOR 2	MAN
DOCTOR 3	KID 1
MOTHER	KID 2
MS. INA SHAW	PREACHER
SUE	TOWNSPERSON 1
LIBBY	TOWNSPERSON 2
PEARL	TOWNSPERSON 3
FRED LUDBERGER	ENSEMBLE includes CHORUS, CLASS
LACEY RUBBERTREE	

A NOTE ON THE TEXT

The tale of this Marsupial Girl is often framed and moved forward
by a character called Dr. Pouch. In the early stages of the development of this work, I wrote the part to be played by Sxip Shirey, the
composer of the music for the play. Dr. Pouch was to be positioned
high above the stage on a special "perch" surrounded by the many
instruments Sxip has used to create the sound world of the play. Dr.
Pouch was to play much of the music live and create sound effects
using Foley devices and musical instruments.

As we approached production, it became clear that Sxip's
schedule would not allow him to perform the role of Dr. Pouch at
Children's Theatre Company. We decided to design and record all of

the sound effects of the piece and allow Dr. Pouch to "trigger" them at certain points in the play. This choice freed the character of Dr. Pouch to come down off his perch and be very near scenes as they occurred on stage.

In this script, Dr. Pouch often "lives" up on a billboard at the entrance of town. He spends time up on the front of the billboard and behind it, where he has set up a kind of hideout for himself, filled with gadgets, toys, and special equipment he uses to aid Marsupial Girl as she comes to terms with who she is. The slogan on the billboard changes from time to time, becoming subject headings for the different chapters in Marsupial Girl's life.

While Dr. Pouch's billboard perch featured prominently in the CTC production, the director chose not to have the billboard be the medium for the subject headings for Marsupial Girl's life. Instead, they were represented with signs that were held by actors or that emerged from unexpected places (such as a sign that rolled out, scroll-like, from an open book). Theatres who produce this work are invited to reimagine the way these subject headings are rendered to suit the needs of their production.

The CTC production also produced the play on a stage nearly devoid of furniture or any kind of naturalistic set requirements: benches became a bed, chairs became a schoolhouse. This minimalist staging helped support the quick changes needed in the play.

A NOTE ON THE POUCH

In the CTC production, Marsupial Girl wore a loose fitting dress with a kind of square "trap door" in the front—almost like the trap door you see in the back of old-fashioned long underwear. When she opened her trap door, the top of her pouch was visible. The pouch was made of a flexible material and looked like the pouch on an animal, with a touch of magic-looking silver fur. Marsupial Girl often moved items in and out of her pouch in full view of the audience.

Other more representational solutions—such as a pocket on the outside of a dress, or a front pocket sewed into some overalls— may also be effective. — *Lisa D'Amour*

A small Texas town surrounded by an expanse of sand and land. A line of telephone poles stretches into a big sky. An old billboard reads: "Welcome to West Texas – Big Sky, Bigger Dreams." *An* OLD MAN *in an old cowboy hat appears beneath the billboard, silhouetted against the sunrise. This is* DR. POUCH. *He wears a coat covered in many pockets. He has a guitar strapped to his back. He walks among the telephone poles down until he finds one with a ratty old power box. He flips the switch. Poof! Crackle! Pop! The lights in town come to life. He swings his guitar to the front and plays a chord. He walks across the stage to a pile of old gadgets and pushes a button or pulls a lever. He creates the sound of wind. Then he finds a ratty old microphone. He leans down into it:*

DR. POUCH: Hey. *(The wind blows.)*
Some stories start a long, long time ago.
Some stories start in your own backyard.
Some stories start in the teeny tiny room
in the center of your head.
And some stories start in Texas.
(The wind blows and the slide guitar slides.)
HOWDY. *(The "Howdys" echo through the space.)*
Ready or not, my big toe, wiggly little Texas town,
here we—

The stage and house instantly black out. Only the "Welcome to West Texas" billboard glows bright. The TOWNSPEOPLE *enter, whispering.*

TOWNSPERSON 1: The day she was born all the lakes dried up.

TOWNSPERSON 2: The day she was born every child in town caught a cold. Achoo!

TOWNSPERSON 3: The day she was born was probably the loneliest day of her life.

TOWNSPERSON 1: The day she was born all the doctors at the hospital quit.

TOWNSPERSON 2: I QUIT!

TOWNSPERSON 3: The day she was born people saw giant kangaroos dancing in the clouds.

TOWNSPERSON 1: That child is *not* a kangaroo!

TOWNSPERSON 2: She is too—

TOWNSPERSON 1: Is not!

TOWNSPERSON 2: Is too!

TOWNSPERSON 1: Is not!

TOWNSPERSON 2: Is too!

DR. POUCH *finds a ratchet in his pocket and cranks it, fast.*

DR. POUCH: Holy puppy on a peach tree, fishy on a dog leash, cow chowin' down at the family dinner table—What is all this fuss about?

The billboard has changed to read: WHAT IN THE WORLD?

The townspeople (Teresa Marie Doran, Nadia Hulett, Kelsie Jepsen, Casey Smart, Gerald Drake, Jessie Shelton, Eva Curland, Ashford J. Thomas, Susanna Stahlmann, and Leigha Horton) wonder about Marsupial Girl (Anna Reichert) in the world premiere of *Tale of a West Texas Marsupial Girl.* Photograph by Rob Levine.

DR. POUCH: Are they afraid of a monster come out of the sea? A giant hairy beast come down out of the sky?

CHORUS: WHAT IN THE WORLD?

A sudden gasp from the townspeople as a girl cuts through the crowd. A quite regular girl.

MARSUPIAL GIRL: Hey.

DR. POUCH: A girl. Just a girl.

MARSUPIAL GIRL: Not *just* a girl.

DR. POUCH: Pardon me, ma'am. This girl is something else entirely.

MARSUPIAL GIRL: Something else entirely.

DR. POUCH: That's clear as a cowbell. (DR. POUCH *hits a cowbell.)*
Been clear since the beginning
When I first spied you with my pigpie eyes.
You certainly stirred up the pot
On that dusty dog-mouth day when:

The billboard changes to read: IT'S A GIRL!

THE OLD MAN: The Marsupial Girl Gets Born

DR. POUCH *reads the billboard to* MARSUPIAL GIRL.

DR. POUCH: It's - A - Girl!

Immediate sound of a new baby crying. DR. POUCH *takes* MARSUPIAL GIRL *up the ladder, onto the billboard. They watch the following from above.*
    Lights on a group of women, crowded together around WOMAN 3, *who holds baby* MARSUPIAL GIRL. *Nearby,* MARSUPIAL GIRL's *mother lies in a hospital bed.*

WOMAN 1: Oooh! Look at her beautiful toes!

WOMAN 2: Oooh! And her beautiful nose!

WOMAN 3: Ooooh! And her earlobes! Stupendous earlobes!

WOMAN 1: And her tiny little fingers—

WOMAN 2: And her teeny little legs—

WOMAN 3: And her teeny tiny soft—OH MY GOD!

WOMAN 3 *practically tosses baby marsupial girl to* WOMAN 2.

WOMAN 2: What on earth is the—OH MY GOD!

WOMAN 2 *practically tosses the baby to* WOMAN 1.

WOMAN 1: Really, now you ladies are being so silly I declare I just
   don't know what all the—*(beat)* Oh. Oh my.

Three DOCTORS *come on stage, dressed in scrubs and masks. They take off
their masks and throw them on the floor.*

THE DOCTORS: I QUIT!

DOCTOR 1: It's an abomination!

DOCTOR 2: A freak of nature!

DOCTOR 3: That child is *not* listed in *any* of the GREAT BOOKS.

MARSUPIAL GIRL's *mother calls out from her room.*

MOTHER: Excuse me . . . is everything all right out here?

Everybody in the room bolts except WOMAN 1, *who looks distressed for a
moment but then gets her act together quickly:*

WOMAN 1: Oh yes, dear, yes everything's fine they're just closing up
   shop for the night—

MOTHER *(overlapping)*: Closing up shop?

WOMAN 1: —yes, closing up shop so here's your little darlin' OK then
   gotta run now sweet dreams!

And she bolts, too. MOTHER *is alone with* MARSUPIAL GIRL.

MOTHER: They act like they've never seen a newborn child before. What on earth could they be—*(beat)* Oh. Oh. You are indeed a special girl aren't you? You are one of a kind. Those silly old raisin-brains can't even pronounce you.

BABY MARSUPIAL GIRL *begins to cry.*

MOTHER: Shhhhhhh. That a girl, mama's precious, special girl . . .

MOTHER *gathers* BABY MARSUPIAL GIRL *against her chest.*

MARSUPIAL GIRL: Something else entirely.
THE OLD MAN: Yup!

MOTHER *stands up.* BABY MARSUPIAL GIRL *is gone.* MOTHER *reads from a reference book.* MARSUPIAL GIRL *watches.*

MOTHER: Pouch. See: Marsupial.
MARSUPIAL GIRL: Marsupial?
DR. POUCH: Marsupial.

The billboard reads "MARSUPIAL."

MOTHER *(reading)*: A Mar-su-pi-al is a mammal. A mammal with a—

DR. POUCH's *voice echoes deep and loud in the space, as the billboard changes to read* "POUCH."

DR. POUCH: POUCH

As MOTHER *continues, the words* "marsupial" *and* "pouch" *continue to appear and disappear on the billboard. The words as spoken by*

DR. POUCH *and* MARSUPIAL GIRL *become a rich bed of sound under-neath* MOTHER'S *speech.*

MOTHER: When a baby—

MARSUPIAL GIRL: Marsuuuuupial

MOTHER: —is born. It comes into the world not quite ready: So the first thing they do when they get here is crawl up into their mother's—

DR. POUCH: POUCH

MOTHER: —and stay there. Until they are ready to hop on out into the world.

DR. POUCH AND MARSUPIAL GIRL: Marsupiiiiiiial.

MOTHER: Mar-su-pi-al?

DR. POUCH: From the Latin Marsupium. And the Greek Marsippion.

MARSUPIAL GIRL: Well, smell you, Dr. Pouch.

DR. POUCH: Ouch. Dr. Pouch?

MARSUPIAL GIRL: Dr. Pouch.

DR. POUCH: At your service, ma'am.

MOTHER: The best known marsupial in the world is, of course, the kangaroo. But there are many other kinds, with names as strange and wondrous as the word—

DR. POUCH AND MARSUPIAL GIRL: Marsupiaaaaaaaal.

MOTHER: —itself. With names like—

MARSUPIAL GIRL: Sugar glider

MOTHER: With names like—

MARSUPIAL GIRL: Tasmanian devil

MOTHER: With names like—

MARSUPIAL GIRL: Agile wallaby

MOTHER: Pig-footed bandicoot?

MARSUPIAL GIRL: Black-striped wallaby.

DR. POUCH: Marsupial mole

MOTHER *disappears.*

DR. POUCH AND MARSUPIAL GIRL: —and the

Boodie boodie
Boodie boodie
Burrowing betons
Wallaby bilby
Brush kangaroo

DR. POUCH *walks over to the pile of gadgets on the side of the stage. He pulls out a record and puts it on a ramshackle record player: it plays the beat to a song.* MARSUPIAL GIRL *helps him turn the record up.* DR. POUCH *goes to the microphone and takes a harmonica out of his pocket. He wails on the harmonica. Then, he sings "Sugar Glider":*

DR. POUCH: *Is she a sugar glider?*
                Is she a wallaroo?
                Or a Tasmanian devil
                Boodie boodie boodie boodie
                Brush kangaroo
                (To marsupial girl)
                Are you a sugar glider?

MARSUPIAL GIRL: *Am I a wallaroo?*

DR. POUCH AND MARSUPIAL GIRL:
                Or a Tasmanian devil
                Boodie boodie boodie boodie
                Brush kangaroo

DR. POUCH: *Agile wallaby*
                Pig-footed bandicoot
                Black-striped wallaby
                Marsupial mole
                Little northern native cat
                Feathertail glide
                Queensland koala
                Long-nosed potoroo
                Cinnamon antechinus
                Red-legged pademelon
                Brushtail possum

MARSUPIAL GIRL: *Wombat*
DR. POUCH: *Wallaroo*
DR. POUCH AND MARSUPIAL GIRL: And the
Boodie boodie
Boodie boodie
Burrowing betons
Wallaby bilby
Brush kangaroo
DR. POUCH: *Agile wallaby!*

MARSUPIAL GIRL *dances the agile wallaby.*

DR. POUCH: *Pig-footed bandicoot!*

MARSUPIAL GIRL *dances the pig-footed bandicoot.*

DR. POUCH: *Black-striped wallaby!*

MARSUPIAL GIRL *dances the black-striped wallaby.*

MARSUPIAL GIRL: *Marsupial mole!*

DR. POUCH *dances the marsupial mole. A pack of kids has been watching. They run on stage, singing, dancing the dances they have just seen.*

CHILDREN: *Agile wallaby*
Pig-footed bandicoot
Black-striped wallaby
Marsupial mole
Little northern native cat
Feathertail glider
Queensland koala

Their parents join, concerned, singing with the kids.

The parents try to push the kids away from MARSUPIAL GIRL *as they sing.*

PARENTS   *Cinnamon antechinus*
                              Red-legged pademelon
                              Brushtail possum
                              Wombat
                              Wallaroo
                              And the
                              Boodie boodie
                              Boodie boodie
                              Burrowing betons
                              Wallaby bilby
                              Brush kangaroo

DR. POUCH: *Macropus robustus—*

MARSUPIAL GIRL: What is that?

DR. POUCH: Another name for wallaroo. Then *Macropus giganteus.*
    Hypsiprymnodon moschatus

MARSUPIAL GIRL: What?

DR. POUCH: Other names for kangaroo.

PARENTS AND KIDS *Is she a sugar glider?*
                              Is she a wallaroo?
                              Or a Tasmanian devil
                              Boodie boodie boodie boodie
                              Brush kangaroo
                              (spoken)
                              Macropus agilis
                              Chaeropus ecaudatus
                              Macropus dorsalis
                              Dasyurus hallucatus
                              And the
                              Boodie boodie boodie boodie
                              Burrowing betons

Wallaby bilby
Brush kangaroo

And the
Boodie Boodie Boodie Boodie
Burrowing betons
Wallaby bilby
Brush kangaroo
And the
Boodie boodie boodie boodie
Burrowing betons
Wallaby bilby
What in the world are you?

The song is over. DR. POUCH *ratchets his ratchet.*

DR. POUCH: Which brings us right back to—The girl with the pouch.

The billboard changes to read: WHAT IN THE WORLD?

MARSUPIAL GIRL: Hey.
DR. POUCH: Now I've heard of pouches on possums and pouches on
    pretty little hairy-nosed wombats, but never have I ever heard of
    a pouch on a girl. (MARSUPIAL GIRL *opens up her pouch and pulls
    out a rose.*) Ohhh . . . this is gonna make people nervous.

The billboard changes to read: MARSUPIAL GIRL: THE EARLY YEARS.

DR. POUCH: Marsupial Girl, the Early Years.

MOTHER *appears, sitting in her house.*

MARSUPIAL GIRL: For you, mother!
MOTHER: Why thank you, my girl.

MARSUPIAL GIRL *pulls another flower out of her pouch.*

MARSUPIAL GIRL: For you, mother!
MOTHER: Why—thank you!

MARSUPIAL GIRL *pulls flower after flower out of her pouch.*

MARSUPIAL GIRL: For you and for you and for you!

MOTHER *is a bit dismayed.*

MOTHER: Where did you get all these flowers, girl?

INA SHAW *calls from off stage.*

INA SHAW: Neighbor! Neighbor! Oh neeeeeighbor!

INA *runs in, out of breath.*

INA SHAW: I believe I just saw your girl running from my garden.
    (INA *takes a sniff of the roses in* MOTHER'S *hands.)* And, yes, those
    are my roses. I'd know their scent anywhere.
MOTHER: Girl, did you get these roses from Ms. Shaw's garden?
MARSUPIAL GIRL: Yes! You should see them all! Enough for the
    whole town!
INA SHAW: Little girl, do you know how LONG it takes to CULTIVATE
    the perfect rose? Especially in the heat of Texas?
MARSUPIAL GIRL: No.
INA SHAW: My roses are older than YOU. And better groomed, I
    might add.

MOTHER *hands* INA *the roses.*

MOTHER: Here's your roses back, Ms. Shaw. They'll look pretty in
    a vase.

INA SHAW: Thank you.

MARSUPIAL GIRL *pulls another rose out of her pouch.*

MARSUPIAL GIRL: And here's another.
INA SHAW: Eek! (INA *shields her eyes.*)
MARSUPIAL GIRL: And another.
INA SHAW: Eek!
MARSUPIAL GIRL: Don't you want them, Ms. Shaw?
INA SHAW: Do you really think I'd want them after they've been in your . . . in your . . . (INA SHAW *turns to* MOTHER.) Really, neighbor, it's time to teach your girl some MANNERS. She'll be grown soon and then what? Hmmmm?

INA SHAW *storms off.* MOTHER *speaks gently and firmly to* MARSUPIAL GIRL.

MOTHER: Now girl, you can't take other people's things. Stealing is wrong.
MARSUPIAL GIRL: I wasn't stealing. I was collecting.
MOTHER: Girl.
MARSUPIAL GIRL: Isn't that what this thing is for, Ma? Holding things like—(MARSUPIAL GIRL *pulls a smooth stone out of her pouch.*) Magic Rocks pulled from the mud of Town Lake. (MARSUPIAL GIRL *pulls a handful of bottle caps from her pouch.*) And bottle caps from the beginning of time that I will sell for one billion dollars.
MOTHER: These are plain ole Coke tops.
MARSUPIAL GIRL: Shh! (MARSUPIAL GIRL *pulls a folded piece of paper out of her pouch.*) A take-out menu from the pizza place.

MOTHER *takes the menu: she could use that, actually.* MARSUPIAL GIRL *pulls another rose from her pouch.*

MARSUPIAL GIRL: And of course roses! I could fit a whole house full of roses in this thing!

MOTHER: Just because you can doesn't mean you should. Picking up rocks—

MARSUPIAL GIRL: Magic rocks—

MOTHER: —and bottle caps is fine, girl, but you can't take things that belong to other people. Not without asking. Understand?

MARSUPIAL GIRL: Got it. Never take roses from that mouse-faced, icy-hearted busybody named Ina Shaw!

MOTHER *runs to grab* MARSUPIAL GIRL.

MOTHER: Girl!

MARSUPIAL GIRL: That's what you call her, Ma!

MOTHER: Girl, I am going to tickle you all the way to La-La Land!

DR. POUCH: Like a pretty parakeet who barks like a dog.
          Or a truck that runs on ice cream.
          Like your Daddy playing tennis with big fat frog.
          This girl, she leaped right out of a dream.

MARSUPIAL GIRL *and her best friend,* SUE, *are playing in the dust. They have recently abandoned their game of jacks.*

SUE: What is it?

MARSUPIAL GIRL: It's like a backpack, only better.

SUE: And located conveniently in the front. We've totally got to play something with that thing.

MARSUPIAL GIRL: Like what?

SUE: Like, like, like—detectives! And your pouch can hold all the clues we find!

MARSUPIAL GIRL: Or superheroes! And my pouch can hold our superhero special effects!

SUE: Brilliant! Maybe Batman and Robin—

MARSUPIAL GIRL: No, no, no! (MARSUPIAL GIRL *closes her eyes and thinks. She points to* SUE.) Sandwoman—(*She points to herself.*) And The Wind.

SUE: Yes! I'll point my finger at the bad guy and POOF! Turn him into a pile of sand.

MARSUPIAL GIRL: Or hide under the big table where the bad guys eat, and turn every bowl of soup to sand.

SUE: But what does the wind do?

MARSUPIAL GIRL: Well.

SUE: What?

MARSUPIAL GIRL: Come here.

SUE *crosses to* MARSUPIAL GIRL. MARSUPIAL GIRL *opens her pouch just a little bit. We hear the faint sound of wind.* MARSUPIAL GIRL *closes it.* SUE *looks at her.*

SUE: Whoa.

MARSUPIAL GIRL: I know. I open it up, and I hear sounds. Words even.

SUE: What kind of words?

MARSUPIAL GIRL: Shivery-inside-out words. Run-to-your-mom words.

SUE: Can I listen?

MARSUPIAL GIRL: You won't be scared?

SUE: Of course not. We're superheroes. Sandwoman and The Wind.

MARSUPIAL GIRL: OK.

MARSUPIAL GIRL *opens her pouch.* SUE *puts her ear close to it.*

MARSUPIAL GIRL: What do you hear?

SUE: I hear . . . shhhhhhhhooooooo . . .

MARSUPIAL GIRL: Yes?

SUE: Shhhhhooooopialius pop top.

MARSUPIAL GIRL: Shoopialus pop top.

SUE: Abbamara pip shop

MARSUPIAL GIRL: Abbamara pip shop

SUE: Abba-da

MARSUPIAL GIRL: Abba-dee

MARSUPIAL GIRL AND SUE: Abba-dip-dip-dip-dip doo.

DR. POUCH *accompanies the two girls on his slide guitar. They sing* "Shoopialus Pop Top."

MARSUPIAL GIRL AND SUE: *Liputmanish hyi op*
Double unc unc q
Q q double mop
Shoopialus pop top
Shoopialus pop top
Fie wop sue!

MARSUPIAL GIRL *and* SUE *crack up laughing.* MARSUPIAL GIRL *closes her pouch.*

SUE: It's like, it's like, it's like—a secret language!

MARSUPIAL GIRL: What do you think it means?

SUE: Shoopialus pop top?

MARSUPIAL GIRL: Yes.

SUE: Shoopialus equals . . . secret.

MARSUPIAL GIRL: Yes!

SUE: Pop top equals . . . bicycle.

MARSUPIAL GIRL: Secret Bicycle!

SUE: And Abbamara pip shop?

MARSUPIAL GIRL: Riding on the Wind.

MARSUPIAL GIRL AND SUE: Secret Bicycle Riding on the Wind!

SUE: It talks! Its very own Super Duper language!

MARSUPIAL GIRL: I guess it does! And only you and me understand it.

SUE: You—(SUE *points to* MARSUPIAL GIRL.) Me—(SUE *points to herself.*) and the—

MARSUPIAL GIRL *opens her pouch. We hear, deep and echoing sound.*

POUCH VOICE: POUCH

The girls crack up laughing.

MARSUPIAL GIRL: Are you ready for more?

MARSUPIAL GIRL *opens her pouch. Slide guitar again, a song emerging,* *"Shoopialus Pop Top."*

MARSUPIAL GIRL: *Abba dabba dip dop*
SUE: *Abba dabba dip dop*
    Shoopialus pop top
MARSUPIAL GIRL: *Shoopialus pop top*
    Marialus possum shoe
SUE: *Marialus possum shoe*
    Abba da
MARSUPIAL GIRL: *Abba dee*
MARSUPIAL GIRL AND SUE: *Abba dip dip dip dip doo.*
    Liputmanish hyi op
    Double unc unc q
    Q q double mop
    Shoopialus pop top
    Shoopialus pop top
    Fie wop sue!
    Liputmanish hyi op
    Double unc unc q
    Q q double mop
    Shoopialus pop top
    Shoopialus—
LIBBY AND PEARL: Suuuuuuuuuusiiiiiiiie.
DR. POUCH: Aw, blast it.

MARSUPIAL GIRL *closes her pouch. Song evaporates like a sparkler doused* *with water. Sue stands.* LIBBY *rounds the corner, with* PEARL. LIBBY *is* *obviously the ring leader, even at age five.*

LIBBY: There you are. Your dad's looking for you.

SUE: I'm coming.

LIBBY: You better, or I'm gonna tell him who you're playing with.

SUE: I'm coming! I gotta go.

MARSUPIAL GIRL: But—

SUE: We'll play later, OK? (*Almost whispered, a pact, just for* MARSUPIAL GIRL.) Shoopialus Pop Top.

MARSUPIAL GIRL: Fie wop Sue.

LIBBY: What's that crazy talk you're talkin' anyway?

PEARL: Yeah, what's that goofy talk?

SUE: Nothing.

MARSUPIAL GIRL: Nothing.

SUE: Let's go.

As the three girls go, MARSUPIAL GIRL *is alone, for a moment. Then, she tucks their jacks into her pouch as she sings.*

MARSUPIAL GIRL: *Liputmanish hyi op*

THE POUCH: *Op op op op . . .*

MARSUPIAL GIRL *stops. She creeps open her pouch. She sings into it. It seems to answer back.*

MARSUPIAL GIRL: *Double unc unc q*

THE POUCH: *q q q q . . .*

MARSUPIAL GIRL: *QQ double mop*
SHOOPIALUS POP TOP
SHOOPIALUS POP TOP
FI WOP SUE . . .

THE POUCH: q q q q
You you you
Ready ready ready
???????

MARSUPIAL GIRL *closes her pouch tight and runs for home, scared and exhilarated.*

MARSUPIAL GIRL: Mooooooommmmmmmm!

MARSUPIAL GIRL *leaps into bed.* MOTHER *by her side, telling her a bedtime story. As* MOTHER *speaks, the people of the town slowly gather around* MOTHER *and* MARSUPIAL GIRL, *one by one, spying.*

MOTHER: The story of my Girl. Chapter one. And so one day I was swimming at Blue Lake. And the water was so clear and cool I just couldn't stop swimmin' even though everybody else had gone home for dinner. I was floating on my back watching the sun set—

MARSUPIAL GIRL: By yourself?

MOTHER: By myself. Gazing up up up into the blue and the purple and the yellow . . . And then—The sky unzipped itself. Unzipped itself and peeled right open. And out of the hole in the sky flew an enormous—

MARSUPIAL GIRL: kangaroo—

MOTHER: That's right. And she reached deep into her Pouch and pulled out—

MARSUPIAL GIRL: Me!

MOTHER: That's right. And she handed you down, down, down and placed you in my arms and said:

MARSUPIAL GIRL: This is a special creature—

MOTHER: Love her and care for her—

MARSUPIAL GIRL: And teach her to be strong—

MOTHER: And then the kangaroo went up—

MARSUPIAL GIRL: —up, up into the clouds . . .

MOTHER: And I had myself a girl.

MARSUPIAL GIRL: That's how it really happened?

MOTHER: That's how it really happened.

The neighbors gossip.

INA SHAW: Such a shame, spinning those wild tales.

FRED LUDBERGER: Now stranger things have happened 'round here, Ina. I've seen 'em . . .

INA SHAW: She's just a GIRL. A girl with an unfortunate deformity that allows her to steal my roses.

FRED LUDBERGER: One time I saw Bill Wiggin's pig save a child from a burning house. Stranger things have happened . . .

MARSUPIAL GIRL: Where'd she go, Mother? The kangaroo from the sky?

MOTHER: I don't know. Back up there, I guess.

LACEY RUBBERTREE: Saw her layin' in the delivery room just hours old. That girl didn't come outta no sky—

INA SHAW: Course it's true there's no sign of a father—

LACEY: Probably why they're both so UNRULY.

MARSUPIAL GIRL *nestles her head in her mother's belly.*

MARSUPIAL GIRL: Can we go up there with her?

MOTHER *(laughs)*: I'm afraid we're doomed to the ground, girl. Here in the big wide world.

MARSUPIAL GIRL: The big wide world—

MOTHER: Whether we like it or not. Now close your eyes . . .

INA SHAW: We all better keep an eye on that un-usual, un-ruly, un-fathomable.

INA AND LACEY: P-O-U-C-H.

They turns their backs. Sounds of doors shutting and locking.

DR. POUCH: Oh the fringe benefits of being
                Of being
                Something Else Entirely
                Even at five years old.

MARSUPIAL GIRL: Tell me about it, Pouch.

DR. POUCH: Mother and Marsupial Girl. Stub yer toe and the whole
    town smarts. *(The townspeople wince.)* Speak a bad word—

MARSUPIAL GIRL: Foosball!

DR. POUCH: And the whole town clicks its tongue. *(The townspeople
    click their tongue.)*

MOTHER *and* MARSUPIAL GIRL *at home, at lessons.*

MOTHER: We'll keep you home, for now. When I'm on the night shift,
    I'll teach you during the day.

MARSUPIAL GIRL: When you're on the day shift, you'll teach me by
    candlelight.

MOTHER *kisses* MARSUPIAL GIRL *on the head, and turns her back to
audience, tending to something else.*

MARSUPIAL GIRL *(to* DR. POUCH*)*: It's better than school. Mama
    has so many books. I read them all day long. History, science,
    reading, math. Days, weeks, months, years. History, science,
    reading, math. Days, weeks, months, years. Until one day . . .
    Until one day—(DR. POUCH *is snoring loudly, fast asleep.)* Hey,
    Pouch. (MARSUPIAL GIRL *walks over to one of* DR. POUCH'S *gadget
    microphones.)* Dr. Pouch!

DR. POUCH *wakes with a start.*

DR. POUCH: What! Hup!

He ratchets his ratchet, and the billboard changes to read: HAPPY
BIRTHDAY!

MARSUPIAL GIRL: Until one day I am ten years old!
DR. POUCH: Holy puppy in a peach tree. That was some looooong nap.

MOTHER *turns around, holding a cake with ten candles, singing "Happy
Birthday."* MARSUPIAL GIRL *blows out the candles.*

MOTHER: Girl, you're reading me out of house and out of home. I
    can't keep up with you anymore. We've got to stop this.
MARSUPIAL GIRL *(a little distressed)*: I don't get to learn anymore?
MOTHER: No, sweet thing. It's time to go to school.

The billboard changes to read: MARSUPIAL GIRL GOES TO SCHOOL!

DR. POUCH: MARSUPIAL GIRL GOES TO SCHOOL!

As DR. POUCH *speaks, we see pairs of parents seeing their kids off to
school. Kiss Mom, Kiss Dad, go to school. Sometimes a dad leaves for
work, sometimes a mom leaves for work, sometimes both.*

DR. POUCH: School Days, School Days
                    Follow all the rule days
                    No time to worry—
                    No time to pout—

MARSUPIAL GIRL *and* MOTHER, *brushing* MARSUPIAL GIRL'S *hair.*
MOTHER *is nervous.*

MARSUPIAL GIRL: Ow! Ma! You're pulling my brains out!
MOTHER: Smooth your dress.
MARSUPIAL GIRL: Ma, we gotta go. (MARSUPIAL GIRL *dumps her book
    bag out on the floor.)* Hey look! I can carry my notebooks and pen-
    cils right here in my pouch. (MARSUPIAL GIRL *opens her pouch.)*
MOTHER: No!

MARSUPIAL GIRL: Why not?

MOTHER: I got you a backpack, see?

MARSUPIAL GIRL: But this is better than a backpack.

MOTHER: School rules. (MOTHER *puts* MARSUPIAL GIRL'S *supplies into the bag.*) Now let's see, three pencils, one, two, three, two notebooks, one—

MARSUPIAL GIRL: Mom. MOM. I'm going to be fine.

MOTHER: Really?

MARSUPIAL GIRL: Come on. I'll let you walk me to the corner.

MOTHER: Oh, you'll let me, will you . . .

MARSUPIAL GIRL *squeals with laughter, grabs her book bag, and runs out the door.*

DR. POUCH: School Days, School Days
                   Throw your teacher in the pool days . . .

MARSUPIAL GIRL *and* MOTHER *walk to school. They walk by the grocery store. Bins of candy stand outside. A pack of kids passes them.*

MARSUPIAL GIRL: Hey. (*They ignore her and walk by.* MOTHER *stops walking and looks at her.*) How bout a gum ball, Ma. In honor of my first day of school? Pleeeeze?

MOTHER *opens up her change purse, counts her change, closes it.*

MOTHER: No gum balls in class. School rules.

LIBBY *and* PEARL *walk arm in arm.* SUE *walks next to them.* SUE *is carrying* LIBBY'S *and* PEARL'S *book bags.*

MARSUPIAL GIRL: Hey, Susie!

LIBBY *and* PEARL *giggle.* SUE *breaks the chain and goes over to* MARSUPIAL GIRL. LIBBY *goes to the grocer and buys three gum balls.*

SUE: It's Sue. People call me Sue now.

MARSUPIAL GIRL: Hey, Sue.

SUE: You're going to school?

MARSUPIAL GIRL: I'm going to school.

SUE: But you go to school at home.

MARSUPIAL GIRL: Not any more!

LIBBY: Come on, Sue—

LIBBY *hands gum balls to* SUE *and* PEARL.

PEARL: Come on, Sue—

LIBBY: I thought you wanted to walk with us.

MARSUPIAL GIRL: That's alright. I know the way.

SUE *looks at* MARSUPIAL GIRL, *then at* LIBBY *and* PEARL.

SUE: Y'all go ahead.

She gives LIBBY *and* SUE *back their book bags.*

LIBBY: Sue!

SUE: I'll see you there.

SUE *puts the gum ball in her mouth.*

LIBBY: Then give me back my gum ball.

SUE *spits it out and gives it to* LIBBY.

SUE: You're just going to have to spit it out when you get to school.
    (SUE *speaks in a lower voice to* MARSUPIAL GIRL: *a secret plan.*)
    Come on, girl. Let's take the short cut, through Ina Shaw's gar-
    den. We have to be quiet, though . . . (*She speaks or sings quietly.*)
    Liputmanish Hyi Op?

MARSUPIAL GIRL: Double Unc Unc Q

MARSUPIAL GIRL AND SUE: Q Q Double Mop Shoopialus Pop Top
Shoopialus Pop Top—

MARSUPIAL GIRL *and* SUE *take off.*

LIBBY: HEY! WHICH WAY ARE YOU GOING! HEY! WAIT FOR US!

LIBBY *and* PEARL *follow.* MOTHER *waves. All four girls slide into their
school desks in the nick of time.* MRS. PENNYWHISTLE, *the fifth-grade
teacher, addresses them.*

MRS. PENNYWHISTLE: OK, class, as you know my name is Mrs.—
THE CLASS: Pennywhistle!

A smart aleck blows a pennywhistle.

MRS. PENNYWHISTLE: Now that's enough of that. My name is Mrs.
Pennywhistle, and I'm new in town, and I will be your English
teacher for the entire fifth-grade year. Now you were all asked to
bring in a brief essay for the first day of class. Who would like to
go first?
PEARL: I'll go first!
MRS. PENNYWHISTLE: Thank you, Pearl.
PEARL: What I want to be when I grow up: When I grow up, I would
like to be a teacher. I would like to be able to teach students as
well as Mrs. Pennywhistle, the best teacher I ever had. I like to
learn. That is why I want to be a teacher. *(The class claps.)*
MRS. PENNYWHISTLE: Why thank you, Pearl. I think it is lovely that
you want to be a teacher. But remember: studying will help you
go far; flattery will get you nowhere.

The class groans: PEARL'S *just been dissed.*

MRS. PENNYWHISTLE: Who's next?
MARSUPIAL GIRL: I'll go, Mrs. Pennywhistle.

MRS. PENNYWHISTLE: Wonderful. Go right ahead.

MARSUPIAL GIRL: What I want to be when I grow up. Nt ng shoopialus en ruppa hup too nnd farfarht pepper, liputmannish hyi op
thug seroop por fhj jk larty. Bmt vghing grtshyt couirdft rom-
pavatyr est furtivliking nmc unc cedrid fe fe hyt. Waaa! uiyyyt
shooopialus ui ui ui quarb, quarb hutti pa putti pop top. cd jh gk
vw axz. Mii uno yatrokler frudbunner wohnk. yret bah.

Silence. No one dares speak.

MARSUPIAL GIRL: Well?

MRS. PENNYWHISTLE: Well . . . I think it is just wonderful that you
want to be an astronaut when you grow up. *(silence.)*

MARSUPIAL GIRL: An astronaut?

MRS. PENNYWHISTLE: Now who would like to go next?

MARSUPIAL GIRL: I'm sorry, Mrs. Pennywhistle, but I believe you
misunderstood me. Susie, could you help me explain? *(silence.)*

LIBBY: Come on, Susie. Tell us what she said.

SUE *stands up, looks at* MARSUPIAL GIRL.

MARSUPIAL GIRL: I'm sorry, Mrs. Pennywhistle, I forgot that I was
speaking a different language. Very few people understand it.
Only me, Sue and the—

SUE: No!

SUE *stops* MARSUPIAL GIRL *from opening her pouch.*

MARSUPIAL GIRL: No?

SUE *(low, to* MARSUPIAL GIRL*)*: Not here, girl, not now.

MRS. PENNYWHISTLE: Girls!

LIBBY: Forget it, Mrs. Pennywhistle. Nobody can understand her.
Ever since she was a little girl, she's been DIFFERENT from the
rest of US. My dad says she should be put in a "home," but the
"homes" probably wouldn't even take her.

MARSUPIAL GIRL: Stop it.

LIBBY: When my dad heard you were coming to school, well, you should have heard him, you should have heard him. You don't belong here. You don't belong here. You don't—

MARSUPIAL GIRL: Stop it!

And poof! MARSUPIAL GIRL *impulsively reaches toward* LIBBY'S *mouth and grabs her voice. She pulls it out of* LIBBY'S *mouth, and puts it in her pouch.* LIBBY *continues to talk, though we only see her mouth move.*

MRS. PENNYWHISTLE: What . . . What is going on here?

Marsupial Girl (Anna Reichert) has taken Libby's (Jessie Shelton) voice in front of her classmates (Teresa Marie Doran, Susanna Stahlmann, and Eva Curland) and teacher (Kelsie Jepsen). Photograph by Rob Levine.

MARSUPIAL GIRL *is terrified—she's never done this before.*

MARSUPIAL GIRL: I I I I don't know.
MRS. PENNYWHISTLE: Where . . . where is her VOICE.
PEARL: She's got it—that girl! She's got it in her . . . her pouch!
MRS. PENNYWHISTLE: Don't be ridiculous.
MARSUPIAL GIRL: I didn't mean it.

LIBBY, *realizing what has happened, starts to freak.*

PEARL: Give it back, girl! I said give it back!

PEARL *and several other kids run toward* MARSUPIAL GIRL.

MRS. PENNYWHISTLE: Children, stand back! Don't touch it, DON'T
   GET NEAR IT! *(The kids recoil.* MRS. PENNYWHISTLE *speaks to*
   MARSUPIAL GIRL.*)* Is it really in, in, in there?
SUE: Girl, you've got to give it back.
MARSUPIAL GIRL: Hold on. I think I can fix it.

MARSUPIAL *reaches inside her dress and throws* LIBBY'S *voice back into
her mouth.*

LIBBY: I WANT MY MOMMY!!!! *(beat)* Oh. *(testing her voice)* Hello.
   Helllooooo. *(to* MARSUPIAL GIRL*)* You're gonna pay for this one
   day. Just you wait.
PEARL: Just you wait.
MRS. PENNYWHISTLE: Back in your seats! And you, new girl—
MARSUPIAL GIRL: Yes?

MRS. PENNYWHISTLE *whips out her red "detention" notebook.*

MRS. PENNYWHISTLE: Detention.
MARSUPIAL GIRL: Detention!
DR. POUCH: Aw, Double Blast It!

MRS. PENNYWHISTLE: I'll see you in detention. This afternoon.

The stage is filled with whispers from the town. Pieces of words emerge from the whispers.

INA SHAW: —Reached right down that little girl's throat—
LACEY: In the middle of class—
INA SHAW: —Right down her throat and tried to take her breath away—
LACEY: I'm telling you she's not all human—she's one part girl, one part crafty kangaroo!
FRED LUDBERGER: Now wait just a minute—

MARSUPIAL GIRL *at detention.* MARSUPIAL GIRL *is working.* MRS. PENNYWHISTLE *is nearby. Outside the window, several kids chant a nasty rhyme.* SUE *sits apart from them, alone.*

KIDS   Fee Fie Fo Fouch
                 There's the girl with the creepy AHHH.
                 Fee Fie Fo Foo
                 Smelly as a kangaroo!

The kids continue their chant while the neighbors speak.

INA SHAW: And she keeps an army in there, a crafty kangaroo army—
LACEY: No!
INA SHAW: She speaks their language! An up-to-no-good kangaroo language—

MRS. PENNYWHISTLE *places a hand on* MARSUPIAL GIRL'S *shoulder.* MARSUPIAL GIRL *covers her ears.*

MRS. PENNYWHISTLE: Don't listen to them.
MARSUPIAL GIRL: How can I not listen? All they do is talk about me.
MRS. PENNYWHISTLE: You've got to learn to shut them out, girl.
You've got a whole life to live, and nobody can stop you.

LACEY RUBBERTREE: What if she is planning a rebellion?

INA *and* LACEY *gasp.*

INA AND LACEY: A crafty kangaroo rebellion!
FRED LUDBERGER: Oh please.
LACEY: She and that momma of hers—
INA SHAW: They're gonna crawl out of there, hopping all over town, dozens of kangaroo girls, crushing the post office and even the school with their hop hop hop.

MRS. PENNYWHISTLE *sends* MARSUPIAL GIRL *on her way. The chants and gossip continue.*

LACEY: Never, never turn your back on that wiggly, squiggly, girl!
INA SHAW: Amen, Brother Ben, Shot a Goose and Killed a Hen.

MARSUPIAL GIRL *opens her pouch. A whimper comes out, a sad little whimper.*

MARSUPIAL GIRL: Shhhh, it's OK.

The pouch cries softly. MARSUPIAL GIRL *walks toward home, comforting it. She sees* SUE *sitting alone.* MARSUPIAL GIRL *walks over to her and sits down. They share a cautious smile.* LIBBY *and* PEARL *enter and walk up to* SUE. SUE *ignores them at first.* LIBBY *holds out the gum ball.* SUE *ignores her.* LIBBY *holds it out again.* SUE *looks at it. Finally,* SUE *takes it, and the three girls run off stage.*
    MARSUPIAL GIRL, *alone now, opens her pouch. It is crying like a baby, now.*

MARSUPIAL GIRL: There you go. Just let it all out . . . Shhh . . .

The pouch cries. We see DR. POUCH *holding up a large book from his perch. Using some gadget—a fishing pole? a mechanical hand?—he drops the book from a great height at* MARSUPIAL GIRL'S *feet. The book lands—poof!—stirring up the dust on the ground. Immediately, the pouch stops crying.* MARSUPIAL GIRL *closes her pouch and picks up the book.*

MARSUPIAL GIRL: Imaginary Creatures and Mythic Beasts. Huh.

The pouch seems placated.

DR. POUCH: Heh heh heh.
MARSUPIAL GIRL: Huh.

MARSUPIAL GIRL *arrives at home.* MOTHER *waits for her in the front yard.*

MOTHER: A detention!
MARSUPIAL GIRL: I can explain—
MOTHER: News spread round the factory faster than a fire in a field
    of dry wheat—
MARSUPIAL GIRL: It's my secret language. I was being creative.
MOTHER: Creative? I'll show you creative. Come down to the assem-
    bly line, and watch the cans roll by, now doesn't that sound
    CREATIVE?
MARSUPIAL GIRL: Ma!
MOTHER: And here I was worried about what other kids would do
    to you.
MARSUPIAL GIRL: Come on, Ma. Let's have story time. It'll make us
    feel better.
MOTHER: I don't think even a kangaroo from the sky can get us out of
    this one.
MARSUPIAL GIRL: I'm sorry, Ma. Really sorry.

Pause. MOTHER *sighs. She puts her hands on* MARSUPIAL GIRL'S *pouch.*

MOTHER: What are we going to do with this thing?
MARSUPIAL GIRL: They say I'm not human, Ma. They say I'm some
    kind of—

MOTHER: Hush. (MARSUPIAL GIRL *hugs mother.*) Did you really try and choke that girl?

MARSUPIAL GIRL: No! I don't know what happened.

MOTHER: You want to go back?

MARSUPIAL GIRL: Yes.

The clock chimes nine o'clock.

MOTHER: Get to bed and wake up early. We'll talk about it in the morning.

MOTHER *picks up her things.*

MARSUPIAL GIRL: You're on the night shift?

MOTHER: Yes.

MARSUPIAL GIRL: But you just worked the day shift.

MOTHER: I couldn't say no.

MARSUPIAL GIRL: You couldn't?

MOTHER: Some people have to work twice as hard just to keep from being called lazy. (MOTHER *kisses* MARSUPIAL GIRL.) Keep the door locked tight, OK, sugar?

MOTHER *leaves.* MARSUPIAL GIRL *turns out the light.* FRED LUDBERGER, *alone.*

FRED LUDBERGER: I'm tellin' you it's all in the way you cast your eye. My cousin the mechanic knows the butcher who knows the postman, and the postman told the butcher that he has seen her, get this, he has seen her fill her pouch full to burstin' with cool water from Town Lake—

MARSUPIAL GIRL, *in bed. She is reading by the light of her bedside lamp. The book: "Imaginary Creatures, Mythic Beasts."*

FRED LUDBERGER: —fill it full to burstin' and bring it to Old Lady Willins in the trailer park cuz Old Lady Willins don't have no running water. Now you tell me, does that sound like a monster to you?

MOTHER *at the factory, working on the assembly line.*

FRED LUDBERGER: It's all in the way you cast your eye. I been castin' mine about for years now. I've seen miracles, and I've seen abominations. That girl is not an abomination. I don't know what she is, but she ain't that.

MARSUPIAL GIRL *looks at her hands. Music begins for the song "What Am I."*

THE TOWN:	*Centaur*
	Minotaur
MARSUPIAL GIRL:	*What am I?*
THE TOWN:	*Cyclops*
	Unicorn
MARSUPIAL GIRL:	*What am I?*
THE TOWN:	*Centaur*
MARSUPIAL GIRL:	*What am I?*
THE TOWN:	*Minotaur*
MARSUPIAL GIRL:	*What am I?*
	What am I?
	With my fingers five
	And again makes ten
	It's all that I need
	What am I?
	With my two eyes open wide
	And again
	To see all I can see
THE TOWN:	*Feet—*

MARSUPIAL GIRL:	*To climb to the mountains*
THE TOWN:	*Arms—*
MARSUPIAL GIRL:	*To swim through the sea.*
	I'd walk I'd walk I'd walk every desert
	To find
	What am I
THE TOWN:	*Boom boom diddy da*
	Boom boom ba diddy diddy
	Boom boom diddy da
	Boom boom ba diddy diddy
	Boom boom diddy da
	Boom boom ba diddy diddy
	Boom boom diddy da
	Boom boom ba diddy diddy
	Boom boom diddy da
	Boom boom ba diddy diddy
MARSUPIAL GIRL:	*I am not an astronaut*
	I am inside out
	I am stopped in my tracks
	I am right side down

Lights rise on MOTHER, *working in the factory.*

MOTHER:	*I am not an astronaut*
	I am inside out
	I have two hands
	One heart
	One mind
	But these will not put my girl's
	Troubles behind her

The following section is sung in syllables, with each actress singing a single syllable in each word. Slashes indicate alternating syllables. Non-slashed lines are sung together. The effect is fluid, like one voice singing.

MARSUPIAL GIRL AND MOTHER: *Wha/t am/ I?*
Wi/th my/ fin/gers /five
An/d a/gain /make/s ten

It's all that I need

Wha/t am/ I?
Wi/th my/ two /eye/s o/pen /wide
An/d a/gain

To see all I can see
THE TOWN: *Feet—*
MARSUPIAL GIRL: *To climb to the mountains*
THE TOWN: *Arms—*
MARSUPIAL GIRL: *To swim through the sea.*
I'd walk I'd walk I'd walk every desert
To find
What am I
THE TOWN *(chanted)*: Centaur Minotaur Cyclops Unicorn
Boom boom diddy da
Boom boom ba diddy diddy
Centaur Minotaur Cyclops Unicorn
Boom boom diddy da
Boom boom ba diddy diddy . . .
(continues underneath the following dialogue)

MOTHER *walks over to* MARSUPIAL GIRL. *She's just come home from the late shift.* MARSUPIAL GIRL *closes the book and places it under the table.*

MOTHER: It's late.
MARSUPIAL GIRL: I know.

MOTHER *pulls an ace bandage out of her bag.*

MOTHER: We're going to keep you safe.

MARSUPIAL GIRL: OK.

MOTHER *starts wrapping the ace bandage around* MARSUPIAL GIRL'S *middle. A whimper from the pouch.*

MOTHER: This will keep you out of trouble. Nothing goes in your pouch, nothing comes out.

A sharp intake of breath from MARSUPIAL GIRL—*the ace bandage is tight.*

MARSUPIAL GIRL: OK.
MOTHER: People will forget.
MARSUPIAL GIRL: Will they?

A shared look: They both know that's not true. The pouch is silent.

MARSUPIAL GIRL: I'll keep really quiet. I'll blend right in.

MOTHER *and* MARSUPIAL GIRL *embrace.*

MOTHER: My precious girl. My little Marsu—

MARSUPIAL GIRL *places her fingers on* MOTHER'S *lips.*

MARSUPIAL GIRL: I'll blend right in.
CHORUS: Boom Boom ba Diddy Diddy Boom.

*Please see addendum at end of script for a one-act option for *Marsupial Girl*.

ACT TWO

Slow, slide guitar. Lights up. The town is quiet. DR. POUCH *is kicked back in his lawn chair, reading a book and drinking iced tea. He looks up at us.*

DR. POUCH: Welcome back to Marpoopsial Girl.
                  I mean, welcome back to Girlsipial Mar.
                  Marpipsupal Girl?
                  Supipsimal Whirl?
                  Hold on a minute.

He stands up, opens his coat, and pulls out a record from one of his inside pockets. He walks over to his record player gadget and puts it on. The record plays a warped, looped version of the word: Marsupial Girl.

DR. POUCH: Marsupial Girl!

He turns up the volume, and we hear beat boxing and a harmonica melody.

DR. POUCH: OK all you sugar gliders. We're going to do a little call and response. A little I say it—you say it, alright? Alright.

DR. POUCH *sings "Opening Rap."*

DR. POUCH: *When I say mar*
                  You say supial
                  Mar

(supial)
Mar
(supial)

When I say mar
You say supial
Mar
(supial)
Mar
(supial)

Mmmm
Now I think you all can do a little better than that.
Am I right? This is Texas.
And I know you all can do a little better than that.

So when I say mar
You say supial
Mar
(supial)
Mar
(supial)

So when I say mar
You say supial
Mar
(supial)
Mar
(supial)

Now we're hopping!
Yip yip yip yippie!

Everybody say pouuuuuuch.
(pouuuuuch)

Pouuuuuuch.
(pouuuuuch)

Every day it's pouuuuuuch.
(pouuuuuch)

All the children say pouuuuuuch.
(pouuuuuch)

It's not a pickled pepper
Or funny flying squirrel
It's just a little tale
Of a marsupial girl

It's not a pickled pepper
Or a funny flying squirrel
It's just a little tale
Of a marsupial girl

DR. POUCH *comes into the audience and asks individual kids to repeat.*

And shoopialus pop top
(Shoopialus Pop Top)

Abba marra pip shop
(Abba Marra Pip Shop)

Double unc unc q
(Double Unc Unc Q)

Double unc unc q
(Double Unc Unc Q)

DR. POUCH *speaks.*

Now I want to hear you all say *Y'all.*
(y'all)

Now I want y'all all to say *All Y'all.*
(all y'all)

The music is over.

DR. POUCH: Well alright! Now, where were we?

The billboard cranks to read: WHAT IN THE WORLD! *The town floods the stage.* MARSUPIAL GIRL *appears in her dress with the ace bandage carefully wrapped around her midsection.*

DR. POUCH: Oh, right. (DR. POUCH *pulls out a megaphone from his coat, or from his gadgets. He speaks into it.*) MARSUPIAL GIRL BLENDS RIGHT IN!

MARSUPIAL GIRL: Shhhhhhhh! That's not how you blend in! You blend in by being very, very quiet, and never being noticed. Like this.

MARSUPIAL GIRL *at school, with* MRS. PENNYWHISTLE *and the kids.*

MARSUPIAL GIRL: What I want to be when I grow up. When I grow up, I would like to be a teacher. I would like to be able to teach students as well as Mrs. Pennywhistle, the best teacher I ever had . . .

MRS. PENNYWHISTLE: Now girl, is that the truth? Is that really what you want to be?

MARSUPIAL GIRL: It's really what I want to be.

DR. POUCH (*to* MARSUPIAL GIRL): What are you talking about?

MARSUPIAL GIRL (*to* DR. POUCH): WAIT. Like this.

SUE *approaches* MARSUPIAL GIRL. LIBBY *and* SUE *wait nearby. The three wear shirts or dresses of the same style, only in different colors.*

SUE: Wanna come to my house and listen to music?

MARSUPIAL GIRL: Who's going?

SUE: Pearl. And Libby.

MARSUPIAL GIRL: I don't think I can.

SUE: Remember when we used to play superheroes? Sandwoman and The Wind!

SUE *starts to laugh.* MARSUPIAL GIRL *does not.*

MARSUPIAL GIRL: Yeah. So.

SUE: And we'd sing along with your—with your—

MARSUPIAL GIRL: It doesn't talk anymore.

SUE: It doesn't?

MARSUPIAL GIRL: Nope.

SUE: Some days, I wish we could go back in time. And be little girls again.

MARSUPIAL GIRL: Yeah, well, we can't, Sue.

SUE: So you wanna come over?

LIBBY *and* PEARL *enter the stage, away from the girls, arm in arm.*

MARSUPIAL GIRL: Thanks, Sue. But I have to study tonight.

SUE: Wait!

MARSUPIAL GIRL: Bye!

DR. POUCH: Aw, Blast it all to—

MARSUPIAL GIRL *leaves.* SUE *hesitates for a moment, then leaves.*
MARSUPIAL GIRL *walks home. The neighbors gossip.*

FRED LUDBERGER: That girl's so quiet now she's like the moon in the sky.

INA SHAW: Yes, but who knows what she's brewing in there.

FRED LUDBERGER: Now, Ina, really, have you ever looked in there?

INA SHAW: Fred! Please!

LACEY: My cousin knows the lady knows the doctor who was there on the day, on the day the girl was born, and my cousin says the

doctor looked inside it on that morning, looked inside it and—
BAM—he couldn't see no more!

FRED LUDBERGER: Hogwash!

LACEY: BLIND! Got the white cane and all!

FRED LUDBERGER: Pig ears!

LACEY AND INA: It's true!

FRED LUDBERGER: I must say I miss that old smile a hers, loud as the horn on an eighteen-wheeler. Haven't seen that smile for a while now . . .

MARSUPIAL GIRL, *at home in her room. She opens* Macbeth *by William Shakespeare.*

MARSUPIAL GIRL *(reading)*: When will we three meet again
                  In thunder, lightning, and in rain.

MOTHER *enters.*

MOTHER: Whatcha doing?

MARSUPIAL GIRL: Reading.

MOTHER: Shakespeare. For school?

MARSUPIAL GIRL: Yup.

MOTHER: You want some help?

MARSUPIAL GIRL: Nope.

MOTHER: OK then.

MOTHER *shuts the door.* MARSUPIAL GIRL'S *pouch grumbles and rumbles.*

MARSUPIAL GIRL: Double Double Toil and Trouble

THE POUCH: Fire Burn and Cauldron Bubble!

MARSUPIAL GIRL: Quiet!

THE POUCH: Quiet quiet quiet.

MARSUPIAL GIRL: I said shhhhhh.

THE POUCH: Shooooopialus pop top.

MOTHER *(outside her door)*: Is everything alright in there?

MARSUPIAL GIRL: Fine, Ma! Just singing a little song, that's all.
Boom Boom Boom Boom

THE POUCH: Boom boom diddy da boom boom ba diddy diddy
(repeat)

MOTHER: That doesn't sound like Shakespeare!

MARSUPIAL GIRL: Sorry, Ma!

THE POUCH: Sorry Ma Sorry Ma Sorry Ma!

MARSUPIAL GIRL *starts to like this singing, and dances along for a
moment.* MOTHER *knocks on the door. The pouch stops.*

MOTHER: Girl! I mean it!

MARSUPIAL GIRL *stops the pouch from singing. She opens the ace bandage a bit, peeks through.*

THE POUCH: Q Q Q Q
You You You
Ready Ready Ready
??????

MARSUPIAL GIRL *presses down the ace bandage.*

MARSUPIAL GIRL: Shhhhhhhhhhhhhh.

DR. POUCH: And so life goes, safe and sound—

The billboard cranks to read: SAFE AND SOUND

DR. POUCH: —in your teenincy town.

MARSUPIAL GIRL: You got it, Pouch.

DR. POUCH: Ooohh don't say that word!

MARSUPIAL GIRL: Right. If I don't say it, it will just go away.

The pouch makes a noise like a stomach growling noise.

DR. POUCH: Whatever you say, ma'am.

The billboard cranks to read: YEAH, RIGHT. DR. POUCH *whispers to the audience.*

DR. POUCH: Yeah, right.

MARSUPIAL GIRL: I'm going to walk like any other girl. I'm going to talk like any other girl. I'm going to eat and sleep and fold my little hands—

MARSUPIAL GIRL *folds her hands daintily over her bandaged pouch. The pouch makes a stomach growling noise.*

DR. POUCH: Sounds to me like the POUCH has other plans.

The billboard cranks to read: THE POUCH HAS OTHER PLANS.

INA SHAW, LACEY RUBBERTREE *and* MRS. PENNYWHISTLE *stuff envelopes in the church basement.* MARSUPIAL GIRL *and* MOTHER *at home.* MARSUPIAL GIRL *paces.*

INA SHAW *(to* MRS. PENNYWHISTLE*)*: Cross my heart, Penny, it's trouble. Trouble with a capital P – O – U – C – H.

LACEY: You know Shelley Lee's daughter was born with six fingers on her right hand. Do you remember that? She wore a glove on that hand all the way through the seventh grade—

INA SHAW: When she saved up the money to have it removed. Now she's got the prettiest hands in the whole city, have you seen those hands?

MRS. PENNYWHISTLE: Everybody's got something. Look at me, my pinky toe juts out at a ninety degree angle from when my brother dropped a bowling ball on it by accident. Now the doctor wanted to cut the toe clean off, but my mother wouldn't hear of it, and look at me today, can you even see a limp?

INA SHAW: Nope.

LACEY: Maybe a little.

INA SHAW: We can't see it at all.

MRS. PENNYWHISTLE: Everybody's got a little something different on them. That's what makes a body a body.

INA SHAW: Now really, Penny, why are you suddenly this girl's best friend?

MRS. PENNYWHISTLE: She needs a friend, Ina. And she's smart. One of my smartest. She nearly jumped out of her seat when she heard we were going. Most kids think Shakespeare is some kind of dance move.

MRS. PENNYWHISTLE *demonstrates the Shake-spear.*

INA SHAW *(to* LACEY*)*: The girl wants to go on the field trip. The folks from Dallas are driving over to do one of their little Shakespeare plays in the park.

MARSUPIAL GIRL: Mom, it's for school. Can I please, please, please, please, please go?

MOTHER: No.

MRS. PENNYWHISTLE: It's just on the outskirts of town.

LACEY: But that's lovely! Maybe a little culture will do her some good!

INA SHAW: It's *Macbeth*.

LACEY: Oh.

INA SHAW: And it's a sleepover.

LACEY: OH.

MARSUPIAL GIRL: Mom, it's my most favorite play ever. *Macbeth*. There's a King and a Ghost and even Witches.

MOTHER: Definitely no.

MARSUPIAL GIRL: But Mom! I'm blending right in!

LACEY: That girl hasn't been invited to one sleepover in all of her thirteen years.

INA SHAW: That's what I'm talking about.

MARSUPIAL GIRL: Mom, it's only for one night!

MOTHER: We'll talk about it in the morning. Now go to sleep. Go.

MRS. PENNYWHISTLE: Ladies, please! She's just a girl.

LACEY RUBBERTREE *speaks the words in all caps along with* INA SHAW.

INA SHAW: NOT just a girl. (MRS. PENNYWHISTLE *tries to interject. No luck.*) They say there's feathers on the inside of it, feathers made of stick pins and glass. And when she opens it up, a wind pours out, the winds of a thousand animal wars past. If you want to take her, Penny, fine, but don't come askin' us about it. Don't come askin' us because you KNOW what we'll SAY.

MRS. PENNYWHISTLE *exits.*
      MOTHER *sleeps in her bed.* MARSUPIAL GIRL *lies in bed, or kneels by her bedside, saying over and over.*

MARSUPIAL GIRL: Yes say yes
                     Say yes Say yes
                     Yes say yes
                     Say yes say yes.

DR. POUCH *watches from his billboard perch.* DR. POUCH *fashions some kind of strange, twisting tube out of the gutter pipe from his shack. He reaches it down, down, down so the end is at sleeping* MOTHER'S *ear.*

MARSUPIAL GIRL AND DR. POUCH: Yes say yes
                     Say yes Say yes
                     Yes say yes
                     Say yes Say yes.

MOTHER *sits up, stretches, yawns. The sun is up, and it is morning.*
DR. POUCH *quickly pulls the gadget back into his perch.* MARSUPIAL GIRL *stands at her mother's door, in great anticipation.*

MOTHER: Oh. It's such a lovely day out. I think I'll say yes.
MARSUPIAL GIRL AND DR. POUCH: YES!
DR. POUCH: Your momma's in the river catching tap-dancing
                     trout

The sun is made of butter and
Marsupial Girl CAMPS OUT!

The billboard reads: MARSUPIAL GIRL CAMPS OUT!
　　MARSUPIAL GIRL *and* DR. POUCH *whoop with joy.* MARSUPIAL GIRL
runs into her mother's room and jumps into her mother's arms.

MARSUPIAL GIRL (*singsong*): I'm going to a sleepover.
　　　　　　　　　　I'm going to a pla-ay
　　　　　　　　　　I'm going to a sleepover
　　　　　　　　　　I'm going to a pla-ay.

MOTHER *drops* MARSUPIAL GIRL *off at the park, handing* MRS.
PENNYWHISTLE *the permission slip.* MRS. PENNYWHISTLE *takes*
MARSUPIAL GIRL'S *hand.*

MRS. PENNYWHISTLE: Don't worry, I'll keep my eye on her.

MRS. PENNYWHISTLE *leads* MARSUPIAL GIRL *over to a line of kids.* SUE
stands in line behind LIBBY *and* PEARL. MARSUPIAL GIRL *passes* SUE,
LIBBY, *and* PEARL.

MARSUPIAL GIRL: Hey, Sue.
SUE: Hey.

LIBBY *suppresses a snicker.* PEARL *whispers something to* LIBBY. LIBBY
whispers something to SUE. SUE *shrugs them off.* MARSUPIAL GIRL *looks*
at SUE.

SUE: Hey.
MARSUPIAL GIRL: You said that already, Sue.
MRS. PENNYWHISTLE: Children! We have arrived! The campsite with
　　our tents is over there. The stage where the actors will appear is
　　right here. And over there are the woods. And who is allowed to
　　go into the woods?

ALL KIDS (*mopey, complaining*): NOBODY is allowed to go in the woods.

MRS. PENNYWHISTLE: Brilliant. Now the play is about to start. Quiet, and quick let's take our seats. If it were done when 'tis done 'twere best it were done quickly! Let's go . . .

MARSUPIAL GIRL *and a group of kids are watching the opening scene from* Macbeth. MRS. PENNYWHISTLE *sits nearby, keeping an eye on* MARSUPIAL GIRL.

ACTRESS 1:	When will we three meet again
	In thunder, lightning, or in rain?
ACTRESS 2:	When the hurly-burly's done,
	When the battle's lost and won.
ACTRESS 3:	That will be ere the set of the sun.
ACTRESS 1:	Where the place?
ACTRESS 2:	Upon the heath.
ACTRESS 3:	There to meet with
ALL THREE:	Macbeth!

LIBBY *and* PEARL *enter. They are in another part of the park.* SUE *enters with a flashlight.*

LIBBY: Here we are—in the woods! (LIBBY *and* PEARL *high-five.*) Where have you been, sister?

SUE: Killing Swine. (*The three girls crack up.*)

LIBBY: We've got no time to waste. We've got to get back before the intermission, or we'll get totally creamed.

PEARL: Yeah, double, double totally in trouble.

PEARL *cracks up. Nobody else does.* LIBBY *shoots her a look.* LIBBY *and* PEARL *straighten up and get serious.*

LIBBY: Sue.

PEARL: Sue.

LIBBY: Are you ready?

SUE: Yes.

LIBBY: Tonight is the night that you become a sister. A sister to me and to Pearl. We told you how this works. You bring us something that you STOLE. Something very IMPORTANT that you STOLE in a very DANGEROUS way. And you must SHOW it to us. That means we can TRUST you. Understand?

PEARL: Understand?

SUE: I think so.

LIBBY: Good. (LIBBY *looks at* PEARL.) We're ready.

SUE *pulls out a small, sharp pocketknife.*

SUE: This is my daddy's special pocketknife. Passed down to him from his daddy. He sharpens it every Sunday, after church. He's gonna go completely nuts when he finds out its gone.

LIBBY: A knife?

SUE: A knife.

PEARL *takes the knife. Inspects it. Hands it to* LIBBY. LIBBY *looks it over, then looks at* PEARL. *Then:*

LIBBY: I'm sorry, Sue.

SUE: What?

LIBBY: We think you can do better.

PEARL: We think you can do better.

LIBBY: We think you can steal something more dangerous.

SUE: More dangerous than my daddy's knife? Do you know how hard it was for me to—

PEARL *whispers something in* SUE'S *ear.* SUE *looks at* LIBBY.

LIBBY: Understand? Just bring it here and show it to us, that's all.

PEARL: And make it talk. I want to hear it talk.

LIBBY *punches* PEARL *in the arm.*

LIBBY: Just show it to us. Then we'll know you are a real sister.

SUE: Forget it.

LIBBY: Then forget you. Let's go, Pearl.

PEARL: Let's go.

LIBBY: So long, Sue. And tell your dad thanks for the knife.

LIBBY *takes the knife and links arms with* PEARL.

SUE: Wait. (LIBBY *and* PEARL *turn around.)* Wait right here. I'll go get her.

SUE *runs off.* LIBBY *and* SUE *giggle and high-five each other. As* SUE *makes her way back to the play,* DR. POUCH *keeps close watch.*

DR. POUCH: No no no no—

MARSUPIAL GIRL *is watching the play with the other kids.* MRS. PENNYWHISTLE *is enrapt in the action, practically mouthing the words along with the actors.* SUE *sneaks over to* MARSUPIAL GIRL, *taps her on the shoulder.*

ACTOR 1: Is this a dagger which I see before me,
The handle towards my hand? Come, let me
clutch thee!
I have thee not, and yet I see thee still.

SUE: Hey.

DR. POUCH: No say no say no say no—

MARSUPIAL GIRL: Hey.

SUE: I need your help.

MARSUPIAL GIRL: What do you mean?

SUE: I can't explain right now. I just—*(from the kids in the crowd: shh-hhhh!)* I need you to come with me.

DR. POUCH: No say no say—

MARSUPIAL GIRL: But the play . . .

SUE: It'll just take a minute. I need your help. And when we're done . . . (MARSUPIAL GIRL *is skeptical.* SUE *looks her in the eye.*) Maybe we can ride our Secret Bicycle out onto the wind and ride far, far, far away from here . . . (MARSUPIAL GIRL *and* SUE *look at each other.*) Please?

DR. POUCH: No say no say no say—

MARSUPIAL GIRL: OK.

DR. POUCH: *(Defeated.)* No.

A bell rings on the stage where the play is taking place. MARSUPIAL GIRL *and* SUE *steal away.* MRS. PENNYWHISTLE *watches.*

ACTOR 1: I go, and it is done. The bell invites me.
Hear it not, Duncan, for it is a knell
That summons thee to heaven, or to hell.

LIBBY *and* PEARL, *in the woods. We hear* SUE *and* MARSUPIAL GIRL, *running toward them.*

MARSUPIAL GIRL: Wow. Where are we going?

SUE: Just a little farther . . .

SUE *runs in with* MARSUPIAL GIRL.

LIBBY: Well, well, well. Nice work, Sue.

MARSUPIAL GIRL: Libby.

SUE *stands behind* MARSUPIAL GIRL, *hands on her shoulders.*

SUE: Here There you go. I brought her. And I showed her. That's what you wanted, right? Let's go, girl.

LIBBY: Hold on, Sue. IT. We want to see IT. Not HER. Who cares about HER.

MARSUPIAL GIRL: Sue?

LIBBY: Sue's trying to become a sister. Our sister. But she needs to show us something first. Something dangerous. Something she's got, that we DON'T got.

MARSUPIAL GIRL (*to* SUE): This is why you brought me here?

SUE: I don't . . . I don't know.

LIBBY: Alright, Sue. We're ready. You want the knife? (LIBBY *takes out the knife.*) Show us.

MARSUPIAL GIRL: Sue.

LIBBY: Well, Sue?

SUE *looks at* MARSUPIAL GIRL, *then unwraps the bandage. A rumble emanates from the pouch.*

LIBBY: Whoa. Look at that.

PEARL: Make it talk! Make it talk!

MARSUPIAL GIRL *holds out her arms, resigned and defiant.*

MARSUPIAL GIRL: Go ahead, Sue. Show them what kind of monster I am.

LIBBY *and* PEARL *look at* SUE.

SUE: No.

LIBBY: Open it!

SUE: It's not true. She's not a—

MARSUPIAL GIRL: Hush. I'll open it for you. Everybody ready?

SUE: No. Please. Girl, I made a mistake. I was wrong to bring you here. You're my friend. You're the best friend I've ever ha— (MARSUPIAL GIRL *reaches out her hand and grabs a "piece" of* SUE'S *voice.*) Ah. Ahhhh—

MARSUPIAL GIRL *pulls and pulls, until she has* SUE'S *voice in her hand.*

MARSUPIAL GIRL: You're not my friend. I don't have any friends.

Then, she opens her pouch. A yawning, windy sound comes out. She puts SUE'S *voice in her pouch.* SUE *opens and closes her mouth. She can't speak anymore.*

MARSUPIAL GIRL: There you go, Libby. I opened it. WHAT ELSE DO YOU WANT?

MARSUPIAL GIRL'S *pouch rumbles and echoes as she speaks.* LIBBY *drops the knife.* PEARL *runs off, taking* SUE *with her.*

LIBBY *(to* PEARL*)*: Hey, come back! Don't leave me here with—Pearl! Sue! I said come back! (MARSUPIAL GIRL *picks up the knife.)* Hey. That's not yours.
MARSUPIAL GIRL: Oh yeah? (MARSUPIAL GIRL *closes the knife. She opens her pouch and puts it in. Closes the pouch.)* Come and get it.
LIBBY: Look at you. You really think you're somebody.
MARSUPIAL GIRL: Get out.
LIBBY: You're nobody. NOBODY.
MARSUPIAL GIRL: I said, GET OUT!

The pouch wails "Get out" with her. LIBBY *yells as she runs off.*

LIBBY: Mrs. Pennywhistle! She's got a knife!

MARSUPIAL GIRL *yells. Her pouch moans.* DR. POUCH *wails.*
MARSUPIAL GIRL *yells. Her pouch moans back.* DR. POUCH *wails.*
MARSUPIAL GIRL *yells. Her pouch moans back.* DR. POUCH *wails.*
As this trio continues, MARSUPIAL GIRL *wanders through the dust.*

MARSUPIAL GIRL: Fi Fie Foe Fouch
                    Who's the girl
                    with the creepy—ahhhhh
                    Fi Fie Fo Foo
                    Smelly as a kangaroo.

She begins gathering things out of the dust—sticks, old bike spokes, sage-brush, colored telephone wires, pop-tops. As she continues her chant, we see MRS. PENNYWHISTLE *looking for her, calling "Girl? Where are you, girl? Girl? Where are you?" We hear the cries of other kids looking for her, too, floating through the air.*

MARSUPIAL GIRL: Fi Fie Foe Fouch
                    Who's the girl
                    with the creepy—ahhhhh
                    Fi Fie Fo Foo
                    Smelly as a kangaroo.

MARSUPIAL GIRL *repeats her chant two, maybe three times. Day begins to break.* MRS. PENNYWHISTLE *and* SUE *stand before* MARSUPIAL GIRL'S *mother.* LIBBY, PEARL *and* SUE *are there. We don't see* MARSUPIAL GIRL.

MRS. PENNYWHISTLE: I was watching her like a hawk and then . . .

MOTHER: Where's my girl?

LIBBY: She had a knife. It was THIS BIG—(LIBBY *indicates a HUGE knife, much bigger than the tiny, unopened pocketknife.*)—and she was holding us all at knife point.

LACEY: A barbarian.

INA SHAW: A danger to this community, I'm telling you!

LACEY: I don't know where she belongs, but she DON'T belong HERE.

FRED LUDBERGER: Can we all just calm down for a hare's breath of a minute—

MOTHER: This has got to be a mistake. Sue. Where is my girl? Speak to me, Sue.

LIBBY: She can't speak. Your girl took her VOICE.

INA SHAW *and* LACEY RUBBERTREE *gasp.*

MOTHER: That's crazy talk. She wouldn't do that. Not intentionally. Not to Sue.

MRS. PENNYWHISTLE: I searched all night.

FRED LUDBERGER: And we'll keep searching. She can't be far, that little critter.

INA SHAW: Maybe we should stop searching. Did you ever think of that? Maybe that girl is better off far, far, FAR away.

MARSUPIAL GIRL *walks into the crowd, hair wild, pouch untamed. She has woven the items she picked up in the dust into a kind of armor, or cape. She might even have a tin can tail.*

MARSUPIAL GIRL: Hey.

The townspeople gasp and hush up.

MRS. PENNYWHISTLE: Girl! I was so worried about you!

MRS. PENNYWHISTLE *moves forward to hug* MARSUPIAL GIRL.

MARSUPIAL GIRL: Stand back.

MARSUPIAL GIRL *bends her knees and brings up her hands like paws. Then, she hops like a kangaroo: one, two, three times. The townspeople gasp.*

FRED LUDBERGER: Easy now. Easy now.

MARSUPIAL GIRL: Hi, Sue. Tell your dad I said thanks for the knife, Sue. Oh right. I forgot. You can't tell your dad anything.

MARSUPIAL GIRL *opens her pouch—a loud roar comes out "at"* SUE. *The crowd is silent and aghast.*

MARSUPIAL GIRL: Well, well, well. For once this town has nothing to say.

SUE *steps forward. She puts her hand on her own stomach, where her "pouch" would be.*

MARSUPIAL GIRL: I'm sorry, what?

SUE *points back and forth between herself and* MARSUPIAL GIRL, *then places her hand where her "pouch" would be.*

MARSUPIAL GIRL: I don't understand you, Sue. Maybe your sisters
    can help you out. Ma?
MOTHER: Yes, girl.

MARSUPIAL GIRL *takes her mother's hand.*

MARSUPIAL GIRL: I'm tired. Let's go home.

As MARSUPIAL GIRL *walks with* MOTHER, DR. POUCH *speaks into a microphone.*

DR. POUCH: Q Q Q Q
                U U U U
                Ready Ready Ready Ready?
MARSUPIAL GIRL: Ha. What do you think?
DR. POUCH: Marsupial Girl rebels!
MARSUPIAL GIRL: I rebel!

Phat guitar from DR. POUCH.
    MARSUPIAL GIRL *at home, the next school day. Her hair is still wild.*
MOTHER *hands* MARSUPIAL GIRL *her lunch.*

MOTHER: You're going to school like that?
MARSUPIAL GIRL: Yes. (*guitar*)
MOTHER: Are you sure?
MARSUPIAL GIRL: Yes.

MARSUPIAL GIRL *puts her notebook and pencils in her pouch.*

MOTHER: Are you going to get in trouble?

MARSUPIAL GIRL: Yes. (*guitar*)

MARSUPIAL GIRL heads out to school. We see her pass some kids with their parents. The parents guide the kids to the other side of the street.

MARSUPIAL GIRL: WHAT'S THE MATTER? NEVER SEEN A POUCH BEFORE? (*The parents whisper to their children and shield their eyes.*) They wish they had a pouch. A pouch that can carry everything they need. Everything they ever wanted . . .

MARSUPIAL GIRL passes the grocery store with the bin of bubble gum out front. We see her stop in front of the bin of bubble gum.
   Guitar tension raises as MARSUPIAL GIRL stands next to the bin of gum. MARSUPIAL GIRL opens her eyes and reaches toward the gum, then pulls her hand back, nervous. Does the pouch whimper? She puts her hands on her pouch.

MARSUPIAL GIRL: Who cares that it doesn't belong to me? We can just take it. Take it and keep it right here.

MARSUPIAL GIRL reaches out and takes a gum ball. She opens her pouch and puts it in. The GROCER comes outside. She looks him right in the eye.

Marsupial Girl (Anna Reichert) puts a gum ball in her pouch. Photograph by Rob Levine.

And takes another gum ball. She puts the gum ball in her pouch.

GROCER: Can I help you?
DR. POUCH: Some people called this her Blue Period.

She pours the whole jar of gum balls into her pouch and hands the empty jar to the GROCER.

DR. POUCH: Some people called these her dark days.

The GROCER *runs off, scared.*

DR. POUCH: But unless things turn sour, I called this period incredibly cool.

MARSUPIAL GIRL *watches the grocer run off.*

MARSUPIAL GIRL: Huh, look at that, he's scared of me. Run everybody, run!

DR. POUCH *sings "Not This Girl." As he sings, we see a line of plump and eager five-year-old kids.* MARSUPIAL GIRL *hands them each a gum ball. They chew.*

DR. POUCH: *She walks around the town.*
                 Head held high, lips turned down.
                 No one can put her down.
                 Not this girl.

The scrawny kids are all blowing big pink bubbles now. MARSUPIAL GIRL *sees* LIBBY, SUE, *and* PEARL *looking at a teen magazine.*

DR. POUCH: *She struts her way to school.*
                 She doesn't mind the rules.
                 She takes from all the fools

MARSUPIAL GIRL *takes the magazine and puts it in her pouch.*

MARSUPIAL GIRL: *This new girl*
You don't like me coming round to call?
I just want your little Barbie doll.
New jacks and shiny red ball.
I take it all I take it all I take it all I take it all.

She takes the microphone from DR. POUCH.

Say say say
Too much talk
I just don't care
I take what I want.
MARSUPIAL GIRL AND TOWN: *Say say say*
Too much talk
I just don't care
I take what I want.
DR. POUCH: *Answers from a test—*
MARSUPIAL GIRL: *I steal*
Candy bars from a vest—
DR. POUCH: *She steals—*

We see a row of "pretty" girls. MARSUPIAL GIRL *takes the ribbons from their hair.*

MARSUPIAL GIRL: *I steal ribbons from the pretty girls' hair.*
THE GIRLS: *Ouch! Ouch! Ouch!*
MARSUPIAL GIRL: *You want them back? Reach in my POUCH!*
THE GIRLS: *AAAAHHHHH!*

The pretty girls run away. We see and hear LACEY RUBBERTREE *and another person from town whispering.*

MARSUPIAL GIRL: *You sneer at who I am?*
I'll snatch your whispers—bam!

She steals INA *and* LACEY'S *whispers.*

> *And feast on whisper jam.*
> *For my supper.*
>
> *They call me freak and so I freak.*
> *Forget the shy, the mild, the meek.*
> *I'll have the whole town crying—*

WHOLE TOWN: *Eek!*

MARSUPIAL GIRL AND TOWN: *Say say say*
> *Too much talk*
> *I just don't care*
> *I take what I want.*
>
> *Say say say*
> *Too much talk*
> *I just don't care*
> *I take what I want.*

DR. POUCH: *Taking what she needs.*

MARSUPIAL GIRL: *This new girl.*

DR. POUCH: *Dirty little deeds.*

MARSUPIAL GIRL: *This new girl.*

DR. POUCH: *What's she got to lose.*

MARSUPIAL GIRL: *This new girl.*

DR. POUCH: *She has 'em shaking in their shoes.*

MARSUPIAL GIRL *leads the frightened town in this last chorus, almost like she is hypnotizing them into being her "backup" singers.*

CHORUS: *Na na na na na na na*
> *Na na na na na na*
> *Na na na na na na na*
> *Uh-oh uh-oh*

Na na na na na na na
Na na na na na na
Na na na na na na na
Uh-oh uh-oh

Na na na na na na na
Na na na na na na
Na na na na na na na
Uh-oh uh-oh

Na na na na na na na
Na na na na na na
Na na na na na na na
Uh-oh uh-oh

She walks around the town
Head held high lips turned down
No one can put her down.

MARSUPIAL GIRL: *This new girl.*

DR. POUCH: So you take what you want.

MARSUPIAL GIRL: Yep.

A man walks by reading the newspaper. MARSUPIAL GIRL *snatches it and puts it in her pouch.*

DR. POUCH: Or at least, what you think you want.

MARSUPIAL GIRL: That's right.

A woman walks by looking in her compact mirror. MARSUPIAL GIRL *snatches it and checks her own hair. The woman waits for the mirror back.* MARSUPIAL GIRL *puts the mirror in her pouch. The woman meekly walks away.*

MARSUPIAL GIRL: And sometimes—(*A girl walks by listening to a walk-man or iPod. She takes it.*) I just take. (*speaking to her pouch*) Look at that, nobody is going to bother us now. This is going to be great! (SUE *runs up to* MARSUPIAL GIRL.) Stay away.

As a crowd gathers, SUE *rubs the place on her belly where her pouch would be, then points back and forth between herself and* MARSUPIAL GIRL. MARSUPIAL GIRL *puts her hands over her ears.*

MARSUPIAL GIRL: I don't have anything to say to you, Sue. I said stay away!

LIBBY *appears and puts her arm around* SUE.

LIBBY (*to* SUE): Get away from her, Sue. Go on, keep shoving that thing full of everybody's stuff. You're such a loser.
MARSUPIAL GIRL: What's that, Libby?
LIBBY: You will never be normal. You will always be a monster, you freak. You're gonna be alone forever with your big, fat, ugly Pouc—

MARSUPIAL GIRL *pulls the voice from* LIBBY'S *mouth and puts it in her pouch.*

MARSUPIAL GIRL: Maybe I am. But I don't have to hear that from you anymore.
TOWNSPERSON 1: Look at her! That's no girl, that's an a—

MARSUPIAL GIRL *takes the* TOWNSPERSON'S *voice.*

TOWNSPERSON 2: Abomination. She's not normal. I've been telling you all that for—

MARSUPIAL GIRL *takes the* TOWNSPERSON'S *voice.*

TOWNSPERSON 3: Years and years. Ever since I first laid eyes on that girl I knew exactly what she was. A true blue, certified FREE EEE EEE—

MARSUPIAL GIRL *takes the* TOWNSPERSON'S *voice.*

MRS. PENNYWHISTLE: Girl, please. (MARSUPIAL GIRL *is out of breath. She looks at* MRS. PENNYWHISTLE.) This is not the way to make things better.

MARSUPIAL GIRL: Oh yeah? And what do you suggest, Mrs. Pennywhistle? Another sleepover?

MRS. PENNYWHISTLE: If you'd just sit still and talk to me for a minute I might be able to—ah—ahhhh!

But MARSUPIAL GIRL *has stolen* MRS. PENNYWHISTLE'S *voice. She puts it in her pouch.*

MARSUPIAL GIRL: I'm going to shut you out. I've got a whole life to live, and nobody can stop me.

A group of townspeople approaches, all talking at once.

TOWNSPERSON: Put her in a cage! (MARSUPIAL GIRL *steals the voice.*)

TOWNSPERSON: Run her out of town! (MARSUPIAL GIRL *steals the voice.*)

TOWNSPERSON: Kangaroo! (MARSUPIAL GIRL *steals the voice.*)

MARSUPIAL GIRL: QUIET! (*We hear the sound of a dog barking.*) You too. (MARSUPIAL GIRL *takes the sound. We hear the sound of cars beeping their horns.*) ALL OF YOU! (*She steals the sound of the car horns. We hear the sound of church bells.*) ENOUGH!

MARSUPIAL GIRL *takes the church bell sounds, one by one. We hear the sound of a plane zooming overhead.*

MARSUPIAL GIRL: YOU TOO! (MARSUPIAL GIRL *steals the sound.*)

The last townspeople with voices begin to babble. The town cowers in a group near the edge of town. As they babble, MARSUPIAL GIRL *steals all their voices in one enormous swipe. It is a physically difficult gesture— stealing all those voices is hard for her.*

MARSUPIAL GIRL: QUIET!

She puts them in her pouch. A bird flutters overhead, singing.

MARSUPIAL GIRL: I said QUIET!

She reaches up to steal the sound. She steals the birdsong, but the little bird is tough. MARSUPIAL GIRL *pulls at the sound, the little bird pulls back. Finally,* MARSUPIAL GIRL *pulls the sound out of the bird's mouth, and shoves it in her pouch.*

We hear the sound of a bug buzzing. MARSUPIAL GIRL *focuses in on the bug.*

MARSUPIAL GIRL: You too.
She snatches the sound, and puts it in her pouch. MOTHER *enters.*

MOTHER: Girl.

MARSUPIAL GIRL *looks at* MOTHER.

MARSUPIAL GIRL: Stay away, Ma.
MOTHER: Girl, please—
MARSUPIAL GIRL: I've got everything under control.

MOTHER *holds out her arms.*

MOTHER: The world is big and wide—
MARSUPIAL GIRL: And UGLY. Just like me.
MOTHER: That's not what I see.
MARSUPIAL GIRL: Mom, don't start.
MOTHER: And so one day I was swimming at Blue Lake
MARSUPIAL GIRL: Mother, please. I'm warning you—

MOTHER *slowly approaches* MARSUPIAL GIRL.

MOTHER: And I looked up and the sky unzipped itself. And that Giant Kangaroo handed you down, down, down and gave you to me. And she said

MARSUPIAL GIRL: This is a special creature.

MOTHER: Love her and care for her.

MARSUPIAL GIRL: Teach her to be strong.

MOTHER: And then she went back up into the sky. And I had myself a—

On the word "girl," MARSUPIAL GIRL *steals her mother's voice.*

MARSUPIAL GIRL: You think I ever really believed that stupid story?

Silence. MOTHER *backs away, with her hand on her lips.*

MARSUPIAL GIRL: Wow. I did it. I shut them all out. Hey, pouch, I—

She looks up at DR. POUCH. *His mouth moves open and shut: she's taken his voice too.*

MARSUPIAL GIRL: Huh. I guess I REALLY did it. Hello!
Her "Hello" ricochets through the space. A flat, hollow echo. From the pouch we hear a garbled, grumbled "Hello." Her pouch has grown quite large, filled to the point of bursting with sound and the objects she stole.

MARSUPIAL GIRL: It's just you and me. Like in the beginning. ISN'T THIS GREAT! *(The pouch groans a ghastly groan.)* Whoa, whoa now. Shhhhhhh. You're fine. *(another pouch groan: pleading, imploring)* No, I can't. Do you want it to be like before? People calling us names? Whispering behind our back? *(another pouch groan)* NO. Can't you see how great this is? We won! We shut them out! WE'VE GOT A WHOLE LIFE TO LIVE.

MARSUPIAL GIRL'S *angry shout echoes through the space. The pouch implores her.*

MARSUPIAL GIRL: NO. This is it. Forever. Me and you. Me and my— (*She bangs on her pouch.*) Me and my—(*She bangs on her pouch again.*) Me and my—

She bangs on her pouch three times: gong, gong, GROAN. She places her hands on her pouch and looks at it.

MARSUPIAL GIRL: Oh.
THE POUCH (*groans*): Feet—
MARSUPIAL GIRL: To climb to the mountains
THE POUCH (*groans*): Arms—
MARSUPIAL GIRL: To swim through the sea.

MOTHER *appears in the distance. She mouths the following words along with* MARSUPIAL GIRL.

MARSUPIAL GIRL: I'd walk I'd walk I'd walk every desert to find—

MOTHER *disappears.* MARSUPIAL GIRL *places her hands on her pouch, as though recognizing what she has done to it for the first time.*
MARSUPIAL GIRL: What am I?

The pouch continues to groan and rumble. MARSUPIAL GIRL *sings softly.*

MARSUPIAL GIRL: *Lipputmannish hyi op*
(*The pouch groans back a barely audible "Op Op Op Op Op."*)
MARSUPIAL GIRL: *Shoopialus pop top*
(*The pouch groans back, a grotesquely distorted "Pop top Pop top."*)
MARSUPIAL GIRL: *Shoopialus pop top*
Fie wop—
(*The pouch answers "Sue Sue Sue Sue." It turns into a pouch cry.* SUE *appears.*)
MARSUPIAL GIRL: Sue!

SUE *approaches her.*

MARSUPIAL GIRL: Stay away. You shouldn't see me like this. (SUE *shakes her head.* SUE *points back and forth between her and* MARSUPIAL GIRL.) What? (SUE *makes the motion again.*) You and me? (SUE *points to herself.*) You. (SUE *points to* MARSUPIAL GIRL.) Me. (SUE *points to herself.*) You. (SUE *points to* MARSUPIAL GIRL.) Me. (SUE *rubs her own belly, where her pouch would be.*) And the pouch. (*Then,* SUE *mimes opening her pouch.*) Oh no, Sue, I can't. I really can't. (SUE *mimes opening it again.* MARSUPIAL GIRL'*s pouch moans and groans.*) I'm a monster. And that's just the way it's going to be.

SUE *points her fingers toward her own mouth as if to say "Give me my voice back" to* MARSUPIAL GIRL *and puts her hands on the pouch.*

MARSUPIAL GIRL: I can't. (SUE *rubs her hands on* MARSUPIAL GIRL'S *pouch: a healing gesture.*) Sue, I—

SUE *puts a finger to her lips. Shhhh.* SUE *puts her hands on the opening of* MARSUPIAL GIRL'S *pouch.* MARSUPIAL GIRL *opens the pouch just a tiny bit. First, we hear the sound of wind. Then we see* SUE *breathe in deep.* MARSUPIAL GIRL *is scared and closes the pouch tight.*

SUE: Hey.
MARSUPIAL GIRL: Hey.
SUE: You got a lot of stuff in there.
MARSUPIAL GIRL: Yep.

SUE *puts her hand on the pouch. It whimpers.*

SUE: Does it hurt?
MARSUPIAL GIRL: No, no it's fine. We're just getting used to it.
    (*a growl from the pouch*)
SUE: Maybe you should put some of it back.
MARSUPIAL GIRL: No way! Everybody says I'm a monster. So now, I'm a monster with a little peace and quiet. (*The pouch groans.*)

SUE: You're not a monster.

MARSUPIAL GIRL: Then why did you do what you did, Sue? Why?

SUE: I was scared. And stupid.

MARSUPIAL GIRL: Well, maybe not. Maybe this is how things are supposed to be.

SUE: No. It's supposed to be like when we were little, when it was just us, when we didn't care what anybody thought.

MARSUPIAL GIRL: Grow up, Sue. We can't go back in time. *(big pouch groan)*

SUE: I remember the first time you showed it to me. It was the most amazing thing in the world. We need to make everybody see what we see.

MARSUPIAL GIRL: I see a monster.

SUE: I see my friend. Who is a girl. With a pouch. (SUE *puts her hands on* MARSUPIAL GIRL'S *pouch.* MARSUPIAL GIRL *looks scared.)* I'm here, girl. I'm right here by your side.

Together, they open the pouch a little more. We hear the sound of DR. POUCH's *guitar.* DR. POUCH *plays. The pouch continues to grunt and groan, and* MARSUPIAL GIRL *guards it. She looks at her pouch, and sings: bluesy, grungy, like Macy Gray. Song "What's That Thumpin' with the Boom Bang."*

MARSUPIAL GIRL: *What's that, thumpin' with the boom bang?*
What is at the bottom of this thang?

MARSUPIAL GIRL AND SUE: *What's that, thumpin' with the boom bang?*
What is at the bottom of this thang?

MARSUPIAL GIRL: *If they call me monster freak*
Am I just a monster freak
What is at the bottom of this thang?
If I say that I'm a master thief
Does that make me a master thief?

SUE: *What is at the bottom of this?*

MARSUPIAL GIRL *places her hands on her pouch.*

MARSUPIAL GIRL: *This is my, this is my, this is my, this is my . . .*

She seems like she is going to open it. She bails. She starts over.

SUE: *What's that, thumpin' with the boom bang?*
                    What is at the bottom of this thang?
MARSUPIAL GIRL AND SUE: *What's that, thumpin' with the boom bang?*
                    What is at the bottom of this thang?
SUE: *If you hide it all away.*
                    Does it really go away?
MARSUPIAL GIRL: *What is at the bottom of this thang?*
                    This is my, this is my, this is my, this is my . . .

MARSUPIAL GIRL *opens her pouch. She almost reaches in, then bails. The pouch groans.*

SUE: Girl, you have to do it.
MARSUPIAL GIRL: Can't do it.
SUE: Girl, you're gonna blow!
MARSUPIAL GIRL: I KNOW!
SUE: We've got to get to the bottom. Put it all back.

The pouch groans.

MARSUPIAL GIRL: Too late.
SUE: No! Never too late.

The pouch groans a big groan.

MARSUPIAL GIRL: I CAN'T DO IT!
SUE: I'm going to help you. I'm going to count to three. Ready?
MARSUPIAL GIRL: No!
SUE: Ready or not—
MARSUPIAL GIRL: Wait!

The pouch is groaning louder, it's really quite frightening.

SUE: One. Two. Three.

SUE opens the pouch. MARSUPIAL GIRL *reaches inside and throws out a sound. Silence, then we see* MOTHER *and hear her voice.*

MOTHER:	*What am—*
MARSUPIAL GIRL:	*—I? Am I who they say I am?*
	What is this? Is this what they say it is?
	Do I have the eyes to see,
	To see to the bottom of this thing?
	Do I have the words to say
	All the things I've been thinking—hey.

Music stops. DR. POUCH *appears and speaks.*

DR. POUCH: Hey. You've had it from the beginning. And you will have it until the bitter, beautiful, dog-day end. Come on, Girl.

MARSUPIAL GIRL *throws out the sound of birdsong. Music starts again.*

DR. POUCH: Birds flying.

MARSUPIAL GIRL *throws out the sound of babies crying. She continues to throw out sounds that weave into the mix.*

MARSUPIAL GIRL:	*My oh my, babies my crying*
DR. POUCH:	*Kids on the bicycles blowing their horns*
MARSUPIAL GIRL:	*Bubble gum poppin*
DR. POUCH:	*Old ladies swappin gossip*
MARSUPIAL GIRL:	*Something strange and beautiful being born?*
DR. POUCH:	*What could it be?*
MARSUPIAL GIRL, SUE, AND MOTHER:	
	Something strange and beautiful being born?

DR. POUCH *creates the pouch crescendo, as* MARSUPIAL GIRL *lets the sounds pour out of her pouch.*

MARSUPIAL GIRL AND SUE: *What am I? Am I who they say I am?*
What is this? Is this what they say it is?
Do I have the eyes to see,
To see to the bottom of this thing?
Do I have the words to say
All the things I've been thinking—hey.

ALL: *What am I? Am I who they say I am?*
What is this? Is this what they say it is?
Do I have the eyes to see,
To see to the bottom of this thing?
Do I have the words to say
All the things I've been thinking—hey.
This is my, this is my, this is my, this is my
This is my, this is my, this is my, this is my
This is my, this is my, this is my, this is my
This is my, this is my, this is my, this is my
This is my, this is my, this is my, this is my
This is my, this is my, this is my, this is my
This is my, this is my, this is my, this is my—

TOWNSPERSON (*over the top of the chorus*): *What am I?*

TOWNSPERSON (*over the top of the chorus*): *What is this?*

TOWNSPERSON (*over the top of the chorus*): *What am I?*

MARSUPIAL GIRL (*over the top of the chorus*): *Do I have the eyes to see?*

TOWNSPERSON (*over the top of the chorus*): *What is this?*

MARSUPIAL GIRL (*over the top of the chorus*): *Do I have the words to say?*

TOWNSPERSON (*over the top of the chorus*): *What am I?*

CHORUS: *This is my, this is my, this is my, this is my—(abrupt silence)*

The song ends. MARSUPIAL GIRL *is surrounded by the people of her town. Her pouch is back to normal size.*

MARSUPIAL GIRL: Libby.

The crowd gasps, jumps back. LIBBY *and* PEARL *turn to* MARSUPIAL GIRL. *She speaks, simply and plainly.*

MARSUPIAL GIRL: This is my pouch. Here. *(She shows them her pouch.)* It opens at the top, like this. *(She opens it. The crowd gasps.)*

INA SHAW: Keep talking, everybody! Keep talking! If we all talk at once, she can't take our voices away!

Everyone starts talking, loudly.

MARSUPIAL GIRL: No! Listen! Please!
FRED LUDBERGER: EVERYBODY HUSH! You got eyes in your head, right? Zip yer lips and LOOK for once. *(They stop.)*
MARSUPIAL GIRL: Thanks. *(beat)* Miss Ina Shaw, this is my pouch. There's something I've been meaning to give back to you. From way back when. It's way down at the bottom. Just a second—Just a—

She pulls a rose out of her pouch: one of the roses we saw in the beginning of the play. INA *shies away.*

MARSUPIAL GIRL: No, please, take it. It belongs to you. It's been here. Right here. In my pouch. (INA *takes the rose. A gasp from the crowd.)* This is my pouch. *(A wince from the crowd but not the gasp like before.)* As you all know, I can keep things in it. Lots of things. Sometimes, too many things.

She reaches in and pulls out SUE'S *pocket knife. Another wince from the crowd.* SUE *walks over to* MARSUPIAL GIRL. MARSUPIAL GIRL *hands her the knife.*

MARSUPIAL GIRL: I'm really sorry, Sue.
SUE: I'm sorry too.

SUE *takes the knife. A murmur runs through the crowd. A few people inch their way forward, to get a closer look.* LACEY RUBBERTREE *leaves in a huff, making a dramatic cross through the crowd. A voice calls out from the crowd.*

TOWNSPERSON 1: Were you really born with that that that . . .

MARSUPIAL GIRL: This pouch? Yes.

TOWNSPERSON 2: Does it hurt?

MARSUPIAL GIRL: The pouch?

TOWNSPERSON 2: Yes.

MARSUPIAL GIRL: Sometimes. If I don't take care of it.

TOWNSPERSON 1: Is that fur on the outside?

MARSUPIAL GIRL: Yes. My mother and I wash it like you wash your hair.

Laughter from the crowd, but a laughter of understanding, not mockery. MOTHER *comes to* MARSUPIAL GIRL'S *side.*

TOWNSPERSON 3: Is it true that your pouch talks?

SUE: Oh. You mean this?

SUE *opens* MARSUPIAL GIRL'S *pouch.*

THE POUCH: Shoopialus Pop Top!

INA SHAW *faints. Someone in the crowd catches her.*

TOWNSPERSON 3: Yeah, that. What kind of hocus pocus is that?

MARSUPIAL GIRL: Well, I think it's just . . . a voice. Do you ever hear a voice inside you? And you can't make it be quiet no matter how hard you try? A voice that tells you everything's going to be OK?

DR. POUCH: OK.

MARSUPIAL GIRL: A voice that warns you when you're getting ready to do the wrong thing?

DR. POUCH: Yeah, don't do that.

TOWNSPERSON 3: Nope. Never.

MARSUPIAL GIRL: Really?

MRS. PENNYWHISTLE: Don't listen to her, girl. We all have that voice.

TOWNSPERSON 3: Not coming out into the open air like that!

MARSUPIAL GIRL: Well, that's how I'm different. I'm different. From you. Sue, tell your dad I'm sorry for taking his knife. Tell him I was scared back then. I'm not scared anymore.

MOTHER *comes to* MARSUPIAL GIRL'S *side.*

MOTHER: Tell him she'll never be scared again.

MARSUPIAL GIRL: No. I can't say I'll never be scared. I'm just . . . ready. *(She opens her pouch.)*

THE POUCH: READY

SUE *comes to* MARSUPIAL GIRL'S *side.*

MARSUPIAL GIRL: Ready?

SUE *puts a hand on her shoulder.*

SUE AND MOTHER: Ready.

DR. POUCH: She's ready!

DR. POUCH *changes the billboard to read:* SHE'S READY!

ALL: She's ready.

DR. POUCH *wails on the harmonica, then reprise of "Sugar Glider."*

DR. POUCH: *She's not a sugar glider.*

MARSUPIAL GIRL: *I'm not a wallaroo.*

DR. POUCH AND MARSUPIAL GIRL: *Or a Tasmanian devil*
                    Boodie boodie boodie boodie
                    Brush kangaroo

ALL:	*Agile wallaby*
	Pig-footed bandicoot
	Black-striped wallaby
	Marsupial mole
	Little northern native cat
	Feathertail glider
	Queensland koala
	Long-nosed potoroo
	Cinnamon antechinus
	Red-legged pademelon
	Brushtail possum
	Wombat
	Wallaroo
	And the
	Boodie boodie
	Boodie boodie
	Burrowing betons
	Wallaby bilby
	Brush kangaroo
DR. POUCH:	*She's not a sugar glider.*
MARSUPIAL GIRL:	*I'm not a wallaroo.*
ALL:	*Or a Tasmanian devil*
	She's a marsupial girl
	She's a marsupial girl
	She's a marsupial girl
	She's—

And all singing and music stops as MARSUPIAL GIRL *finishes the last line of the song. Her a cappella voice rings out plain and simple, loud and clear.*

MARSUPIAL GIRL: *A marsupial girl*

THE END

At the end of Act One, MARSUPIAL GIRL *is speaking her lines to* MOTHER, *who is wrapping her up:*

MARSUPIAL GIRL: I'll keep really quiet. I'll blend right in.

MOTHER *and* MARSUPIAL GIRL *embrace.*

MOTHER: My precious girl. My little Marsu—

MARSUPIAL GIRL *places her fingers on* MOTHER'S *lips.*

MARSUPIAL GIRL: I'll blend right in.

DR. POUCH *pulls out a megaphone from his coat or from his gadgets. He speaks into it.*

DR. POUCH: MARSUPIAL GIRL BLENDS RIGHT IN!

Perhaps the billboard cranks to read: MARSUPIAL GIRL BLENDS RIGHT IN!

MARSUPIAL GIRL: Shhhhhhhh! That's not how you blend in! You blend in by being very, very quiet, and never being noticed. Like this.

The act can then continue as written.

Madeline and the Gypsies

Barry Kornhauser

Based on the book by Ludwig Bemelmans

Music by Michael Koerner

Created in collaboration with Circus Juventas
Directed by Peter C. Brosius
Choreography by Joe Chvala

The world premiere of *Madeline and the Gypsies* opened on
September 19, 2008, at Children's Theatre Company, Minneapolis,
Minnesota.

CREATIVE TEAM
Music direction by Andrew Cooke
Scenic design by Joseph D. Dodd
Costume design by Helen Q. Huang
Lighting design by Nancy Shertler
Sound design by Kristian Derek Ball
Dramaturgy by Elissa Adams
Stage management by Erin Tatge
Assistant stage management by Angie Spencer
Assistant direction by Leah Adcock-Starr
Dance captain: Marvette Knight

ORIGINAL CAST

MISS CLAVEL AND GYPSY	Marvette Knight
MADELINE	Francesca Dawis
CLEMENTINE	Kacie Riddle
PEPITO	Jack Wyatt Jue
PEPITO'S SERVANT, SNAKE CHARMER, GYPSY, HUNTER	Gerald Drake
GYPSY MAMA	Autumn Ness
CLOWN	Dean Holt

STRONGMAN	Reed Sigmund
LION AND GYPSY	Xander Cackoski
ELEPHANT, GYPSY ROUSTABOUT, FROG PUPPETEER	Cody Braudt
GYPSY, SEAL PUPPETEER, FARMER'S WIFE, WOMAN IN PARIS, BIRD PUPPETEER	Kathryn Jorgenson
FARMER, HORSE, TRAIN CONDUCTOR, GENDARME, GYPSY, CABBIE	Max Wojtanowicz
FARMER'S DAUGHTER, GYPSY, RABBIT PUPPETEER, CIRCUS VENDOR	Lindsey Alexandra Hartley
FARMER'S BABY, GYPSY	Cole Bacig
FARMER'S SON, HORSE, JEWEL THIEF, BUTTERFLY PUPPETEER, GYPSY, MAN IN PARIS	Anders Nerheim
SCHOOLGIRLS	Kelly Adams, Megan Collins, Lexis Galba, Emilee Hassanzadeh, Megan Hernick, Grace Kibira, Simone Kolander, Elaine Patterson, Allison Van Siclen, Rebecca Wilton
CIRCUS JUVENTAS PERFORMERS	Rachel Butler, Travis Curren, Nick Dahlen, Anwar Hassouni, Mostapha Hassouni, Gemma Kirby, Zach Morgan, and Anna Ostroushko

ORCHESTRA

violin	Carolyn Boulay
woodwinds	Brian Grivna
bass	Bruce Heine
percussion	Jay Johnson
keyboard and conduction	Andrew Cooke

CAST OF CHARACTERS

MISS CLAVEL

MADELINE

CLEMENTINE

PEPITO

PEPITO'S SERVANT

SNAKE CHARMER

HUNTER

GYPSY MAMA

CLOWN

STRONGMAN

LION

PETRONELLA

STREET SWEEPER

ELEPHANT

FARMER'S WIFE

FARMER'S DAUGHTER

FARMER'S SON

FARMER'S BABY

FARMER

HORSE

TRAIN CONDUCTOR

GENDARME

CABBIE

CIRCUS VENDOR

JEWEL THIEF

MAN IN PARIS

WOMAN IN PARIS

ENSEMBLE INCLUDES GYPSIES,
CIRCUS PERFORMERS, ANIMAL
PUPPETEERS, AND SCHOOLGIRLS

The illustrations in Ludwig Bemelmans's *Madeline and the Gypsies* (1958) were as informative to this play as was his text, perhaps even more so. There are only a few written lines at best per page, but those charming pictures speak a thousand words. A close look at them will prove not only delightful but quite telling. To this end, the page numbers from the book that served as each scene's source material will be noted at the start of the scene. These numbers refer to the hardcover Viking edition of Bemelmans's book. As much as these illustrations informed the play's dialogue and action, they should also its design. As a visual tribute in the Children's Theatre Company production, the proscenium of the stage was somewhat inspired by the "picture frames" Bemelmans painted on the inside front and back covers of each of his Madeline books. It depicted the walls of an old house in Paris with shuttered windows, serving on one side as Madeline's boarding school and opposite as the Spanish Embassy.

Finally, much of the material that follows was invented during the rehearsal process of the premiere production and often in collaboration with the participating Circus Juventas. Future productions should feel free to take liberties with this business and create original clowning moments as well as particular circus acts that best suit the skills and inclinations of the performers.

ACT ONE

Scene 1

[Page 5] The play opens upon the exterior described above. [Illustrations of the Old House in Paris and the Spanish Embassy can be found in Madeline and the Bad Hat *(1956).] The base of the Eiffel Tower looms in the background. There is music. Out of the front door of the house eleven little* SCHOOLGIRLS *march in two straight lines, followed by* MISS CLAVEL. *[One schoolgirl, who shall be called* CLEMENTINE, *has a slight speech impediment. She says all her v's as f's. This will finally come in handy in Act Two, Scene 1.]*

Song: "Two Straight Lines"

MISS CLAVEL: *In an old house in Paris that is covered with vines*
                          (Vines magically grow on the old house.)
                          Live twelve little girls
SCHOOLGIRLS: *In two straight lines!*
CLEMENTINE: But—
MISS CLAVEL *(attempting to count the* SCHOOLGIRLS *as they "LA, LA, LA . . . " and dance about)*: 1-2-3-4-5-6-7-8-9-10-11—*11*?

One seems to be missing. MISS CLAVEL *tries to recount, a task made impossible by the* SCHOOLGIRLS' *singing and dancing.*

SCHOOLGIRLS: *In two straight lines we break our bread*
                          And brush our teeth
                          And go to bed.
CLEMENTINE: But—
SCHOOLGIRLS: *We smile at the good*

A GENDARME, *as seen in an illustration in the original* Madeline, *enters and tips his hat.*

SCHOOLGIRLS: *And frown at the bad*

A THIEF, *also pictured in the original story, snatches the purse of a pretty young* WOMAN *who is passing by. He is quickly apprehended by the* GENDARME. *But rather than escorting the perpetrator to jail, the* GENDARME *escorts the lovely victim offstage. Ah, Paris!*

CLEMENTINE: *(missing* MADELINE*) And sometimes we are fffery sad.
(She spots her friend in the second-story window of the house.)*
MISS CLAVEL: Regardless,
*We leave the house at half past nine
In rain—*
CLEMENTINE: But, Miss *Clafffel—*
MISS CLAVEL: *Or shine.*
SCHOOLGIRLS: *Yes, we leave the house at half past nine—*
CLEMENTINE *(trying one last time to let* MISS CLAVEL *know that*
MADELINE *is still in the house)*: But please look *abofffe!* It's—
MISS CLAVEL *(NOT singing)*: MADELINE!

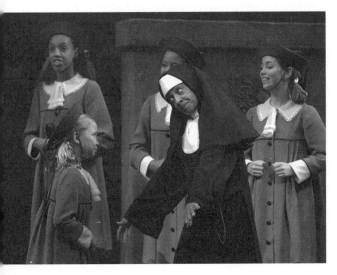

Clementine (Kacie Riddle) urges Miss Clavel (Marvette Knight) to wait for Madeline in the world premiere of *Madeline and the Gypsies*. Photograph by Rob Levine.

MADELINE (*in the window of the old house*): Why, bonjour, my dear
   good Miss Clavel.

MISS CLAVEL: Bonjour, yourself, young mademoiselle. It's half past
   nine. Time to leave the house.

MADELINE: Just as soon as I . . . feed my mouse.

She holds the creature from the original Madeline *book up by the tail. The
eleven* SCHOOLGIRLS *scream, and as* MADELINE *closes her shutters, run
across stage to the front of the Spanish Embassy. Opening his shutters,*
PEPITO *appears in a second-floor window. With a watering can, he sprays
the* SCHOOLGIRLS, *who scream again and run back to where they started,
as he closes his shutters. By now,* MADELINE *has arrived below, and once
again reveals her pet mouse. The* SCHOOLGIRLS *scream once more, this time
running center to* MISS CLAVEL, *where they huddle close to her.* PEPITO
enters the stage riding on the back of a very sore and unhappy SERVANT.

PEPITO: Giddyup and *ándale!* Quickly, before they get away!

SCHOOLGIRLS (*shaking off the water*): Oh, Pepito! You are such a
   bad hat.

PEPITO: I just wanted your attention, only that.

MISS CLAVEL (*to* SCHOOLGIRLS): The Spanish ambassador's son, but
   as bad as he is haughty.

MADELINE (*aside to her mouse*): I must admit, I kind of like that he's
   a little naughty.

MISS CLAVEL: I shall speak, young man, to your father.

SERVANT: Miss Clavel, I shouldn't bother.

PEPITO: You see, an ambassador doesn't have to pay rent, but he
   does have to go wherever he's sent.

SERVANT: Pepito's alone. His parents are away.

PEPITO: And I have no one with whom to play. So, please come, I
   invite you all to a wonderful gypsy carnival!

SCHOOLGIRLS: Please, Miss Clavel!

PEPITO: I'll pay everyone's admission price! And I'm sure they even
   welcome mice.

MADELINE: Please, Miss Clavel!

PEPITO: I'm begging you on my . . . *servant's* knees.

He snaps the SERVANT'S *bowtie and pokes him in the belly, dropping the man to his knees.*

SERVANT: Miss Clavel, *pretty* please! *(All beg.)*

MISS CLAVEL *(to the* SCHOOLGIRLS*)*: Very well. But you must be on your best behavior. I'll have two *straight* lines. Let's not see them waver.

All cheer. MADELINE *blows a whistle loudly. Startled,* MISS CLAVEL *jumps, as the girls salute and take formation in two straight lines.*

MADELINE *(resuming the song)*: Forward ho! *(The parade begins.)*

PEPITO: *Here we go!*

ALL: *In two straight lines!*

"LA, LA, LAs" end the song as all dance off. But underscoring continues into the next scene, becoming pure "gypsy circus."

Scene 2

[Pages 7–11 and 14–15] The carnival comes into view. The SCHOOLGIRLS *gasp at the sights.* GYPSIES *are everywhere. Among other enticements, they set up a "Wheel of Fortune" on one side of the stage, a fortune-telling booth opposite, and at center a small portable stage with a curtain that can be pulled open or closed by hand. Upstage of that is a large structure, perhaps with a sign reading* CIRCUS TONIGHT.

PEPITO: There it is, girls! The carnival at Notre Dame! Do you see the big circus tent?!

They nod excitedly.

MISS CLAVEL: Now, remember, act like proper little ladies and a respectable young gent—

But before she can finish, PEPITO *holds up a fistful of paper francs. With a squeal, the* SCHOOLGIRLS *all grab a share and, along with their young benefactor, noisily scatter every which way, each drawn by a different exciting attraction.*

MISS CLAVEL: Stop! Come back! Show that you are refined. Children! Children! Childr—. . . Oh, never mind.

There is too much commotion, so much to see and do. The GYPSIES, *who now man booths, concessions, and rides, will do double duty, later serving as circus performers. A* GYPSY MAMA, *inside the fortune-telling booth, reads a few* SCHOOLGIRLS' *futures with a crystal ball as hens peck at the ground in time to the music. Other* SCHOOLGIRLS *buy treats from gypsy vendors. A circus* STRONGMAN, *who has carried on a bull tub—that low, round decorative pedestal on which circus animals sit or stand—climbs atop it to get the crowd's attention, but not before being sure to grab a sausage from one of the vendors. The "side show" is about to begin. [The following acts were used in the premiere production. Most should be replicable but can be replaced or eliminated as need be.]*

STRONGMAN (*indicating the portable stage, perhaps barking into a megaphone*): Step right up! Step right up! Here is an act not to be missed—(*The* SCHOOLGIRLS *gather around, handing him francs.*)— the one and only "Human Pretzel," our contortionist!

He draws open the curtain, and music accompanies the brief performance. Applause as he closes the curtain and turns his audiences' attention to another act to one side of the stage, once again collecting francs, of course.

STRONGMAN: You won't believe your eyes! You'll do a double take when you see our real fakir charm his deadly snake.

The STRONGMAN *crosses down center to count his cash as the* SNAKE CHARMER'S *flute lures a snake from a basket. The* SCHOOLGIRLS *are terrified, but then they see that the snake is a fake attached to the hat of a*

CLOWN, *who climbs out of the basket. This* CLOWN *is a silent character. The* SNAKE CHARMER *angrily waves his flute at the* CLOWN, *who runs away, colliding into the* STRONGMAN, *sending all of the paper money he has collected flying into the air. The angry* STRONGMAN *threatens the* CLOWN, *who pulls the man's megaphone or hat over his face and runs. The* STRONGMAN *pursues him offstage, handing the megaphone to another* GYPSY, *who takes over the carnival barking.*

GYPSY BARKER: Wait! Here comes a wild horse, so move aside; make way for our daredevil's brave trick ride!

As the HORSE *crosses down center with its rider standing on its back,* PEPITO *stops it by pulling its tail, causing it to buck and whinny. Then the boy fires his slingshot at it, sending it running off, and its rider hanging on for dear life.* MISS CLAVEL *chases* PEPITO *offstage. The* GYPSY BARKER *draws everyone's attention elsewhere.*

GYPSY BARKER *(at the Wheel of Fortune)*: Come try your luck! Give the wheel a spin! *(displaying a kewpie doll with a striking resemblance to* MADELINE*)* See the fabulous prize you can win!

CLEMENTINE, *the girl with the slight speech impediment, pays a franc and spins the wheel. But she does not win.*

GYPSY BARKER: Too bad. You lose. Sorry, dear.

CLEMENTINE *walks away dejected.* MADELINE, *seeing this, offers her franc and spins the wheel. The pointer stops at the right place, lights flash, and bells ring. The* GYPSY *hands her the doll, as the* CLOWN, *still running from the* STRONGMAN, *reenters and hides behind the curtain of the portable carnival stage.*

GYPSY BARKER: Hey, we have a winner here!
MADELINE: Clemmy dear, a surprise! *(She offers* CLEMENTINE *the prize.)*
CLEMENTINE: You mean it's mine?

MADELINE: Please don't decline.

CLEMENTINE (*embracing the toy*): Oh, I'm *efffer* so grateful. I shall name her . . . Madeline!

GYPSY (*as the* STRONGMAN *reenters looking for the* CLOWN): Now a feat of prestidigitation to give you a rise—miraculous levitation, which always mystifies!

The CLOWN *appears and seems to be floating in air. His head and arms protruding from one side of the curtain, his legs the other. The* STRONGMAN *spots him but is amazed by this ability. The* CLOWN'S *head then appears above the center of the curtain, one of his legs rising on each side of the curtain, ending up upside down on each side of his head. All the* SCHOOLGIRLS *are amazed, but* PEPITO *quickly draws open the curtain, revealing the* CLOWN *holding two false legs on sticks. The* STRONGMAN *roars and resumes his chase. The* CLOWN *uses the false feet to step on each of the* STRONGMAN's *feet, but upon recovering, the* STRONGMAN *grabs those two fake legs and tosses them onto the ground. He starts after the* CLOWN *once again, but* PEPITO *comes to the rescue, tripping the* STRONGMAN *with one of the discarded feet. He falls on his face as the* CLOWN *salutes the boy and runs off.* MISS CLAVEL *reenters and resumes her pursuit of trouble-making* PEPITO. *The carnival action continues. A performing* SEAL *cuddles up to* CLEMENTINE, *who is now sitting on the portable stage playing with her doll. The* GYPSY (*barker*) *gestures for her to give a franc, which buys her a ball to balance on the* SEAL'S *snout. Other* SCHOOLGIRLS *gather to watch. Afterwards, the* SEAL *snuggles with* CLEMENTINE. PEPITO *runs back on stage, still pursued by* MISS CLAVEL. *But now exhausted, the nun plops down on the little stage. The* SEAL *claps and gives the unsuspecting nun a kiss.*

MISS CLAVEL: Ugh!

STRONGMAN (*having given up his pursuit of the* CLOWN): Come now, Sister, don't be such a priss.

MADELINE: That's what we called being "sealed" with a kiss!

The SEAL *is led off by a* GYPSY *juggling fish.*

GYPSY: All the way from exotic India, for the first time in France: The most colossal and stupendous of performing elephants!

The ELEPHANT *enters majestically to many "Oohs" and "Ahhs" and the tune of the "Can-Can," which the* SCHOOLGIRLS *dance along to. He plants one foot on the bull tub and trumpets gloriously.* MADELINE, *eager to share the excitement with her own pet, takes it out of her pocket.*

MADELINE: Look, dear mouse, have you ever seen such a sight?

As the mouse is inadvertently brandished in the ELEPHANT'S *face, the poor beast bellows loudly and begins to run amok. The* STRONGMAN *and other gypsies struggle to get the creature back under control.*

STRONGMAN: It seems your little friend is causing quite the fright.
MADELINE: How surprising to find someone as large as a house afraid of something so little as a mouse. *(to the* ELEPHANT *as she returns the mouse to her pocket)* Sorry. I've put her away, so you can relax.
STRONGMAN: Mice always give elephants panic attacks. So thank you; that's better. Now calm is restored.

An entering LION *roars, and the* SCHOOLGIRLS *scream.*

PEPITO *(jumping into the arms of the* STRONGMAN*)*: That was until your lion just roared.

The STRONGMAN *dumps him on the ground.*

MADELINE *(crossing to the* LION *and the cowering, whimpering* SCHOOLGIRLS*)*: Now, no need to cry in fear, girls—not one single "boo-hoo." Instead, you need only face that lion and say, "Pooh-pooh!"

The beast looks at the audience, shakes its head in disbelief, makes a funny growl, and heads offstage, with all the GYPSIES *following. The*

CLOWN *reenters with a little seat and a newspaper, the* France Soir. *He sits and begins to read the daily news. This is his greatest pleasure. Just then, the Ferris wheel lights up and begins to spin. It is magnificent! Now, the children all have a common destination.*

PEPITO: The Ferris wheel!

MADELINE: Is it for real?! (PEPITO *nods.*) Such a breathtaking height!

ALL SCHOOLGIRLS: Oh, dear Miss Clavel, might . . . ?

MISS CLAVEL: Two in each car, girls. Do you hear? Only two! . . . And if you don't mind, I may even join you.

All run off to board the ride. CLEMENTINE *stops and gives her doll to the* CLOWN *for safekeeping before joining the others. As the* CLOWN *clears the*

The Girls (Kacie Riddle, Kelly Adams, Megan Collins, Lexis Galba, Emilee Hassanzadeh, Megan Hernick, Grace Kibira, Simone Kolander, Elaine Patterson, Allison Van Siclen, and Rebecca Wilton), Pepito (Jack Wyatt Jue), Madeline (Francesca Dawis), and Miss Clavel (Marvette Knight) are excited to ride the Ferris wheel. Photograph by Rob Levine.

stage, all reenter in pairs carrying the lighted bar that would hold them securely in their seat. MADELINE *and* PEPITO *share one "car,"* MISS CLAVEL *and* CLEMENTINE *another. The* SCHOOLGIRLS *are paired up, also. The Ferris wheel ride is performed as a choreographed piece danced between two huge brightly lit spinning wheels.*

Song: "The Ferris Wheel"

ALL (SINGING):   *Down and up and up and down—*
                     We love the way the wheel goes aroun'!
SCHOOLGIRLS IN FIRST CAR: We could ride this for another hour!
SCHOOLGIRLS IN SECOND CAR: Hey, now we're as tall as the Eiffel Tower!
ALL (SINGING):   *High and low and low and high*
                     We touch the ground and then the sky!
SCHOOLGIRLS IN THIRD CAR: This view could only be called
    "bird's-eye."
SCHOOLGIRLS IN FOURTH CAR: Up here you can see right to Versailles!
ALL (SINGING):   *Round we go, bottom to top.*
                     We hope the wheel will never stop!

A sudden gust of wind blows loudly.

SCHOOLGIRLS IN FIFTH CAR: The wind's starting to really blow!

Another loud gust sounds, blowing MADELINE'S *and* PEPITO'S *hats to the ground.*

PEPITO: Oops, there go our hats!
MADELINE: Oh, no!
CLEMENTINE: It *is* getting *offfercast* and breezy.
MISS CLAVEL: And my stomach feels a little queasy.
ALL (*singing*):   *Oooooh!*
                     Spin and spin as the sky turns dark—

A bolt of lightning and a loud clap of thunder.

MISS CLAVEL: Children, it's time to disembark!

As the wheel lets each car off one by one, the storm intensifies, and MADELINE *and* PEPITO *plot.*

MISS CLAVEL: Quickly now, let's get out of the rain. Such a downpour could flood the Seine!
MADELINE: Oh, Pepito. I want just one more ride!
PEPITO: Easy! All we have to do is hide.

They disappear. Just then the CLOWN *returns and hands* CLEMENTINE *back her doll. She runs to join the others. Then the* CLOWN *notices* MADELINE'S *and* PEPITO'S *hats. He picks them up, putting* PEPITO'S *on over his own.*

MISS CLAVEL (*standing by a sign reading* "STATION DE TAXI"): Taxi!

Honking is heard amid the thunder. A wildly careening taxicab pulls up to a screeching halt. [In the CTC production, the cab was simply an actor holding a steering wheel. He wore goggles and a white scarf stiffened to stay stretched out behind him, creating the illusion of his constantly driving at high speed.]

MISS CLAVEL: Come along, children; form two lines! Hurry up, now. No monkeyshines!

She begins counting her charges as they enter the cab in pairs. As she does so, the CLOWN *brings* MADELINE'S *hat to* CLEMENTINE, *who puts it on her doll.*

MISS CLAVEL: 1-2-3-4-5-6-7-8—Come, come, one and all. Don't hesitate! 9-10-

The CLOWN *is swept into the cab by the last several* SCHOOLGIRLS *but is wearing* PEPITO'S *hat.* MISS CLAVEL *hastily counts him by mistake.*

MISS CLAVEL: Pepito. That's 11.

The CLOWN *exits opposite, unseen by* MISS CLAVEL, *who is looking for her last two* SCHOOLGIRLS.

MISS CLAVEL: Oh, but where in heaven—

CLEMENTINE, *carrying the doll wearing* MADELINE'S *hat, is the last to board.*

MISS CLAVEL: Ah, you're 12, sweet Clementine!
CLEMENTINE: And here is *lofffely* Madeline!

In too much of a hurry, MISS CLAVEL *is fooled by the hat and the doll's resemblance to* MADELINE, *and counts the toy.*

MISS CLAVEL: *Très bien,* she makes 13! *(getting in herself)* Oof, I feel
   like a sardine. *(another clap of thunder and bolt of lightning)* Safely
   home, driver, where it's comfy and dry; to Mrs. Murphy's hot
   soup, then sweet beddy-bye.

He steps on the gas and roars off, the girls screaming, the horn honking, the tires screeching all the way. The stage is empty of people. Slowly, MADELINE *and* PEPITO *peer up out of their car, stranded high atop the Ferris wheel. [In the CTC production, the two children were now in a Ferris wheel car high in the air, the lit safety bar they had carried in their hands now attached to their seat.]*

PEPITO: Success, Madeline. We have been forgotten.
MADELINE: Yes, but the weather has turned from bad to rotten.

Another clap of thunder, bolt of lightning. They hug each other involuntarily.

MADELINE: Help!
PEPITO: Silly girl, be like me. I know no fear. *(an even louder crash*

of thunder and brighter bolt of lightning. PEPITO *hugs* MADELINE.)
Help! Please save us!

MADELINE AND PEPITO: Someone get us off of here!!

PEPITO (*spotting the* CLOWN *with an umbrella and the* STRONGMAN, *who is eating his sausage in the shelter of the fortune-telling booth*): Hey! It's us! We're up here, Clown!

MADELINE: Strongman, can you help us down?

PEPITO: Rescue us, please,

MADELINE: before we freeze!

The underscored rescue begins, the attempt beginning with a sequence of the STRONGMAN *trying unsuccessfully to climb onto the* CLOWN *to reach the children. As this occurs:*

PEPITO: Madeline, I'm afraid we may be stuck.

MADELINE (*calling to would-be rescuers*): Excuse me, could you maybe call a fire truck?

The rescuers spot a rope.

PEPITO: Look, it's a rope!

MADELINE: At last, some hope!

PEPITO (*as the* CLOWN *prepares to toss the rope*): Heave ho!

MADELINE (*as the* CLOWN *lassos the* STRONGMAN *instead*): Oh, no.

PEPITO: So much for that great plan.

MADELINE: No, here goes the Strongman!

The STRONGMAN *manages to loop the rope onto the Ferris wheel car and begins to haul it toward the ground, the* CLOWN *securing the opposite end. But this attempt is spoiled when the* CLOWN *gets his foot caught in the rope and is pulled skyward with each tug. The car is released and floats skyward again. The children scream.*

PEPITO: Oh, this scheme is bound to fail. We had best both start to bail.

MADELINE (*to the would-be rescuers*): Please try again, for who knows
    when another thunder boom
PEPITO AND MADELINE: will spell our certain doom!

The STRONGMAN *tries again, and this time he succeeds. After lowering
the car, he lifts each child to safety as the* CLOWN *struggles to hold the car
at ground level. The* STRONGMAN *whisks the children to* GYPSY MAMA,
now waiting to wrap them in warm blankets. They exit as the CLOWN,
*still holding onto the car, is slowly lifted into the air. Blackout. [One
alternative approach is to eliminate all or some of the dialogue above and
have the* GYPSY MAMA *begin shouting orders in an Eastern European–
sounding rhyming gypsy gibberish to the* CLOWN *and* STRONGMAN. *A
slapstick sequence begins as they unsuccessfully attempt a rescue. As this
continues, the* GYPSY MAMA, *beneath an umbrella, rolls her eyes, and
walks over to the ride's control lever. Giving it a simple pull, the children's
car lowers to the ground. She escorts the two offstage, shaking her head.
The* CLOWN *and* STRONGMAN, *trying to climb one another, look out
toward the audience, collapse in a heap. Blackout.]*

Scene 3
[Pages 12–13] The SCHOOLGIRLS' *bedroom in the old house covered with
vines. The* SCHOOLGIRLS, *some still drying their hair with towels, are
already dressed for bed.* MISS CLAVEL *enters wheeling a cart. On it are
twelve bowls of hot soup.*

MISS CLAVEL: Ooh la la la la la la la la la. *Mes pauvre petites.* Hurry,
    now, get under your sheets. Be warm and cozy. You'll eat in bed.
    You'll stay well, if you're well fed. (*as she begins serving hot soup
    down the line of beds*) And happy if you plan ahead. That's what
    one does when one's well-bred. So, that carnival visit will be
    our last (*the* SCHOOLGIRLS *groan*) . . . without first checking the
    weather forecast.
SCHOOLGIRL: But we had such fun at the fairground!
MISS CLAVEL: Just be grateful you're home safe and sound. (*serv-
    ing* CLEMENTINE, *who still holds her doll*) In fact, dear children,

let us offer a humble grace, thankful for *everything*, not just this bouillabaisse.

CLEMENTINE (*troubled by the potential duration of the grace*): Gracing *effferything*? Oh, but that will take so long!

MISS CLAVEL (*continuing to serve the soup*): Come, girls, let us sing. I believe you know the song.

Song: "We Are Thankful"

SCHOOLGIRLS:	*We are thankful*
	For the food upon our table,
	And for lives so very stable
	That we find ourselves quite able
	To function
	Without pause or compunction.
MISS CLAVEL: Yes,	
	Bow your heads, girls, and genuflect
	'Cause we've been blessed to come to know what to expect.
SCHOOLGIRLS:	*Our daily lives are set—in every last respect—*
	So, in effect, our life's correct, indeed perfect.

The SCHOOLGIRLS *lift their spoons to their mouths but are stopped from tasting the welcomed soup by* MISS CLAVEL'S *continuation of the song.*

MISS CLAVEL:	*We take great comfort in routine.*
	In two straight lines.
SCHOOLGIRLS:	*No in-between? (They are given a nonverbal reply by their teacher.)*
	We are thankful
	For such consistency
	And regularity.
CLEMENTINE:	*Oh, Miss Clafel, I hafffe to pee!*
MISS CLAVEL:	*Potty time,*
	Dear Clementine, is ten of three.

(CLEMENTINE *cringes and squirms.) Just—*
Cross your legs, girls, and genuflect
'Cause we've been blessed to come to know what
    to expect.
SCHOOLGIRLS: *Our daily lives are set—in every last respect—*
So, in effect, our life's correct, indeed perfect.

They once again eagerly raise their spoons to their mouths, but, alas, are once again stopped by MISS CLAVEL.

MISS CLAVEL: Ahem!
SCHOOLGIRL *(each taking one)*: AMEN! AMEN! AMEN! AMEN!
    AMEN! AMEN! AMEN! AMEN! AMEN! AMEN! AMEN!

After that eleventh "Amen," they all briefly glance at the last empty bed, then quickly slurp down their soup before stopped yet again.

MISS CLAVEL *(collecting the spoons and empty bowls as she wheels the
    cart from bed to bed)*: Girls, the reason that you are so secure
    is that we follow standard procedure. Now, you were just one
    "Amen" shy.
CLEMENTINE: But—
MISS CLAVEL: This time I will not ask you why.
HALF OF THE SCHOOLGIRLS: But Miss—
MISS CLAVEL: Now, you've finished supper, and it is half past nine.
OTHER HALF: But Miss Clavel—
MISS CLAVEL: Not now, children!
ALL SCHOOLGIRLS: But you've lost—
MISS CLAVEL *(reaching the last bed, finding it empty)*: Madeline!?!
    (musical button)

Scene 4
[Pages 16–17] The CLOWN *and* STRONGMAN *ride in on a gypsy wagon
pulled by two* HORSES. *The* STRONGMAN *is happily enjoying noshing on a
sausage. Opposite,* GYPSY MAMA *enters with the two children, wrapped
in blankets.*

GYPSY MAMA: *Madeline.* That is such a lovely name. But you're soaked to the bone, dear; what a shame. *(and to the boy)* And you are?

PEPITO *(arrogantly)*: Pepito, of course! From Spain.

GYPSY MAMA: Well, come in, both of you, from the rain.

MADELINE: It's so good to get out of the cold and wet.

GYPSY MAMA *(handing the children circus garb taken from the wagon)*: Change into these, my dears; you'll feel better yet.

PEPITO: And who will be my servant to help me dress?

The CLOWN *and* STRONGMAN, *standing side by side, look at each other. The* STRONGMAN *points to the* CLOWN *with his sausage. The* CLOWN *slaps it away. He does so again. The* CLOWN *slaps it away harder, and it swings and hits him on the head. Both the* CLOWN *and* STRONGMAN *point to the production's orchestra conductor in the pit. He just shrugs.*

GYPSY MAMA *(to* PEPITO*)*: We're a bit shorthanded right now, I confess. You'll have to try, on your own, to do your best.

PEPITO: Hmpf! This is no way to treat a special guest.

He haughtily grabs the garb. MADELINE *takes hers, and they step behind the wagon to change, as the* CLOWN *and* STRONGMAN *hang a makeshift drape.*

STRONGMAN: I say we sell that boy—no matter the pay! Heck, let's just give the spoiled monster away!

GYPSY MAMA: Hush! Don't you see? It was destiny that sent the torrential downpour that brought these children to my door. I'll hold them close forevermore; they're just what I've been praying for!

STRONGMAN: Oh, but why such a fuss? After all, you've got us!

He gives GYPSY MAMA *a crushing bear hug and kiss on the cheek.* CLOWN *intercedes trying to get into it and inadvertently separates* GYPSY MAMA *from the huddle, which leaves* STRONGMAN *kissing him.*

GYPSY MAMA: Ah, I rest my case!

The STRONGMAN *realizes what he is doing, and pulls away in disgust.*
The CLOWN *gives him a quick kiss back. The* STRONGMAN *repels him.*

GYPSY MAMA: . . . And detect a trace of jealousy.

STRONGMAN: Jealous? Not me! Of who? Children without the brain
to come inside out of the rain?

GYPSY MAMA: Hush! They're coming! Another word and I will see red!

MADELINE *appears from behind the drape in her gypsy circus garb.* GYPSY
MAMA *fusses over her. Then* PEPITO *enters from around the wagon. His
new clothing is put on a bit funny. But* GYPSY MAMA *likes it even more.
She squeals with joy, pinches his cheeks, and plants a big, loud raspberry
of a kiss on the side of his face.*

GYPSY MAMA: My, you look . . . perfect! Now quickly, climb into bed,
while I fix you something . . . soothing.

MADELINE (*as* PEPITO *joins her on the wagon*): Like Miss Clavel's
chamomile tea!?

GYPSY MAMA: Oh, even better than that, my dear Madeline, so you
will see. My homemade "potent" medicine.

*Helping the children settle into bed, handing them each a steaming glass
of brew.*

GYPSY MAMA: So drink it down before I tuck you in.

PEPITO: It tastes funny.

The CLOWN *takes* PEPITO'S *cup, takes a drink, gargles with it, indicates to
self that it is fine, spits it back into the cup, and returns it to* PEPITO, *who,
unaware of what just happened, finishes it.*

MADELINE (*to* GYPSY MAMA, *questioning the efficacy and safety of the
brew*): Are you sure—?

GYPSY MAMA (*interrupting*): Your Gypsy Mama knows every cure. A
fine prescription, believe you me! So finish it all—*Tout de suite!*

The children swallow it down quickly. The CLOWN *and* STRONGMAN *take their empty glasses, as* GYPSY MAMA *boards the wagon, places two pillows on her lap, and signals the children to rest their heads.*

GYPSY MAMA: Now, dear children, close your eyes. All will be better when you arise.

Song: "Gypsy Lullaby"

Gently, as the STRONGMAN *silently mocks her singing but soon gets caught up in the music.*

GYPSY MAMA: *Aaaaaaaaaaah.*
                     Dream gypsy dreams of new horizons,
                     New adventures, new surprisin's.
                     Ah, sleep is near. May dreams take you far
                     As we now follow the evening star.
STRONGMAN (*loudly, up-tempo, out of control, jarring the children awake, as the* CLOWN *tries to quiet him*):
                     Bonsoir! Goodnight! Bonsoir!
                     Bonsoir! Goodnight! Bonsoir!
                     As we now follow the evening star!
                     Bonsoir! Goodnight! Bon—!
GYPSY MAMA (*spoken angrily*): Shhhah!!! You woke them! That's all wrong!
STRONGMAN: Can I help it? Even my voice is strong!

The CLOWN *steadies the nervous* HORSES *and* GYPSY MAMA *tries again, the children putting their heads back down.*

GYPSY MAMA (*gently, as the* STRONGMAN *struggles to contain his growing exuberance*):   *Aaaaaaaaaaaah.*
                     We fold the big wheel and the tent,
                     Pack our wagon, and never lament.
                     A hasty "adieu" as away we steal,

For the life mobile is the life ideal.
Let others cry "they came and went!"
We travel to our heart's content!

STRONGMAN (*again up-tempo and loud, once again waking the children*):
Somnolent! Go to sleep! Somnolent!
Somnolent! Go to sleep! Somnolent!
We travel to our heart's content!
Som—

GYPSY MAMA (*furious*): Noooo!!!!!! How many times must I tell you to be quiet?!

STRONGMAN: Forgive me, Mama. I really did try it. But I'm a gypsy. Music makes my head spin!

GYPSY MAMA: Nonsense! All you need is some self-discipline.

Now the CLOWN *starts the "Aaaaaaaah" incantation to resume the music. He and* GYPSY MAMA *sit the* STRONGMAN *down on the wagon and place pillows on his lap. The* STRONGMAN *is taken aback, clearly uncomfortable when the children rest their heads once again on those pillows, but soon picks up the chant begun by the* CLOWN.

STRONGMAN (*gently, as slowly but surely* GYPSY MAMA *now finds herself fighting to maintain control as the music stirs her gypsy blood*):
—Aaaaaaaaah.
It doesn't take a crystal ball
To know the sleep in which you fall
Will fill with dreams that will enthrall
With visions of new ports of call,
For gypsies do not like to stay.
They only come . . . to go away.

GYPSY MAMA (*unable to contain herself any longer, way up-tempo and really loud, startling not only the children, who cover their ears, but the* HORSES, *who bolt away*):
Allez! Go 'way! Allez!
Allez! Go 'way! Allez!
They only come to go away!
Allez! Go 'way! Allez!

STRONGMAN (*with* CLOWN *gesturing the same*): SHHHHHHHH!

GYPSY MAMA: Who? Me? (CLOWN *and* STRONGMAN *nod.*) Oopsy!
She tucks the children back in, and all finish the song as the lullaby it was
meant to be. As they sing, the CLOWN *gestures for the* STRONGMAN *to pull*
the wagon in place of the missing horses. To encourage him, the CLOWN,
sitting in the driver's seat, attaches the sausage to a fishing pole and
dangles it just out of reach in front of the now-hitched STRONGMAN, *who*
pursues it offstage, wagon in tow.

GYPSY MAMA *and* STRONGMAN: *Sweet gypsy dreams to both of you.*
When you awake, you'll see the world anew.

Scene 5
[No source pages for this scene.] The "cab" pulls up to the now deserted
fairgrounds at Notre Dame, with MISS CLAVEL *and Pepito's* SERVANT *as*
the CABBIE'S *passengers. A street sweeper is sweeping away the last bit of*
debris of the gypsy circus as the cab comes to a screeching halt.

CABBIE: You see, the grounds are completely clear.
MISS CLAVEL: It's as if those gypsies were never here! (*to* SERVANT)
    And the children are with them?
SERVANT: Of that I'm quite sure.
MISS CLAVEL: Then you must help me find them, *señor, por favor!*
SERVANT: But how, Sister? Gypsies never stay long in one place.
MISS CLAVEL: Dear heaven, will I never again see Madeline's
    sweet face?
SERVANT: If I know Señor Pepito, he'll soon cause so much *strife—*
CABBIE: the gypsies will want he and Madeline out of their . . . *leaf?*
MISS CLAVEL AND SERVANT: *Life!*
CABBIE: Right!
SERVANT: Señor, pardon. But here we all speak in rhyme, you know.
    Yet I notice—if you do not mind me saying so—that this is some-
    thing you've really managed to bungle.
CABBIE: Alas, rhymes always get stuck on the tip of my . . . *tonguel?*

MISS CLAVEL (*to* SERVANT): Never mind that. You must get word to Pepito's parents.

SERVANT: I don't deny it. . . . But not just yet, Sister.

CABBIE: Why not?

SERVANT (*with a big sigh*): I'm quite enjoying the peace and quiet.

Smiling broadly, he exits with a passerby, the pretty young WOMAN *rescued by the* GENDARME *in the first scene. This is, after all, Paris.*

MISS CLAVEL: Despite the seeming cheer in that remark, for me there has never been a day so dark.

She and the CABBIE *drive off into the night,* MISS CLAVEL *taking one long, last look behind her.*

Scene 6

[Pages 18–19] Dawn of a bright new day. Music change. On the opposite side of the stage, the gypsy wagon rolls onto the grounds of the Chateau de Fontainebleau. The GYPSY MAMA *is gently waking the still-sleeping children. The* CLOWN *plays the tambourine in accompaniment to the music, while also reading his newspaper [as is pictured on pages 18–19 in* Madeline and the Gypsies—*although it is hard to see because he is sitting right on the fold]. Leading the other* GYPSIES, *the* STRONGMAN *enters carrying a barbell. All begin setting up camp.*

Song: "The World Belongs to You"
(interspersed throughout this and the next scene)

GYPSY MAMA: *A bright new day—the sky is blue.*
The storm is gone; the world is new.
This is the castle of Fountainebleau.
Children, come out, enjoy the view!

Much gypsy activity begins as MADELINE *and* PEPITO *climb out of the wagon to marvel at their surroundings and the excitement of the gypsy hustle and bustle. The* CLOWN, *sitting on the bull tub, begins shucking oysters in a bucket.* PEPITO *slaps the* STRONGMAN'S *belly, and the man drops the barbell onto his head, which sends him sprawling to the ground.*

PEPITO: I've never seen a castle quite so splendid

MADELINE: Or so grand!

GYPSY MAMA: See, children. That's what comes from joining up with a gypsy band.

MADELINE (*along with the* STRONGMAN *under his breath*): Joining up?

GYPSY MAMA: Castles for playgrounds. And that's just the start. As for being a gypsy—well, here's the best part:

ALL GYPSIES (*except the* CLOWN *and* STRONGMAN):

>*We tell fortunes; we sing and dance,*
>*With hearts as big as our elephants.*
>*Give us the gypsy life, carefree and wild—*
>*The perfect life for every child!*
>*No rules to follow, no bother or fuss.*
>*We're gypsies! The world belongs to us!*
>*Hey!*

STRONGMAN (*to the* CLOWN): But is it "perfect" for me? No, indeed! Now I've got two more hungry mouths to feed. Argh! We've traveled too far; can't send them back. (*But he gets an idea.*) . . . Unless we ship them off . . . in a gunnysack!

The GYPSY MAMA *attacks the* CLOWN—*not the* STRONGMAN—*for this, knocking off his hat and berating him with gypsy gibberish curses.*

STRONGMAN (*to* CLOWN): Now look what you've done. You've gotten Gypsy Mama mad! She wouldn't be angry if you weren't so bad!

He knocks the CLOWN *off of the bull tub and dumps the bucket of oysters into the* CLOWN'S *hat.*

MADELINE: Pepito, I'm not sure if this should scare us, but we might be a *million* miles from Paris.

GYPSY MAMA: There, there now, A little something for you to ponder: Gypsies are home wherever they wander. So no matter where we dwell, the world is your oyster—

STRONGMAN: Break open its shell!

The CLOWN *dumps the hatful of oysters on the* STRONGMAN'S *head. Joyful chaos! All the* GYPSIES *dance as the* STRONGMAN *takes off in pursuit of the* CLOWN, *who eventually ducks into the orchestra pit, grabs the conductor's baton, and begins conducting the band. This fools the* STRONGMAN *for a moment only. The* CLOWN *escapes his clutches with a distraction— tossing the show's score into the air.*

GYPSIES (ending the dance break and the song): HEY! (lights out)

Scene 7

[No source pages for this scene.] On one side of the stage, lights up on MISS CLAVEL, *who sits on* MADELINE'S *empty bed, sadly stroking the covers. She is holding a candle. Slowly throughout the scene, the other* SCHOOLGIRLS *join her, each carrying a candle, and* CLEMENTINE, *her doll, as well.*

MISS CLAVEL: Our precious pearls lost! They could be a million miles from here! Oh, we may never see the two of them again, I fear!

SCHOOLGIRL: Dear Miss Clavel, I must exclaim: "*Au contraire.*" They will both return *tout de suite;* so don't despair.

MISS CLAVEL: And just what makes you so certain, *ma chéri?*

SCHOOLGIRL: Easy. They forgot a change of underwear!

There is a funny little musical "plink." MISS CLAVEL *touches her scalp beneath her wimple.*

MISS CLAVEL (*aside*): I think I just got another gray hair. Perhaps, dear children, we had best say a prayer. (*All the* SCHOOLGIRLS *are onstage by now, and all here bow their heads.*)

Dear Lord,
The gypsy life is carefree and wild,
The worst sort of life for any child.

SCHOOLGIRLS (*joining* MISS CLAVEL):
so if it's not too inopportune,
Please bring our strays home to us soon.
We miss the way Madeline smiled, plus
The way that Pepito oft' beguiled us.

MISS CLAVEL: *so may these simple words suffice,*
And float straight up to paradise.

ALL: *Amen.*

All blow out their candles. Lights and music change. Opposite now is
PEPITO'S SERVANT *on the telephone inside the Spanish Embassy. He is*
dressed quite inappropriately. On the phone table is a vase with a rose, a
small tablecloth, and a fruit bowl.

SERVANT: I'm afraid you can't speak with him just now, Señor
Ambassador. . . . Uh, he's with Madeline. You know, that little
girl who lives next door . . . . Oh, no. Pepito's been no trouble.
No trouble at all. . . . Of course. If there is any problem, I'll be
sure to call. . . . No! No need to hurry back. After all, you are duty
bound. Everything is fine, Señor (*He hangs up the phone.*) . . . so
long as Pepito's not around.
A servant is quite reconciled
To a life seldom carefree or wild.

He wraps the tablecloth around his waist and puts the fruit bowl on
his head.

SERVANT: *But say "adios" to one bad hat,*
And everything changes (He snaps his fingers.)
Just like that!

He snaps his fingers again. And again. And is soon doing a flamenco
dance of joy, ending with the rose in his teeth.

SERVANT: OLE!
                Hey-hey.

Exit. Lights out.

Scene 8

*[Pages 24–27] Gypsy music. The full stage now becomes Carcassonne,
the newest camp. The large upstage structure holds multiple clotheslines,
where, among other items,* MADELINE *and* PEPITO'S *regular clothing
hangs, as does one of the umbrellas used at the rained-out carnival. A
tightrope is being rigged up center. [The tightrope in the CTC production
was only about four feet off the ground and had mats placed beneath it as
part of the setup.] To one side of the stage, bubbles float out of a bathtub,
where the* SEAL *and fully dressed* CLOWN *bathe. Opposite the* ELEPHANT
*and a trainer wash clothing in a washtub. Circus paraphernalia is scat-
tered about, as everyone is preparing for the day ahead.* MADELINE
approaches the ELEPHANT.

MADELINE: Hello, dear sir; I hope you won't mind some advice,
    which has to do with your attitude toward . . . mice.

She reveals her pet. The ELEPHANT *panics, squirting the audience with its
trunk, the orchestra conductor wisely holding an umbrella over his head.
But* MADELINE *tenderly persists.*

MADELINE: You're too big a fellow and a mouse way too small for
    you to have cause to be frightened at all. In fact, you'd be wise to
    befriend this cute creature. He can scratch every itch your trunk
    can't quite reach, sir.

She carefully places the mouse on the ELEPHANT. *It scurries about, and
the* ELEPHANT *lets loose with a great happy sigh before giving* MADELINE
a big kiss with its trunk. The GYPSY MAMA *observes this and is pleased.*

GYPSY MAMA: Madeline and Pepito, I think at last you are ready to
    join our gypsy cast. *(to* STRONGMAN *and* CLOWN*)* They've traveled

with us to many a town, so what do you say, Strongman and Clown, time we teach these children our circus skills?

STRONGMAN (*as the* CLOWN *begins climbing out of the tub*): Us?! Why, the very thought gives me the chills! I won't! (*and pushing the* CLOWN *back into the bath)* Him neither! We don't know how!

GYPSY MAMA (*threatening, as the* CLOWN *climbs out once again)*: You'll teach them, boys. And you'll teach them *now!*

She pushes the innocent CLOWN *back into the tub.*

PEPITO (*crossing to the tightrope)*: Don't be chicken, Madeline, (*The chickens squawk.)* come try the high wire!

MADELINE: I'm not frightened!

Climbing onto the platform at one end of the wire, she attempts—with underscoring—to step onto the tightrope but keeps withdrawing.

MADELINE: OK. So I'm a liar. (PEPITO *laughs. The* STRONGMAN *lifts him out of the way.)* Oh, Gypsy Mama, I can't do this. I can't do it at all!

GYPSY MAMA (*to* STRONGMAN *and* CLOWN): Help her!

STRONGMAN (*to* MADELINE, *referring to the* CLOWN, *who is attempting to mount the platform opposite the girl's)*: Don't worry! He's here to catch you if you fall!

He slaps the CLOWN, *who proceeds to fall. The* GYPSY MAMA *gives the* STRONGMAN *the evil eye, as the* CLOWN *reattempts the climb. The "Eye" does the trick; the* STRONGMAN *backs down. Again, to* MADELINE.

STRONGMAN: But you won't! Here's the secret: Just don't look down! Instead, look straight into the face of the Clown.

He gestures to the CLOWN, *just mounting the platform, but it is not his face staring at* MADELINE, *rather his backside. The* CLOWN *quickly turns around.* GYPSY MAMA *gestures for acrobat* PETRONELLA *to climb onto the wire in front of* MADELINE. *The woman does so, handing the girl the umbrella from the clothesline. [The acrobat may need to use a balance pole that can be handed to her by another gypsy once she is in position.]*

GYPSY MAMA (*to* MADELINE): And, Madeline, this is Petronella. Hold on to her—and that umbrella. She'll help to guide your every stride. Her expertise is certified.

The CLOWN *reveals a certificate.*

STRONGMAN: Now, to help you keep your balance, stick your arm out straight. (MADELINE *does so, extending the arm holding the umbrella.*) And it's on your back leg that you will want to put your weight. Step.

Following PETRONELLA, *her free hand on the woman's shoulder,* MADELINE *hesitantly takes that step.*

STRONGMAN: Pause. (*She pauses.*) Again.

With the CLOWN *beckoning encouragement,* MADELINE *continues on her way, stepping then pausing between each forward motion, following the footsteps of* PETRONELLA. *And she does so with growing assurance.*

STRONGMAN: Now you're getting it!
MADELINE: Soon I'll be an acrobat!
GYPSY MAMA: Yes, you will, my dear!
PEPITO: Phooey, I was hoping she'd go splat!

GYPSY MAMA *shoos him off.* MADELINE, *having made it across the length of the wire, collapses into the waiting arms of the* CLOWN, *who lowers her down to the* STRONGMAN. *She is not just relieved but ecstatic.*

STRONGMAN: Congratulations, dear Madeline!
CLOWN: Hurray!

MADELINE (*to the* CLOWN): You can talk?!

STRONGMAN: Oh, he talks fine. Our stubborn Clown here just refuses to rhyme.

The CLOWN *nods his head very seriously.*

GYPSY MAMA: Why do you think we gypsies invented mime?

CLOWN *builds a mime wall, walks into it, and falls down.* GYPSY MAMA *continues, to all the* GYPSIES.

GYPSY MAMA: So, what do you think now of our Madeline!?

PEPITO (*returning*): What's the big deal? So she showed a little spine by walking 'cross some old clothesline. Why, anyone can do it. Rather obviously, there is nothing at all to it. Let me demonstrate with an encore.

He has mounted a platform, and now, with underscoring, takes a step onto the tightrope. But he withdraws. Again. And again. He is clearly terrified. Finally, he grabs the rope with both hands and attempts to shimmy across but flips upside down, hanging on for dear life, though he is only a few feet off the ground.

PEPITO: Help! Give me a hand! (*The* CLOWN *begins to clap.*) Please! *Au secours!* I'm going to die! Oh cruel world, good-bye!

The STRONGMAN, *rolling his eyes, "rescues" the boy, taking him in his arms.*

STRONGMAN: There, safe and sound. (*He drops him on a mat.*) Back on the ground.

PEPITO (*genuinely relieved, shaking hands with the* STRONGMAN): Thank you, thank you so very much.

He offers his hand to the CLOWN, *who is now sitting on the tightrope, but pulls it away at the last moment, causing the* CLOWN *to fall off.*

MADELINE (*hugging the* CLOWN *and* STRONGMAN): You both must have the magic touch!

GYPSY MAMA: But let us see if you truly have the gypsy knack. It is time for both of you to try to ride bareback!

There is a huge collective gasp as all of the other GYPSIES *enter to see this, and two wild* HORSES *gallop noisily onto the stage. Music as the* CLOWN *and* STRONGMAN *comically try to gain control of the raucous creatures. Both are finally subdued, and* MADELINE *is the first to find the courage to approach one. She bravely pets the* HORSE *and wins its favor. The* CLOWN *kneels at the* HORSE'S *side, and* MADELINE *climbs on his back to mount the steed. Then* PEPITO *tries. He approaches the second* HORSE *with even more trepidation than he showed on the tightrope. Hands shaking, he too pets the* HORSE, *is accepted, and is lifted onto its back by the* STRONGMAN. *Music.* MADELINE *confidently stands on her horse as it trots about.* PEPITO *does the same but gets cocky and gives his steed a good slap. Frenetic music as it bolts offstage,* PEPITO *screaming and once again finding himself hanging on for dear life. Happy music returns as* MADELINE *continues her ride, only to be interrupted by the frenetic music as* PEPITO *runs across stage screaming, his* HORSE *in pursuit. Happy music; more* MADELINE *riding, once again interrupted by the frenetic music as Pepito's* HORSE *returns, dragging the screaming boy behind and off one last time. Happy music, and* MADELINE'S *ride concludes. She is lifted off of her* HORSE *to much cheering.* PEPITO *returns on foot, exhausted and rather shaken.*

GYPSY MAMA: Now, it's time to rehearse our circus show! So come on, Gypsies—Ready, set, go!

The stage fills with performing gypsies, ready to do juggling, trapeze stunts, feats of strength, unicycling, tumbling, balancing on balls, riding the German wheel, plate spinning, tightrope walking on that clothesline, etc. The gypsy band attempts to play circus music, perhaps accompanied by the SEAL *honking horns. But the musicians—*SEAL *included—are not at all together. Neither are the performers. The scene becomes an elaborate* *unintended clown show with pratfalls, collisions, disasters, and disputes. Balls and performers might even fly into the audience. This goes on for some time, until* MADELINE *blows her whistle. Everything stops cold.*

MADELINE: As much as I truly admire how gypsy business does transpire, I'd be remiss if I didn't tell something I learned from Miss Clavel.

GYPSIES (*after a beat*): Well?

MADELINE: Now and again it might be kind of keen to have just a bit of structure and routine.

Madeline (Francesca Dawis) performs in the circus. Photograph by Rob Levine.

GYPSIES: Huh?

MADELINE: Please allow me to show you what I presume can certainly happen if you'll all resume with one straight line here, and one straight line there.

The GYPSIES just stare at her as if she were crazy. MADELINE appeals to GYPSY MAMA.

GYPSY MAMA: You heard her, gypsies! Go right to where you will all need to be.

MADELINE: And just you wait and see!

The GYPSIES reluctantly form two straight lines.

GYPSY MAMA *(to herself)*: One straight line? Maybe two? Sounds crazy. But what the who!

PEPITO steals the conductor's baton and leads the drummer in beating a crisp march. The GYPSIES, driven by the beat, peel off of their lines in a most orderly fashion and sharply take their places. Once all are set, they collectively perform a little bow to the accompaniment of a brief percussive fanfare. MADELINE addresses GYPSY MAMA. With another whistle, MADELINE signals PEPITO to strike up the whole band. Glorious circus music ensues including the SEAL'S horns, and the rehearsal runs like clockwork, everyone successfully practicing their acts. Each different act rehearsal begins with a whistle from MADELINE and ends with the performer(s) bowing, not to the theatre audience, but to MADELINE and the STRONG-MAN, who stands with her now, practicing his ringmaster duties. He has also taken on one further responsibility. Throughout the rehearsal, the CLOWN tries to sit and read his newspaper, but he only seems to get in the way of the performance. For example, in the CTC production, as a fire juggler took his bow, one of his flaming pins caught the newspaper on fire; when the German wheel rolled off, CLOWN was sitting on it, reading. Grabbing hold, he lost his newspaper, only to scoop it up when the wheel rolled back on stage with him in it. The STRONGMAN stays busy, not only supervising along with MADELINE, *but trying to keep the* CLOWN *out of the way—with mixed success. After the final rehearsal concludes.*

MADELINE: There, Gypsy Mama, now do you see what I mean?

Struck speechless, GYPSY MAMA *just nods in amazement.*

STRONGMAN *(finally impressed by* MADELINE*)*: Madeline, one day
    you'll be a great gypsy queen!
GYPSY MAMA *(to* CLOWN *and* STRONGMAN*)*: Indeed, she has taught
    us as much as we have taught her. *(to* MADELINE*)* Madeline, I've
    come to think of you as my own true daughter.
STRONGMAN: Sounds like a cause for celebration, don't you think?
GYPSY MAMA: Yes, I do. Gypsies, let's break out the food and drink!
ALL GYPSIES *(with a cheer, springing into dance)*:
                You're gypsies now! There is no debate.
                So children, time for us to celebrate!
                Give us the gypsy life, carefree and wild—
                The perfect life for every child!
GYPSY MAMA: *No matter where we briefly dwell,*
STRONGMAN: *Chartres Cathedral or Mont Saint-Michel;*
ALL GYPSIES: *From Marly-le-Roi to Fountainebleau,*
                The world, dear children, belongs to you!
                All the world belongs to—
                (catching their breaths) "heh heh heh heh"—You!

End song. Lights out.

INTERMISSION

ACT TWO

Scene 1
[Pages 28–30] Music welcomes us to a split scene. Time has passed. On

one side of the stage, in dim light, MISS CLAVEL *and the* SCHOOLGIRLS *sit on and around* MADELINE'S *empty bed,* MISS CLAVEL *absently but briskly brushing a* SCHOOLGIRL'S *hair—oblivious to the pain she is caus-ing.* CLEMENTINE *has her doll, of course. Opposite, there is full light on a new location—Honfleur. Fully illuminated,* MADELINE *and* PEPITO *are settled in on one side of the stage, she sitting on a trunk, he practicing his "tightrope" walking on the lip of the stage apron. As the introductory music ends.*

MADELINE: I wonder if back home they miss us.

PEPITO: Go on! I truly doubt that they even know we're gone.

MADELINE: Still, Pepito, I think it's about time we sent dear Miss Clavel a line.

PEPITO: Well, then, I'm just the fellow to help you write such a note 'cause I've had plenty of practice. Here, let me quote: "Please excuse Pepito from school yesterday. He was very sick." Then I simply sign my mama's name. It always did the trick!

MADELINE: Oh, Pepito, how exceedingly smart.

PEPITO *(joining her)*: We'll need a pen and postcard for a start.

MADELINE *produces both, and they settle down to write, a bull tub their desk.*

Song: "Dear Miss Clavel"

MADELINE (WRITING): *"Dear Miss Clavel"*

Lights dim on MADELINE *and* PEPITO *and rise up on* MISS CLAVEL *and eleven little* SCHOOLGIRLS.

SCHOOLGIRL 1: *Poor Miss Clavel.*

Lights dim on the dorm room and rise on Honfleur.

MADELINE (TO PEPITO): *How do you spell "Clavel"?*

PEPITO: *Q-L-V-V-V-L*

MADELINE *gives him a funny look, as the lights dim on Honfleur and rise on the dorm room.*

SCHOOLGIRL 2 *(to the others, referring to* MISS CLAVEL*)*:
                She's not looking very well.
SCHOOLGIRL 3:   *Something's wrong, I can tell. (lights shift from*
                dorm to Honfleur)
MADELINE *(writing)*: *"We're in a circus." (to* PEPITO*)*
                How do you spell "circus"?
PEPITO: *S-I-R-K-I-S-S*

MADELINE *looks at him again; lights shift.*

SCHOOLGIRL 4 *(sarcastically to* SCHOOLGIRL 3*)*:
                "Something's wrong"?! How ever did you guess?
                She is the shadow of her former self—
SCHOOLGIRL 5, CLEMENTINE: *(and here's where her speech impediment*
                helps a rhyme)
                —From worrying, because instead of twelfffe—
SCHOOLGIRL 6:   *That's twelve*
SCHOOLGIRL 7:   *—There are only eleven!*
SCHOOLGIRL 8 *(her hair being absently but brusquely brushed)*:
                Ouch! Miss Clavel, you're pulling!
MISS CLAVEL *(now aware of what she's doing)*:
                Oh, good heaven!
                I'm so sorry, dear . . . Poor Madeline! (lights shift)
MADELINE (WRITING): *"Pepito and I are feeling fine."*
                (to PEPITO*) How do you spell "are"?*
PEPITO: *R*

MADELINE *looks at him yet again; lights shift.*

MISS CLAVEL: *We never even said "au revoir."*
MADELINE *(lights switch; writing)*: *"Much love from Pepito and Madeline."*
                (to PEPITO*) How do you spell "much"?*

PEPITO:	*M–U–S–H*
MADELINE:	*S–H?*
PEPITO	*Sure!*
	Spelling, for me, is second nature.

MADELINE *looks one last time; lights shift.*

SCHOOLGIRL 9:	*Dear Miss Clavel, you're looking pale.*
MISS CLAVEL:	*Not one phone call, not even mail. (lights shift)*

MADELINE *(addressing the postcard)*: "To Miss Clavel in Paris, France."

PEPITO *(looking it over)*: Why, a first-class correspondence! I believe I will sign it, too. *(He does so.)* But how shall it be sent? *(an idea)* We have a horse! Pony Express?

MADELINE *(taking back the postcard)*: Better yet, by rodent!

She hands it to her pet mouse, who scurries up and around the proscenium arch, bringing the card across stage to the old house covered with vines, with lights and "music" [some xylophone] following the creature all along the way. In the CTC production, the mouse disappeared into a hole at the top of one side of the proscenium arch, its scurrying silhouette illuminated in a little round window at the top center of the proscenium, and then it reappeared in a hole at the top of the opposite side of the arch, climbing down to the SCHOOLGIRLS. *A surprised* SCHOOLGIRL 10 *retrieves the postcard from the mouse.* MADELINE *and* PEPITO *exit as lights rise on* MISS CLAVEL *and the* SCHOOLGIRLS.

SCHOOLGIRL 10: Miss Clavel, a most "special" of deliveries!

MISS CLAVEL *(crossing center, lights following)*: Did you thank the mailman, dear?

SCHOOLGIRL 10: Do we have some cheese?

MISS CLAVEL *(with the postcard)*: At last, word from Madeline!

SCHOOLGIRL 10: And Pepito, who did cosign.

MISS CLAVEL *(upon reading it)*: *Thank heaven, they're safe!*
But all is not well!

SCHOOLGIRL 11: *What is it? What's wrong, dear Miss Clavel?*

ALL SCHOOLGIRLS: *We must know, we must know! What is it, pray tell?*

MISS CLAVEL: *Poor Madeline . . . has forgotten how to spell!*

(*end song*) I must find her, but that will be hard.

SCHOOLGIRLS: Wait! Check the postmark on the card!

MISS CLAVEL: My clever girls! It reads "Honfleur"! That's where Madeline is, for sure. Unless, of course, they should move on. Oh, we must get there before they're gone! This is a desperate situation. We must quickly head to the train station!

A SCHOOLGIRL: "Quickly." How?

MISS CLAVEL *looks at the* SCHOOLGIRLS. *They look at each other. They all know the answer.*

ALL (*calling*): Taxi, now!

A honking and then the loud screeching of tires is heard. The "cab" appears as MISS CLAVEL *and the* SCHOOLGIRLS *make their way to the street.*

CABBIE: Where to, Sister?

MISS CLAVEL (*as the* SCHOOLGIRLS *begin boarding hurriedly*): To the next train!

CABBIE: What's the rush?

MISS CLAVEL: No time to explain. Here, this postcard exposes the whole terrible caper. Once you drop us off, please take it straight to the newspaper. But right now we need to catch the *Express!*

CABBIE: I'll have you there in two minutes or . . . *fewer?*

SCHOOLGIRLS (*after a collective groan, and as they pile into the cab*): Less!

CABBIE: Right!

MISS CLAVEL: No, left! Then straight. We mustn't be a moment late! So, step on it!

HALF THE SCHOOLGIRLS: Fast!

ALL SCHOOLGIRLS: And faster!

MISS CLAVEL: Off to prevent a disaster!

Just as the cab noisily zooms off, that pretty WOMAN *walks by, and a* GENTLEMAN *opposite. The breeze caused by the exiting taxi blows up her skirt and drops the man's pants. They share a brief moment of embarrassment but then walk off arm and arm. We'll always have Paris! An airplane crosses the sky of the now empty stage, pulling a banner reading:* "MADELINE AND PEPITO, TOO, WHERE ARE THE BOTH OF YOU?" *Leaflets drop from the sky onto the audience. They have a photo of the two missing children and the words:*

> MISSING:
> The two children pictured on this handbill.
> Last seen in circus between Normandy and Deauville.
> Where are they now? Do you know?
> Phone Miss Clavel with info.

Scene 2

[Pages 31–33] The wagon and several trunks are brought on stage by a few GYPSIES. GYPSY MAMA *begins consulting her crystal ball, mumbling to herself in gypsy gibberish. The others leave to retrieve more items as the bespectacled* CLOWN *unfolds his chair and begins reading the latest edition of* France Soir. *An article catches his eye, and it clearly upsets him. He looks at the audience, back at the paper, and then turns the paper around to show the audience a huge headline:* "MISS CLAVEL AND SCHOOLGIRLS TAKE HONFLEUR TRAIN TO FIND MADELINE AND BOY FROM SPAIN!" *He tries to get the* GYPSY MAMA'S *attention. But clearly she does not wish to be disturbed.*

GYPSY MAMA: Not now, I'm getting important information. *(The* CLOWN *gestures a "but . . .")* I said, Hush, clown! You'll spoil my concentration. *(He frantically waves the newspaper.)* There's nothing there I need to see. *(referring to her crystal ball)* All is revealed right here. So leave me be! *(He sticks the paper in her face, but she rips it out of his hands and crumples it.)* Get out of here now, or risk a good gypsy curse! Trust me, my friend, few things could be worse.

She throws the crumpled paper into the orchestra pit and returns to her crystal. The CLOWN *is not ready to give up. Straddling the pit, he tries unsuccessfully to reach for his paper. The orchestra conductor tries to help. He picks up the newspaper and holds it out for the* CLOWN. *But reaching for it, the* CLOWN *loses his balance and falls into the pit, disappearing with a cacophony of smashing instruments. A violin flies out.* GYPSY MAMA *is horrified.*

GYPSY MAMA: Clown? Oh, no. He fell in the pit!

She races to the edge of the pit, drops to her knees, and tries to see the CLOWN. *Then to the conductor.*

GYPSY MAMA: You! This is all your fault, you twit! What's wrong with you? My life you are ruining!

She hits him repeatedly with the violin, destroying it in the process. Then, contritely, returning the ruined instrument to him.

GYPSY MAMA: Here, I think this needs a good tuning.

She lifts herself up, covers her eyes, and begins to weep profusely at the sad fate of her dear CLOWN. *Meanwhile, the* CLOWN *reappears on stage— climbing out of one of the trunks. He has the newspaper with him and gets an idea. Straightening it out, he carefully places it under* GYPSY MAMA'S *crystal ball. Then he notices her crying. That makes him sad, very sad. He starts to cry loudly, too. She crosses to comfort him. They cry in each other's arms for a moment, but then she realizes who it is. Furious, she throws him right back into the pit! There is another cacophony of crashing instruments, but this time the* CLOWN *climbs quickly out and joins* GYPSY MAMA *at her crystal ball.*

GYPSY MAMA: I don't like this. I don't like it at all—what I see in my magic crystal ball. "MISS CLAVEL AND SCHOOLGIRLS TAKE HONFLEUR TRAIN TO FIND MADELINE AND BOY FROM

SPAIN!" Oh, we may lose the children now! (*The* CLOWN *nods sadly.*) No! This I will never allow! (*The* CLOWN *surreptitiously extracts the newspaper.*) Why, the children have only just begun to enjoy our gypsy kinds of fun. And were I to lose them now, *I'd* feel terribly cheated as I've only just begun to feel, at long last . . . needed.

The CLOWN *comes up with another idea. He runs over to the wagon, smears a little axle grease on his fingers, and makes a moustache on his face. He shows his disguise to the desolate heartbroken* GYPSY MAMA.

GYPSY MAMA: No. Go!

He doesn't give up. He runs back and smears a little more on his bald head, and shows GYPSY MAMA.

GYPSY MAMA: You, shoo!

But CLOWN *persists. Heading back to the wagon one last time, he attempts a more brazen disguise, tying a kerchief around his head and a blanket around his waist as a skirt. Once again, he attempts to get his meaning across to* GYPSY MAMA, *who is at her wit's end.*

GYPSY MAMA: I said "skedaddle—or it's the paddle!" Wait! I've got it! (*smearing an axle grease moustache on her own face*) No one would recognize them if we in some way could disguise them! (*The* CLOWN *looks at the audience.*) Yes, we must hide the children at all cost!
STRONGMAN (*entering*): Bad news!
GYPSY MAMA: We know!
STRONGMAN: You know my lion's lost!?
GYPSY MAMA: Oh. (*then realizing the seriousness of the situation*) Oh, no! We have a show tomorrow tonight!
STRONGMAN: He just wandered off and is nowhere in sight!
Whatever was I thinking to have left the beast on his own?
GYPSY MAMA (*struck by an idea*): Never mind that now . . .

CLOWN *pats the* STRONGMAN *on the back. The* STRONGMAN *notices the* CLOWN *is in drag and reacts. In way of explanation, the* CLOWN *shows his colleague the newspaper headline.*

GYPSY MAMA: . . . Perhaps we can kill two birds with one stone. *(calling)* Madeline! Pepito! *(to* CLOWN *and* STRONGMAN*)* Good thing I like to sew.

The children enter along with some of the GYPSIES *continuing to carry in items, which are about to be usefully transformed.*

GYPSY MAMA *(to* MADELINE *and* PEPITO*)*: Dear ones, how would you like to try on a lovely costume of a lion?
MADELINE: Well, no one's ever asked me that before.
PEPITO: It'd be the strangest suit I ever wore.
GYPSY MAMA: Just think of it—a perfect fit, and you can play the beast in tomorrow's show! So come along. Hurry, children. Here we go!

The CLOWN *heads upstage to where the other* GYPSIES *have congregated and begins gathering fabrics and materials that he will use to fashion a makeshift lion costume. Meanwhile,* GYPSY MAMA *begins measuring the children as she sings.*

Song: "Trekniks Ur Relentskee Ingst Shpleen"

GYPSY MAMA: *Children, on my heart is weighing*
                        A very wise old gypsy saying
                        Whispered from Mindanao to Moscow
                        Which may be worth conveying now.
STRONGMAN, MADELINE, AND PEPITO:
                        "Trekniks ur relentskee ingst shpleen."
                        Do tell us please, what does that mean?
GYPSY MAMA: *"Whoever travels the road with me,*
                        is, in my heart, true family."

The children are escorted upstage to where the CLOWN *has set up shop.*
Two GYPSIES *raise a blanket as a screen, and the children are placed*
behind it. Now the CLOWN *really gets down to work. As the song contin-*
ues, bits of fabric and other materials fly into the air as he busily cuts and
shapes his design.

GYPSY MAMA AND STRONGMAN: *And family is everything*
　　　　　　　　　　　　To it we must hold fast and cling,
　　　　　　　　　　　　And do so at whatever cost
　　　　　　　　　　　　For without family we are lost.

CLOWN *sticks his head out above the screen and joins in.*

GYPSY MAMA:　　　　　*Aaaaaaaaaaaaaaaaaaaaaaaaaaaah!*

Back to work for the CLOWN, *and* GYPSY MAMA *and* STRONGMAN *continue*
what has become a dance.

STRONGMAN:　　　　　*A mother needs her children to raise.*
　　　　　　　　　　　They bring sweet music to all her days,
GYPSY MAMA:　　　　　*For a family without its young*
　　　　　　　　　　　is like a song that's left unsung.
STRONGMAN:　　　　　*"Trekniks ur relentskee ingst shpleen."*
　　　　　　　　　　　"Trekniks ur relentskee ingst shpleen."
GYPSY MAMA:　　　　　*"Whoever travels the road with me,*
　　　　　　　　　　　is, in my heart, true family."

The screen is lowered, and the new "lion" is revealed. The costume
very much resembles that of the actual beast, although with a clearly patch-
work, homemade, improvised quality. MADELINE *has heads;* PEPITO, *tails.*

GYPSY MAMA:　　　　　*That's why with needle and some string*
　　　　　　　　　　　I sew the children in this thing.
STRONGMAN:　　　　　*No one will know what is inside*
　　　　　　　　　　　the tough old lion's leathery hide.

GYPSY MAMA: *They will have seemed to disappear,*
STRONGMAN: *At least until the coast is clear.*
GYPSY MAMA: *I'll keep the children on the road*
                And teach them both our gypsy code:
:   *(dancing, including* FAUX LION*)*
                "Eshteem ur relentskee schpott—tite!"
                "Eshteem ur relentskee schpott—tite!"
GYPSY MAMA: *"Honor your family with all your might!"*
                Yes, that's every gypsy's true birthright!
CLOWN *(operatically):* *Aaaaaaaaaaaaaaaaaaaaaaaaaaaaaah—*

GYPSY MAMA *crosses to the* CLOWN *and threatens him for stealing her part.*

CLOWN: —Aaah!
GYPSY MAMA *(sewing the last stitches on the costume herself):*
                Now that the deed is nearly done
                All I can say—in more ways than one—
                is, yes, my dear young kith and kin,
                (and ending to the close of the tune of a popular
                music standard)
                "I'VE GOT YOU UNDER MY SKIN."
ALL: *Aaaaaaaaaaaaaaaaaaaaaaaaaaaaaah!*
                Hey!

End song. GYPSY MAMA *admires her handiwork and bites off the last thread, as the* GYPSIES *exit.*

GYPSY MAMA: There you go; finished. All intact. And now to teach you the lion's act. *(whispering to her compatriots)* For a time that's where they must remain.
MADELINE: What was that?
STRONGMAN: Just that it's time to TRAIN!

Scene 3

[No source pages for this scene. However, MISS CLAVEL *and the* SCHOOL-
GIRLS *are seen on the train on page 42.]* On the Paris–Honfleur Express.
*[In the CTC production the train was depicted by an engineer carrying a
light and wearing a smokestack hat that spewed real smoke. The* SCHOOL-
GIRLS *and* MISS CLAVEL *tap-danced behind him, to a musical theme
marking the "train's" journey. All tapped in place during the lines below.]*

MISS CLAVEL *(to the impatient* SCHOOLGIRLS*)*: The TRAIN is on time!
Just sit back and relax. Listen to the clickety-clacks on the tracks.
CLEMENTINE *(doll in hand)*: But when will we *ariffffe,* dear Miss
Clafffel? When?!
MISS CLAVEL: We'll arrive, Clementine, just as soon as we can.
CLEMENTINE: Miss Clavel, you've *trafffled* by train before?
MISS CLAVEL: That's safe to assume.
CLEMENTINE: Then can you tell me—Do they *hafffe* a ladies' room?
It's ten of three, and I *hafffe* to—
MISS CLAVEL *(making it clear she understands)*: Oui, oui! Some things
are better left unsaid.
OTHER SCHOOLGIRLS *(looking "out the windows")*: Miss Clavel!
Tunnel dead ahead!

The "train" exits into a blackout.

Scene 4

[Pages 34–35] Lights up on the circus space. Enter the FAUX LION.

MADELINE: Well, Pepito, now comes the big test. Let's be sure to do
our very best. After all, you know, a lion has got his pride.
PEPITO: Yes, but how did I get stuck playing his backside?
MADELINE: I would say for that role no one is better qualified.

The STRONGMAN *enters carrying and placing a bull tub. He is followed by
the* CLOWN *pushing a small gypsified baby carriage containing a variety of
paraphernalia.*

STRONGMAN *(referring to himself)*: OK, this lion tamer's ready. It's time your tricks were tried. Let us start with something very simple—Sit!

Underscoring begins. The FAUX LION *heads for the bull tub, and the two children sit upon it, legs crossed, quite casually.*

STRONGMAN: Ay! That pose will *prove* you're a counterfeit! On your haunches, as if to announce: "I am a lion, ready to pounce!" *(The children do so, frightening the* CLOWN.*)* Bravo! Now, I want to see you shake.

The CLOWN *offers his hand. Either* MADELINE *sticks her arm out through the lion mouth to take it, or both children frenetically jiggle their bodies. The* STRONGMAN *shakes his head and addresses the* CLOWN.

STRONGMAN: This plan may have been a big mistake. *(to the children.)* No! "Shake" means that you give me your paw, to show the crowd each razor-sharp claw!

*The lion's paw—*MADELINE'S *foot—slaps the* CLOWN'S *proffered hand.*

STRONGMAN: Now that's what I call a "Shake"! Quite authentic; not at all fake. I think we're ready for a more advanced trick. *(He takes a bullwhip from his belt.)* When I crack my whip, you both jump double-quick.

He cracks the whip. MADELINE *and* PEPITO *"hopscotch" to the* STRONGMAN.

STRONGMAN: What was that?! Hopscotch?!?! *(The* CLOWN *nods and tries it himself.)* Hopscotch is strictly forbidden! You're an eight-hundred-pound lion, not a kitten! If you want to correctly pull off this stunt, then you must crouch and spring like you're on the hunt! *(The* FAUX LION *does so. The* CLOWN *leaps back in fear.)* That's more like it! Now you'll jump through a hoop. *(The* CLOWN *holds* up a very small hoop taken from the baby carriage.) Clown, hold it steady. Lion—alley-oop! (He cracks the whip. The FAUX LION doesn't move.)

PEPITO: I'm afraid . . .

STRONGMAN: Afraid?

MADELINE: . . . that we won't make it.

STRONGMAN: You won't know unless you undertake it.

The CLOWN retrieves a stuffed toy animal from the baby carriage and demonstrates by throwing it through the hoop.

MADELINE (to PEPITO): Wish me luck.

The STRONGMAN cracks his whip. She goes for it but turns away at the last minute, whiplashing PEPITO, whose backside ends up in the hoop.

PEPITO: Hey, I'm stuck!

The CLOWN tries to extricate the tail end of the FAUX LION from the hoop, pushing against PEPITO'S backside with his foot. In doing so, he gets his own leg and head stuck in the hoop instead.

STRONGMAN (to the awkwardly entangled CLOWN): Let's try one in extra-large.

The CLOWN, still stuck in the little hoop, clumsily crosses to the carriage and clumsily returns with a big hoop, which he clumsily holds up for the FAUX LION. The STRONGMAN again addresses the children.

STRONGMAN: On your mark. Get set. And—Charge! (He cracks his whip. The FAUX LION expertly leaps through the hoop.) Magnificent! Encore! But this time even higher! (The CLOWN raises the hoop. A crack of the whip, and the FAUX LION jumps through it again.) Good! Tomorrow again—but with two rings of fire!

The FAUX LION'S *jaw drops. The* STRONGMAN *takes advantage by putting his head in its mouth before continuing. As he speaks the* CLOWN *struggles hopelessly to free himself from the little hoop, only to become even more uncomfortably knotted up inside.*

STRONGMAN: A circus lion earns his bread by filling crowds with fear
    and dread. That's right, by scaring people half to death. Let's
    hear you roar.
MADELINE and PEPITO: Roar.
STRONGMAN: No! Take a deep breath!
MADELINE and PEPITO: *ROARRR!*

Terrified, the CLOWN *jumps into the* STRONGMAN'S *arms.*

STRONGMAN: Ah now, that one was far more ambitious! Remember,
    our real lion is quite vicious.

Satisfied, the STRONGMAN *drops the* CLOWN *and pats the* FAUX LION *on the head.*

STRONGMAN: A job well done; you've earned some tea.

He exits with the bull tub, signaling the CLOWN *to serve. Still in his hoop, the* CLOWN *returns to the carriage, pours a cup of tea, and brings it back to* MADELINE. *But she can't drink it through the mask of the lion. The* CLOWN *has a solution. Reaching into an inside coat pocket, he pulls out a long straw and serves the tea through that.*

PEPITO: Hey, out there. What about me?!

The CLOWN *rolls the carriage to the back of the lion. But now seems absolutely stumped on how to serve it, as there is no mouth at this end. But then he gets an idea. He raises the tail, produces a second straw, shakes it like a thermometer, and is about to insert it, when* GYPSY MAMA *enters.*

GYPSY MAMA: Hey! Put that down, you silly Clown! *(then to the children)* And after a lion's fed, he's tucked safely into bed.

Exits, perhaps singing or humming a bit of "The Gypsy Lullaby." The CLOWN *exits opposite, pushing the baby carriage, hobbling off still fixed in the hoop.*

Scene 5

[Pages 36–39 and 42] Dawn, the following morning. The gypsy wagon rolls in with the FAUX LION *sleeping soundly on it. A rooster crows, waking the children, who climb off, frightening the gypsy camp chickens.*

MADELINE: Shh! It's much too early for such a fuss.

PEPITO: Hey, you chickens, it's only us!

MADELINE: Madeline

PEPITO: and Pepito

MADELINE AND PEPITO: traveling incognito. *(The chickens calm down.)*

PEPITO: Now it's time that this Spaniard—

MADELINE: —and this "Frencher"—

PEPITO: had a lion's share

MADELINE: of bold adventure!

As the two sing and cross away from camp, a large bed of sunflowers appears upstage.

Song: "Au Revoir"

MADELINE: *"Au revoir" to two straight lines!*

MADELINE AND PEPITO: *"Au revoir" to half past nines.*

PEPITO: *To sitting up straight in your chair!*

MADELINE: *And one hundred strokes*
                    When brushing your hair.

MADELINE AND PEPITO: *Give us the gypsy life, carefree and wild,*
                            The perfect life for every child.

No rules to follow, no bother or fuss.
We're gypsies! The world belongs to us!
Hey!

Two crossing farmers, carrying haystacks on their backs, come face to face with the FAUX LION.

FARMER AND WIFE: A lion!!

They hide inside their stacks and run off, shouting.

FARMER : Sound the alarm!
WIFE: And call a gendarme!

They are gone! The FAUX LION *shrugs and continues the walk. After a quiet moment.*

MADELINE: The flowers smell sweet.
PEPITO *(a bit wistfully)*: Yes . . . like my mama's perfume.
MADELINE *(even a little more wistfully)*: The colors remind me of my old school bedroom. . . . But I guess I won't see that soon again.
PEPITO: We'll more likely end up in some lion's den. For we're gypsies now and inside this suit—perhaps forever.
MADELINE: And so we never get to go back home?
PEPITO: No, Madeline . . .
MADELINE AND PEPITO: Never.

The song concludes but now in a very melancholy tone, as the children realize that they are missing the things they are singing about.

MADELINE *(as a* SCHOOLGIRL *appears in the flowers holding a soup tureen)*:   "Au revoir" to Mrs. Murphy's yummy cuisine.
PEPITO *(as another* SCHOOLGIRL *appears in the flowers holding a miniature guillotine)*: "Au revoir" to my tiny toy guillotine.
            (The guillotine blade drops.)

MADELINE (*as yet another* SCHOOLGIRL *appears in the flowers with a dollhouse*):   To playing with the dollhouse Papa sent
PEPITO (*as his* SERVANT *appears in the flowers, with a tormented look*):
And causing the servants eternal torment.
MADELINE AND PEPITO: *Give us the gypsy life. We know every trick*
. . . Except maybe how not to feel homesick.
We miss those who love us, now from afar.
I wish I could see them . . . just to say "au revoir."
If only to say "au revoir."

(End song.)

MADELINE (*with a deep sigh*): I feel as if Miss Clavel today must be a gazillion miles away.

The FAUX LION *slowly, forlornly, exits. Immediately afterwards, the Paris–Honfleur "train" whizzes across stage, accompanied by its musical theme.*

Scene 6
[Pages 44–52] Circus time! The FAUX LION *enters with* GYPSY MAMA.

GYPSY MAMA: I must tell you, I was worried sick. But you made it back just in the nick. You go on soon in the center ring. Until then, let's wait off in the wing.

She escorts the FAUX LION *off. Just then the real* LION *wanders in; ominous underscoring marking its entrance. The beast is quickly spotted by the entering* CLOWN *and* STRONGMAN, *who carries in and places the bull tub.*

STRONGMAN: Oh, there you are, children. Where have you been? Never mind. The show is about to begin. The others are out looking for you, quite worried you'd miss your big debut.

He signals the LION *to jump onto the bull tub. But the creature does not respond. So the* STRONGMAN *begins to drag the recalcitrant beast in place.*

STRONGMAN: This is no time to grow shy. We're in a rush.

Tugging the now angry LION *onto the bull tub, it roars in his face.*

LION: ROARRRRRR!!!!!

STRONGMAN *(responding to its very bad breath)*: The roar's not bad, but, hey, you forgot to brush. *(then to the* CLOWN*)* Now, Clown, I must change into my ringmaster's clothes. Run them through their paces; keep them on their toes.

He hands the CLOWN *his bullwhip and exits. The* CLOWN *has no idea what to do with it. Meanwhile the* LION *starts to wander off again. The* CLOWN *drops the whip and grabs the beast by the tail.*

LION: ROARRRRRRRRRRRRR!!!!

The CLOWN *stops for a moment but then dismisses his thoughts. He finally succeeds in pulling the* LION *back onto the bull tub, and offers his hand in the "Shake" gesture. The* LION *powerfully swats it away. Not to be deterred, the* CLOWN *picks up the whip and taps the* LION'S *front paw with it. The beast swats him even harder, sending him sprawling. That does it. The* CLOWN *decides it is time for a face-to-face talk. He pries opens the* LION'S *jaws and sticks his head into its mouth. There is a long, low growl. The* CLOWN *withdraws his head, closes the jaws, and looks toward the audience. He then cleans his glasses, reopens the jaw, and inserts his head once more. Another scarier growl. The* CLOWN *removes his head again, just before the* LION *snaps shut his mouth. The* CLOWN *looks again toward the audience and back at the* LION*, provoking an even bigger roar.*

LION: ROARRRRRRRRRRRRRRRRRRRRRRRRR!!!!

As the underscoring concludes, the CLOWN *runs off screaming, pursued by the real* LION*. As they exit, the* STRONGMAN *returns in his ringmaster garb to "open the gates" and let in the crowd—*MISS CLAVEL *and the* SCHOOL-GIRLS*, who take front-row center seats.*

STRONGMAN (*as the crowd gets seated*): Please take a seat and with it our thanks . . . (*aside*) . . . while we, in turn, gladly take your francs.

Everyone settled, there is a musical fanfare, and the STRONGMAN, *in his role as ringmaster, introduces the show.*

STRONGMAN: Ladies and gentlemen and children of all sizes,
Welcome to a Gypsy Circus full of surprises!

Still screaming, the CLOWN *comes running back through and off opposite pursued by the roaring* LION; *this underscored.*

STRONGMAN: Not exactly what I had in mind.

Another quick cross by screaming CLOWN *and roaring* LION. *The* STRONGMAN *just looks, but then gets back to business.*

STRONGMAN: No, you'll find this circus one of a kind!

Circus music! The show begins, the gypsy performers in beautiful costumes. The acts earlier seen in rehearsal are now performed in their full glory, each eliciting lots of "oohs" and "aahs" from the crowd. During the first.

MISS CLAVEL: This seems so dangerous, so frightening.
ALL SCHOOLGIRLS: Yes, and ever so *excitening!*

More performances and applause. Then a third cross by CLOWN *and* LION.

A SCHOOLGIRL: But where are Madeline and Pepito?

MISS CLAVEL: They must be here; keep watching the show.

Still more performance, applause, then.

ANOTHER SCHOOLGIRL (*pointing*): Is that him?!

ANOTHER SCHOOLGIRL (*pointing*): Is that her?!

MISS CLAVEL: I can't tell. I'm not sure. (*then realizing that the indicated performers are not the missing two.*) No.

ALL SCHOOLGIRLS (*disappointed*): Ohhhhh. (*But a quick virtuoso stunt distracts them.*) Oooooooh!

CLEMENTINE: *Brafffo!*

The acts continue as the CLOWN appears peeking out of the orchestra pit. It seems the coast is clear. But then the LION slowly rises up behind him. Once the CLOWN notices, he leaps out of the pit, screaming, and runs back onto the stage, the LION ducking back out of sight. Taking refuge at the proscenium arch, the CLOWN catches his breath. But then out of a small window in what was the door to the House in Paris covered in vines, the LION'S paw emerges and swats the CLOWN on the ground.

MISS CLAVEL (*distraught, not seeing any of the above, still only looking out for the missing children*): They're no place at all! Not here nor there!

STRONGMAN: Silence!

MISS CLAVEL *runs off to one side. The circus music comes to a close. The grand finale is about to take place.*

STRONGMAN: Now for the lion act; you had all best beware! He's a bona fide man-eater, so you stay alert. (*directly to the SCHOOLGIRLS, sweetly*) As for little girls, they're his favorite (*then the twist*)—dessert!!! (*The SCHOOLGIRLS scream, run opposite, and tightly hug MISS CLAVEL.*) People, I give you—The King of Beasts!

MISS CLAVEL: Oh, I wish we had brought along a few priests.

Music signals the FAUX LION'S grand entrance. The STRONGMAN cracks his whip, and the FAUX LION leaps up onto the bull tub. Applause and cheers. Now, the STRONGMAN signals for a drum roll, pulls open the beast's jaws, and sticks his head in its mouth. Big gasps and applause. He takes a bow, the FAUX LION'S *mouth still wide-open. Through the opening,* MADELINE *spots* MISS CLAVEL *and the* SCHOOLGIRLS.

MADELINE: Look, Pepito, in the first row!
PEPITO: Oh, yes, there are people we know!

The STRONGMAN *lifts two hoops and is about to have them set aflame when the* FAUX LION *leaps off the bull tub and heads straight toward the audience.* MISS CLAVEL *stands—her arms outstretched and eyes tightly closed—to shield the* SCHOOLGIRLS. *When the* FAUX LION *reaches them, the* SCHOOLGIRLS *also spring into action, remembering* MADELINE'S *lesson.*

SCHOOLGIRLS: Pooh-pooh!

The FAUX LION *stops dead in its tracks. The* SCHOOLGIRLS *are impressed with themselves. Familiar voices emanate from inside the lion hide.*

MADELINE: Miss Clavel, it's us! Madeline!
PEPITO: And Pepito! *(to* MADELINE*)* Well, I guess our adventure is now finito.
MADELINE *(to* MISS CLAVEL*)*: My, are we ever glad to see you arrive!
MISS CLAVEL: Oh, no! We're too late! They've been swallowed alive!!!

She collapses into the mass of SCHOOLGIRLS *as* GYPSY MAMA *reenters.*

MADELINE: Dear Miss Clavel! At last we found you! Please let us put our arms around you.

They embrace, as the CLOWN *reenters. Thinking that the real* LION *is attacking* MISS CLAVEL, *he grabs the beast to pull it off and only succeeds in ripping the costume in half before stopped by the* STRONGMAN. *Perhaps he reveals a new newspaper headline:* "LION ON THE LOOSE!"

STRONGMAN: It's not the lion on the loose! That's just the children, you silly goose.

PEPITO (*revealed, to* MISS CLAVEL): Simply a clever masquerade.

MISS CLAVEL: Oh, thank heaven! I was afraid—

GYPSY MAMA (*to the* CLOWN *and* STRONGMAN, *as* MISS CLAVEL *begins extricating the children out of the lion suit*): I had been keeping all my fingers crossed that they'd not be found because now they're lost. Oh, I fear things will never be the same again once we say "au revoir" to these dear children. (*calling out to her* GYPSIES) Show's over, Gypsies, for my heart has sunk. Time to move on! Elephant, pack your trunk! (*No one budges.*) I said we're leaving! Hop to it! Begin, . . . while I bemoan what might have been.

She exits despondently. The STRONGMAN *and the other* GYPSIES *begin to sadly close up shop. The little* SCHOOLGIRLS *begin to help. The* CLOWN *is bereft. The* STRONGMAN *approaches him.*

STRONGMAN: Is that a tear I see running down your cheek? (*The* CLOWN *nods. The* STRONGMAN *is sympathetic.*) I know. I'm the Strongman, but now I feel weak.

MISS CLAVEL: Oh dear, Madeline, look at you! Such frightful clothes and filthy, too. It's better to be clean than dirty. You'll need a freshly laundered shirty.

ALL OTHERS: "Shirty"?

MISS CLAVEL: OK, it's a wretched rhyme. What can I say? I'm tired, and it has been a very long . . .

SCHOOLGIRLS (*helping her out*): day!

The GYPSY MAMA *returns carrying* MADELINE *and* PEPITO'S *street clothes.*

GYPSY MAMA: Here are your clothes, all cleaned and pressed. (*Handing them their original costumes, she starts to break down but tries to hide this from the children.*) Go into the wagon and get dressed. (*She turns away, crying. Sad gypsy violin music begins.*)

MADELINE: Gypsy Mama?

GYPSY MAMA (*turning back*): Oh, Madeline, it's only that I will miss
     you so!

MADELINE: But remember, a gypsy only comes . . . to go.

GYPSY MAMA: I know!

STRONGMAN (*with* CLOWN *silently concurring*): We know!

They are all crying now. The STRONGMAN *notices a hanky sticking out of
the* CLOWN'S *coat breast pocket. He tries to remove it, only to find that it
is attached to another and another and another ad infinitum [or as long
as the prop budget allows], the chain finally ending with the* CLOWN'S
underpants. The CLOWN, *registering some surprise, grabs them back.*

MADELINE: Good-bye, dear Clown and Strongman. Oh, don't be
     teary-eyed. We could never forget you!

PEPITO: No matter how hard we tried!

The CLOWN *and* PEPITO *share a salute, celebrating the boy's humor. The*
CLOWN *puts his hat on the boy's head. They exit together.*

STRONGMAN (*kissing her on the forehead*): Dearest Madeline, *merci
     beaucoup.*

MADELINE (*to* GYPSY MAMA, *handing her the whistle*): And Gypsy
     Mama, this is for you. Blow it, and you'll think of me.

GYPSY MAMA: No, I couldn't possibly. I have no gift for you both, now
     that it's time to depart.

MADELINE: Oh, but you've already given us one. A gypsy heart.

Song: "Listen to the Rhythm of the Gypsy Heart"

MADELINE: *Some times our paths are all too straight.*
                        We fear getting lost or arriving late.
                        We plan our way with maps and charts,
                        Forgetting it's best to follow our hearts.

GYPSY MAMA: Yes, Madeline.
                        When a gypsy heart beats,

it makes you sing and dance,
Kicks you right in the seat of the pants!
Yes, you'll always take a chance
on a fresh new start
when you listen to the rhythm of the gypsy heart!

PEPITO (*reentering on a* HORSE, *the* CLOWN *alongside*):
Now and again, it's OK to misbehave.
You can't be good from the cradle to the grave.
Instead of always being a "goody two-shoes,"

The CLOWN *gives* PEPITO *a lit firecracker.* PEPITO *tosses it to the* STRONGMAN.

PEPITO: *Be a "bad hat" sometimes—so you don't blow a fuse!*

The firecracker explodes, knocking the STRONGMAN *down.*

ALL: *When a gypsy heart beats,*
it makes you sing and dance,
kicks you right in the seat of the pants!
Yes, you'll always take a chance
on a fresh new start
when you listen to the rhythm of the gypsy heart!

A train whistle sounds.

MISS CLAVEL: The Paris train! Oh dear, it's half past nine. Hurry, everyone, two straight lines!

The SCHOOLGIRLS *line up except* CLEMENTINE, *who, unnoticed by* MISS CLAVEL *runs offstage wriggling.*

GYPSY MAMA: I'm afraid that way you'll never make it. (*to the* STRONGMAN *and* CLOWN) Hitch the horse to the wagon. Let them take it!

She blows the whistle. The wagon, drawn by the two HORSES, *enters the stage and the* SCHOOLGIRLS, *along with* MADELINE *and* PEPITO, *start to board in two straight lines.*

MISS CLAVEL (*counting, as always*): Let' see: 1-2-3-4-5-6-7-8-9-10-11-*12*?! Where's 13?!

CLEMENTINE (*returning much more relaxed, carrying a roll of toilet paper*): Sorry, couldn't wait!

Boarding the wagon, she tosses the roll in the air, and it is caught by the CLOWN, *who uses it to wipe his eyes and blow his nose.* GYPSY MAMA *addresses* MADELINE *one last time, referring to the whistle.*

GYPSY MAMA: I shall treasure this souvenir.

MADELINE (*to the tearful waving* GYPSIES *as the wagon begins to ride off to the station*): Oh, Gypsy Mama, can you hear?!
    My gypsy heart is beating loud and clear.
    It's calling me back to a place I hold dear.

Gypsy Mama (Autumn Ness) and Madeline (Francesca Dawis) say good-bye. Photograph by Rob Levine.

MADELINE AND PEPITO: *The best part of a voyage—by wagon or train—*
is when it's over and you're home again!

ALL SCHOOLGIRLS *Yes, the best part of a voyage—by wagon or train—*
is when it's over and you're home again!

The wagon completes its exit as the SEAL *claps.*

Scene 7

[No source pages for this scene.] In one. GYPSY MAMA, STRONGMAN, *and*
CLOWN *are left alone still waving good-bye to the departed children. They*
sing another chorus at a much slower tempo. As they sing, the CLOWN
picks up a big suitcase and hands it to GYPSY MAMA, *then another for the*
STRONGMAN.

GYPSY MAMA: *When a gypsy heart beats,*
It makes you sing and dance,

STRONGMAN: *Kicks you right in the seat of the pants.*

GYPSY MAMA AND STRONGMAN: *Yes, you'll always take a chance*
on a fresh new start
when you listen to the rhythm of the gypsy heart.

The CLOWN *reaches into his pocket and pulls out the tiniest suitcase one*
could imagine for himself. All three exit the stage.

Scene 8

[Pages 55–56] The music turns up-tempo again. The dorm room back in
the Old House in Paris covered with vines. It has become a veritable circus
as the SCHOOLGIRLS, *now in their nightgowns, frolic about as though*
their beds were trampolines or performing horses. CLEMENTINE *plays*
with her doll, others juggle pillows, two even swing on the chandelier. As
they do so, they sing.

MADELINE AND SCHOOLGIRLS: *When a gypsy heart beats,*
it makes you sing and dance,
kicks you right in the seat of the pants!

Yes, you'll always take a chance
on a fresh new start
when you listen to the rhythm of the gypsy heart!

MISS CLAVEL *enters.*

MISS CLAVEL: Children! Children!

They all scurry into their beds. The chandelier is lowered so those two
SCHOOLGIRLS *can join the others, and then is raised again.*

MISS CLAVEL: Go to sleep right away. Tomorrow, you know, is
    another day. We leave the house at half past nine . . .
MADELINE: In two straight lines . . .
MISS CLAVEL: . . . in rain or shine. Now . . .

Song reprise: Variation on "Gypsy Lullaby" chorus

MISS CLAVEL: *I'll turn out the light and close the door.*
              (She does so. But comes right back in.)
              But first I will count you just once more.
              (sweetly, interacting with each of the SCHOOLGIRLS
              in their beds in turn)
              1-2-3-4-5-6-7-8-9-10-11- . . . 12!
              (That last one is MADELINE.*)*
              Sweet dreams to you, my every dear.
              When you awake . . . We'll all—

GYPSY MAMA, STRONGMAN, CLOWN, PEPITO, his SERVANT, GYPSIES,
and other characters appear in the windows of the proscenium arch, on
the Eiffel Tower upstage, etc., waving to MADELINE.

ALL: *—be here.*

THE END

Buccaneers!

Liz Duffy Adams
Music by Ellen Maddow

Directed by Peter C. Brosius

The North American premiere of *Buccaneers!* opened on September 14, 2012, at Children's Theatre Company, Minneapolis, Minnesota.

CREATIVE TEAM
Choreography by Joe Chvala
Music direction by Victor Zupanc
Scenic design by Joel Sass
Costume design by Mary Anna Culligan
Lighting design by Paul Whitaker
Sound design by Scott Edwards
Dialect coaching by D'Arcy Smith
Fight direction by Annie Enneking
Stage management by Chris Schweiger
Assistant stage management by Danae Schniepp and Stacy McIntosh
Assistant direction by David Caruso and Allie Rekow
Assistant lighting design by Kiki Mead

ORIGINAL CAST

CAPTAIN JOHNNY JOHNÉ	Bradley Greenwald
ENID ARABELLA	Megan Fischer
MOTHER	Autumn Ness
FATHER	Reed Sigmund
MHINA	Dot McDonald
BEVIN	Emilee Hassanzadeh
TOM	Brandon Brooks
TITO ORLANDO	Haden Cadiz
AYANA	Essence Stiggers
LARS	Adam Qualls
ARTEMISIA	Emily Scinto

HARRIET	Caliea Jonessa Koehler
BEGUM	Shefali Bijwadia
PAVEL	Gabe Dale-Gau
ENRIQUE	Roberto Sikaffy
SAYYIDA	Nicole Akingbasote

MUSICIANS

Accordion and percussion by Victor Zupanc

Guitar and mandolin by Joe Cruz

Bagpipes, flutes, and whistles by Dick Hensold

Fiddle by Gabe Dale-Gau (playing PAVEL)

CHARACTERS IN ORDER OF APPEARANCE

ENID ARABELLA, an American girl, ten years old or so

HER MOTHER

HER FATHER

CAPTAIN JOHNNY JOHNÉ, pirate king

BEVIN, pirate, teenaged Irish girl

TITO ORLANDO, pirate, teenaged Spanish boy

MHINA, pirate, African girl ENID ARABELLA'S age or a bit older

AYANA, pirate, MHINA'S younger sister

TOM, pirate, small American boy

PIRATE CHORUS: In roughly descending age from oldest to youngest,
    LARS (Swedish), SAYYIDA (Moroccan), PAVEL (Russian),
    ARTEMISIA (Italian), ENRIQUE (Mexican), BEGUM (Indian), and
    HARRIET (American)

THE BAND: Three or more grown or teenaged musicians (fiddle,
    concertina, Irish and African drums)

Note: Where the script says "PIRATE CREW," that means the principal
child-pirates and the PIRATE CHORUS, all together.

TIME AND PLACE

Early Victorian. First, on a beach. After and for most of it, out at sea
on a pirate ship.

ENID ARABELLA *is alone on a beach, barefoot and shabbily dressed in clothes that were once fine but that are now faded, threadbare, and patched and that she is noticeably growing out of. She has a stick—a pretend sword—with which she menaces an unseen adversary.*

ENID ARABELLA: Avast, ye spotted lubbers! Avast ye and yield, else ye be cut down where ye stand, arr! Aye, ye have underestimated me, villain, have ye not? Ye looked at me in these grimy rags and thought I was a nameless pauper, a nobody, a poor, powerless, helpless beggar girl, and nothing to fear. But ye have mistaken the matter entirely. Ye have been fooled by my disguise, like so many afore ye. For behold: I am Enid Arabella, Pirate Queen: scourge of the south, nemesis of the north, and absolute bloody horror of every point between. HA!

FATHER *(distantly off)*: Enid Arabella!

ENID ARABELLA: Oh no.

MOTHER *(distantly off)*: Enid Arabelllaaa!

ENID ARABELLA *runs to the opposite side of the stage from where the voices are coming.*

ENID ARABELLA: Perhaps it is wrong to evade my parents and to shun their company. But even as we are sinking into desperate poverty, they must constantly tell me to be quiet and ladylike and appropriate. To be invisible and as silent as the grave. To the devil with their suffocating notions! If they would only trust me, I could yet save us all!

Song: "I Could."

> *Though my family's in need*
> *And our bellies sore are shrinking*
> *My own gifts they never heed*

Though great thoughts I'm always thinking
I could save us all so well
If they only once would hear me
Scatter trouble straight to—
(an instrument supplies the syllable)
I could make ill fortune fear me
I could be a bonny buccaneer
Slash away! Sail away!
Till with piles of loot I'd homeward steer
But they never let me
I could be a spy all debonair
Stealing secrets! Mocking death!
Bringing home all the money from my lair
But they never let me
I could be a highway robber bold
Blast away! Race away!
Build them both a palace made of gold
But they never let me
There is nothing much I could not do
I'd be brave! I'd be quick!
I could make them rich and happy too
But they never let me
Oh! They never let me
Have they even met me?
No, they never let me

FATHER AND MOTHER (*off, but nearer*): Enid Arabella!

ENID ARABELLA *hides, and we can see her listen to the following. Her parents enter. They are tense and unhappy, and it is not bringing out the best in them.*

FATHER: Where can she be?
MOTHER: I can almost wish we may not find her.
FATHER: My dear!
MOTHER: I know. I know. But—

FATHER: We have agreed. There is nothing else to be done.

MOTHER: I know. But when I think of sending her away—

FATHER: We cannot allow sentiment to direct us.

MOTHER: Oh! You torment me with your heartless logic!

FATHER: And you torment me with your reproaches!

MOTHER: I have never reproached you!

FATHER: Oh, you've made it plain enough how you blame me for our predicament. And I cannot deny that you are right to do so—I have failed, failed miserably and completely at every venture, and the result is all our money gone, nowhere left to turn, driven first to this lonely and forsaken shore, and now forced to send our only child away to lead a miserable life as a charity case. Believe me, I feel the shame of my failures as keenly as ever you could wish!

MOTHER: I have never blamed you, I have never complained. When we had to sell our house and come to this desolate, grim, déclassé place, I did not complain. When we had to set up housekeeping in a cheap, nasty rented flat where the chimney kippers us all with smoke, I did not utter a single word of complaint. Even when I suffered the shame and distress of having to let go all of the servants and make do with a single slatternly maid-of-all-work who has the breath of an inebriated codfish, I did not dream of complaining. And even when that degradation has aggravated my delicate constitution to the point where I needs must spend six hours of every day lying down with a lavender compress on my forehead, not the faintest breath of complaint passed my lips.

FATHER (*scoffing*): Delicate constitution.

MOTHER: Pardon me? What was that?

FATHER: Oh, nothing, my dear. I only observe that it is remarkable your delicate constitution has stood the strain of all your heroic noncomplaining.

MOTHER: Oh!

FATHER: Enough, I beg. We must calm ourselves. Miss Craggy is waiting. We must find Enid Arabella.

MOTHER: Yes. We must find her and bring her back to the house and give her away to a stranger with a hard face.

FATHER: She is not a stranger, she is my third cousin once removed. And she cannot help that her features are . . . austere.

MOTHER: She may resemble a seraphim for all I care. You know very well what sort of life our child is facing as a charity student at Miss Craggy's School for Girls. She shall be the lowest girl there, scorned and bullied and probably beaten, sent to sleep on a hard little bed in a rat-infested attic, freezing in winter and sweltering in summer—it is scarcely a step above the workhouse!

FATHER: We cannot afford to keep her another day—if we do not send her away, we will all end in the workhouse! We are very fortunate Miss Craggy has agreed to take her upon such terms. I hope I have the proper fatherly regard for our Enid Arabella, but a little girl—especially a wild and willful one—can be of no help to us. With one less burden, I may yet be able to mend our fortunes and bring us back together at last, don't you see?

MOTHER: Burden, oh yes, burden, is it?

FATHER: I beg your pardon?

MOTHER: With no burdens at all you'd do very well indeed, I suppose. Perhaps you would like to send me off to a Home for Burdensome Wives!

FATHER: There's a charming thought!

MOTHER: Oh!

FATHER: I am sorry, my dear, but you try my patience.

MOTHER: Oh, enough, enough. If it must be done, let us have it over with. (calling) Enid Arabella! (ENID ARABELLA steps out and stares at them.) Oh! Enid Arabella, there you are.

FATHER: What were you doing?

MOTHER: Did you not hear us calling?

FATHER: Why did you not answer?

MOTHER: Why did you not come?

FATHER: Good little girls come when called.

MOTHER: Do you understand us, Enid Arabella?

FATHER: And where are your shoes?

MOTHER: Oh! Indeed! What is this?

FATHER: Running about barefoot like a ragamuffin! Why are you not wearing your shoes?

MOTHER: Answer your father at once.

ENID ARABELLA: They have grown too small, they pinch me. It is all right. I am perfectly comfortable.

FATHER: That is not the point!

MOTHER: Shoes are for decent appearances, not comfort! Do you suppose my shoes are comfortable?

FATHER: What on earth will Miss Craggy say to your bare and filthy feet?

ENID ARABELLA: Miss Craggy?

FATHER: Oh.

MOTHER: Oh.

FATHER: Oh, Miss Craggy . . . Miss Craggy is a friend—a distant relation.

MOTHER: She . . . she is come to visit. That is why we were looking for you.

FATHER: It is particularly important that you impress Miss Craggy as a good girl.

MOTHER: A very good girl.

ENID ARABELLA: Why?

FATHER: Perhaps I had better express myself more clearly. You have run about freely of late. But circumstances have become far too serious, and it is high time for you to learn to behave correctly.

ENID ARABELLA: But Father, if you would only let me help, I could—

FATHER: A young lady does not interrupt. A young lady does not make impertinent suggestions. My dear girl, what earthly good do you suppose unbridled spirit or a clever imagination will ever do you?

MOTHER: None at all, I assure you, as you will understand when you are older.

FATHER: Why are you holding that stick?

ENID ARABELLA: It is a pirate sword.

FATHER: There. Exactly. Put it down at once. You must learn to stay indoors and make yourself quietly useful. That is the place that the world has decreed for you. That is where you belong. Do you understand? (Enid Arabella nods.) Very well. Now we must go back. Miss Craggy is waiting.

MOTHER *and* FATHER *turn to go, but* ENID ARABELLA *doesn't move. She gives them a chance to tell her the truth, observing them closely as they prevaricate uneasily.*

ENID ARABELLA: Does Miss Craggy have a nice face?

MOTHER: What a question! Miss Craggy is . . . an honorable and refined lady.

ENID ARABELLA: Why is Miss Craggy here? It is very remote to come for a visit.

FATHER: Miss Craggy is . . . partial to the ocean air.

ENID ARABELLA: How long is Miss Craggy staying?

MOTHER: Oh, just until after luncheon. Miss Craggy has a long . . . a long journey ahead of her—

She breaks off with a muffled sob and turns away. ENID ARABELLA *observes her coldly.*

ENID ARABELLA: I see. And is Miss Craggy—

FATHER: Enough of these questions! Come along at once.

ENID ARABELLA: Pardon me, Father. May I look for my shoes? I believe I left them just along the beach. I am sure you do not wish me to meet Miss Craggy in my bare feet.

FATHER: No indeed. Very well. You may find your shoes and come inside directly. (*to* MOTHER) Come along, my dear.

MOTHER *suddenly stoops down and awkwardly embraces* ENID ARABELLA, *who endures it.* FATHER *gently tugs* MOTHER *away.*

FATHER: Come, my dear, come.

He leads her off, as she muffles her tears in a handkerchief. ENID ARABELLA *looks after them.*

ENID ARABELLA: Traitors. Traitors and liars. You would betray me into the hands of the hard-faced Miss Craggy, deliver me to a life of ignominy and exile. Because I am a burden.

Well. I shall not be a burden anymore. Nor shall I go meekly off to my fate. I will not be sensible and obedient, I will not be sent away to be a scorned and maltreated charity girl. I will seize my own destiny. I will be the master of my own fate. I—I will run away! I will run away to sea and become a pirate.

I am surprised they would have betrayed me so. I thought they loved me better than that . . . at least a little . . .

But farewell, regret. If they do not want my help, I will consider myself free to help myself. From this moment on I am an orphan, ready to make my own way in the world and put my stamp upon it. But now that I think of it, how does one go about running away to sea? I suppose I should find a pirate crew to volunteer for. But where? *(She hears a sound off.)* What's that?

The noise quickly gets louder. She runs and hides behind something to watch. Enter JOHNNY JOHNÉ, *the pirate king, and his crew of young but rough-looking pirates carrying shovels and a heavy-looking chest.*

PIRATE CREW *(chanting, starting off)*:
>What d' y' do with a hog's eye crew?
>Spit 'em and roast 'em and put 'em a stew!
>Y' do! Y' do!
>Y' put 'em a hog's eye stew!

JOHNNY JOHNÉ: Come on, ye pestilent dogs, or it's the rope's end for ye!

PIRATE CREW: Aye, your majesty!

JOHNNY JOHNÉ: Curse ye for a parcel of useless lubbers!

PIRATE CREW: Aye, your majesty!

JOHNNY JOHNÉ: Hop to it, I tell ye!

TITO ORLANDO: Aye, Captain!

JOHNNY JOHNÉ *collars* TITO ORLANDO.

JOHNNY JOHNÉ: Captain, did ye say? The pox take ye, boy, mere captain, is it?

TITO ORLANDO: No, it's, it's, your majesty—

JOHNNY JOHNÉ: It's yer Most Feared and Dreaded Majesty, Glorious King of Pirates from Tenerife to Timbuktu, ye witless hound!

TITO ORLANDO: Aye, your most dreadful majesty—

JOHNNY JOHNÉ *(tossing him aside)*: Nay, ye false dog!

ENID ARABELLA *(aside)*: I believe I will wait for the next pirate crew opportunity. This one does not look at all promising.

JOHNNY JOHNÉ: Feared and dreaded! Feared and dreaded! Is't so curséd hard to remember? *(to Tom)* What say ye, boy?

TOM *(with real enthusiasm)*: Your Most Feared and Dreaded Majesty, Glorious King of Pirates from Tenerife to Timbuktu!

JOHNNY JOHNÉ: Aye, if the scrawniest of ye can remember, the rest of you bloody well can!

TOM: Yes, you bloody well can! Arrr!

JOHNNY JOHNÉ: Now dig! Dig, curse ye!

They all dig, while he sits on the chest, swigging from a bottle, very much at his ease. He leads them in a work song.

Song: "Dig, Boys, Dig"

JOHNNY JOHNÉ:	*When pirate gold we aim to bury*
PIRATES:	*Oh, it's dig, boys, dig*
JOHNNY JOHNÉ:	*It's here's your shovel and what's your hurry*
PIRATES:	*For it's dig, boys, dig!*
JOHNNY JOHNÉ:	*We can't deposit it in the bank*
PIRATES:	*Oh, it's dig, boys, dig*
JOHNNY JOHNÉ:	*When we get our loot from actions rank*
PIRATES:	*So it's dig, boys, dig!*
JOHNNY JOHNÉ:	*Someday in need I'll reappear*
PIRATES:	*Oh, it's dig, boys, dig*
JOHNNY JOHNÉ:	*To dig back up what's buried here*
PIRATES:	*For it's dig, boys, dig!*
JOHNNY JOHNÉ:	*And then I'll lead a life of ease*
PIRATES:	*Oh, it's dig, boys, dig*
JOHNNY JOHNÉ:	*Plundering only when I please*

PIRATES: *For it's dig, boys, dig!*

JOHNNY JOHNÉ: *You may by then be in your grave*

PIRATES: *Dig, boys, dig*

JOHNNY JOHNÉ: *But I will ne'er be fortune's slave*

PIRATES: Dig, boys, dig!!

JOHNNY JOHNÉ: That'll do, that'll do, that's deep enough. Throw her in, and cover her over. (LARS *attempts to lift* BEGUM *over the hole.*) Not her, the chest!

PIRATE CREW: Aye, Your Most Feared and Dreaded Majesty, Glorious King of Pirates from Tenerife to Timbuktu.

JOHNNY JOHNÉ: On second thought, ye may address me as "yer majesty." It takes too bloody long to do the whole bloody thing every bloody time.

PIRATE CREW: Aye, your majesty, thank you, your majesty.

JOHNNY JOHNÉ: Get on with it, ye lazy mongrels! (*They bury the chest as* JOHNÉ *goes on.*) I'll be best pleased to get off this parlous hard land and back on the sea roads where we belong. There be ships to sink and merchants to rob and towns to plunder and burn! Oh, how I dearly love a burning town, the flames gleaming so pretty upon the water as we sail away! Har har!

PIRATE CREW: Har har, your majesty.

BEVIN: The treasure's buried, your majesty sir.

JOHNNY JOHNÉ: Then back to the ship,

PIRATE CREW: Aye, your majesty!

JOHNNY JOHNÉ: Away, ye odiferous curs, go!

They all trudge off with their shovels, followed by JOHNNY JOHNÉ. ENID ARABELLA *comes out and goes to where the treasure was buried.*

ENID ARABELLA: Pirate treasure! Oh, we are saved! With all these riches, we won't be poor anymore. I won't have to run away to escape Miss Craggy and her horrible school. We will be together and happy again at last. And I won't be a burden, just the opposite—I will be the one who found the treasure and saved us all. They will never want to get rid of me anymore. And—AHHH!

JOHNNY JOHNÉ *has snuck back in, crept up, and seized her.*

JOHNNY JOHNÉ: Ah ha! Did ye think ye'd live to rob Johnny Johné?
(*calling to his crew*) Back, back, ye malodorous dolts! See what yer
king has captured!
PIRATE CREW (*running back on*): Aye, your majesty!

JOHNNY JOHNÉ *throws* ENID ARABELLA *to the crew, who throw her
from one to another—maybe swinging her up in the air—as they shout
in rhythm.*

JOHNNY JOHNÉ: Take her and hold her, the thieving wretch!
PIRATE CREW: THE WRETCH!
ENID ARABELLA: Stop!
JOHNNY JOHNÉ: We'll teach her to meddle with pirates' chests!
PIRATE CREW: OUR CHEST!
ENID ARABELLA (*a shriek*): EEH!
JOHNNY JOHNÉ: To think she could steal our hard-won loot!
PIRATE CREW: OUR LOOT!
ENID ARABELLA: Help!
JOHNNY JOHNÉ: Without being captured and caught to boot!
PIRATE CREW: TO BOOT!

They put her down, facing JOHNÉ.

JOHNNY JOHNÉ: Aye, now, let's see what sort of sneaking rat we've
caught! What's yer name, little rat?
ENID ARABELLA: I am not a rat!

*Everyone gasps; even Johnny is taken aback for a second by her daring. His
tone changes; she doesn't know it, but she is in more danger than ever.*

JOHNNY JOHNÉ: Not a rat? No, there ye may be right. For now I take
a closer look, ye be nothing but a mouse. A tiny, squeaking,
gnawing pest of a mouse, are ye not?

ENID ARABELLA: I am not a mouse or a rat or any sort of animal. I am Enid Arabella, and you do not frighten me.

JOHNNY JOHNÉ *pulls his sword out and points it at her.*

JOHNNY JOHNÉ: I don't frighten ye, do I not, Enid Arabella? Then ye be too foolish to live. I'll leave no foolish wench alive to boast of outfacing Johnny Johné. Look yer fill at my majestic self, for it's the last sight ye'll have in this world.

He grabs her by the hair, the better to cut off her head. He lifts his sword.

ENID ARABELLA *(a hasty gasp)*: Ransom!

He pauses, his sword high, and stares at her.

JOHNNY JOHNÉ: What's that?
ENID ARABELLA: Money—parents—ransom—I mean—
JOHNNY JOHNÉ: Spit it out afore I spit you like a goose!
ENID ARABELLA: If you do not kill me, you may ransom me for a handsome price. My family values me highly and will pay any amount for my safe return.

JOHNNY JOHNÉ: Har! A ragged, beggarly bit like you? Who'd part with a counterfeit ha'penny to see your dirty face once more?

ENID ARABELLA: I—I am in disguise. I am more than I look.

JOHNNY JOHNÉ: What you look is like a filthy little liar. Yet it be true, there be no accounting for taste, and there may be some who'd pay ransom for even such a sad scrap as you. Aye, I'll grant ye a stay of execution. I shall be merciful now—only to be crueler later, I promise ye, if ye prove false. Bring her! We've stayed too long on this nastiferous shore. Away!

PIRATE CREW: Aye, majesty, away!

JOHNNY JOHNÉ *exits, and all follow, carrying a struggling* ENID ARABELLA *above their heads, chanting loudly as they go:*

> *Take her and hold her, the thieving wretch!*
> *We'll teach her to meddle with pirates' chest!*
> *To think she could steal our hard-won loot!*
> *Without being captured and caught, to boot!*
> *To boot, to boot, to boot, to boot, to boot!*

They are gone, and all is silent for a second, then:

MOTHER AND FATHER (*off, calling*): Enid Arabella! Eeenid Aaarabeeeeelaaaa!

Music, and the scene changes to the deck of the pirate ship the Jolly Robert. *It is gloomy looking, its sails hanging limply, and it is much and ill repaired; the deck is filthy and littered with crates and barrels of random loot. The flag is a classic white-on-black skull and crossbones, but the skull has an expression of surprise and dismay. There is a boy hanging upside down by his ankles from one of the masts.*
    ENID ARABELLA *is wrapped in chains and hanging by one long chain over the side of the deck, directly over the water.* JOHNÉ *controls the other end of the chain, maybe with some kind of winch or pulley. Or perhaps she is tied up and standing at the end of a plank. The* PIRATE CREW *gives*

JOHNÉ *a wide berth, climbing up into the rigging, edging to the sides of the deck.* BEVIN *is at the wheel.*

JOHNNY JOHNÉ: Well, wench! Welcome to me ship, the *Jolly Robert*! What think ye of it?

ENID ARABELLA (*trying to be brave*): Should it not be the *Jolly Roger*?

JOHNNY JOHNÉ: Roger? Who the devil is Roger? This ship be named after me darling brother Robert, who be jolly indeed, or anyhow he was afore I scuttled him for watering me rum. To Robert!

PIRATE CREW (*promptly*): Huzzah.

JOHNNY JOHNÉ: Where e'er he may be, heaven or the hotter place, the rum-watering devil.

BEVIN: Pardon me, your most feared and dreaded majesty . . .

JOHNNY JOHNÉ: Well?

BEVIN: Requesting permission to cut Enrique down. He's been hanging all day—

JOHNNY JOHNÉ: And what's that to me, curse yer eyes!

BEVIN: Only, he's the one knows where the extra crates of rum are stowed, your majesty.

JOHNNY JOHNÉ: Fair enough, cut the scoundrel down.

ENID ARABELLA: What did he do?

JOHNNY JOHNÉ: He spoke without being spoken to. Ye won't have another warning. Now, tell me, wee rodent, be it true? Be yer people wealthy? Will they pay a kingly ransom for yer safe return?

ENID ARABELLA: Well . . . AHH!

JOHNÉ *has suddenly lowered the chain, and* ENID ARABELLA *has uttered a short scream. He stops her with a jerk just above the water and brings her back up to eye level.*

JOHNNY JOHNÉ: I warn ye, answer me true or you'll be in a shark's belly before the lie is out of your throat. Do ye see them down there? They be hungry lean monsters, they'll tear ye to ribbons in an instant. So what be ye answer?

ENID ARABELLA: My family has no money.

JOHNNY JOHNÉ *(roaring)*: ADDRESS ME AS YOUR MAJESTY, YE DOG OF A RAT!

ENID ARABELLA: Your majesty. My family has no money, your majesty.

JOHNNY JOHNÉ: Aye, 'tis as I thought, and no surprise. Well, then, I be a generous soul, so I'll offer ye a choice. I'll hang ye by yer heels from the yardarm for many a long day, let ye dangle there whilst I laugh myself sick, till ye slowly die. Or I'll grant ye the favor of a quick death in the teeth of those great beasts down there. What say ye? I give ye leave to speak.

ENID ARABELLA: Your, your most feared and dreaded majesty, glorious king of all the pirates from Tenerife to Timbuktu. I am deeply grateful to you for allowing me to choose between a quick and terrible death, and a slow and terrible death. But I would like most humbly to suggest that there may be a third way, one more to your own glorious advantage.

JOHNNY JOHNÉ: Well?

ENID ARABELLA: Might I not be more useful kept alive as a member of your crew? I cannot help but notice that many of them are as young as I, or younger.

JOHNNY JOHNÉ: Aye. But none of these ever tried to steal from me. None of them ever dared to answer me back. Why should I make an exception of you?

ENID ARABELLA: I do not know, your majesty. But surely you are as wise as you are powerful. Can you not think of a reason?

JOHNNY JOHNÉ: Hah! Ye think ye'self a brave lass, don't ye? But are ye as brave in deed as ye are in clever words?

ENID ARABELLA: Try me, your majesty.

JOHNÉ *pulls the chain and brings her down on the deck.*

JOHNNY JOHNÉ: Release her.

They do. He grabs TOM *and throws him down at* ENID ARABELLA'S *feet, then hands her a large and ugly knife.*

JOHNNY JOHNÉ: Someone must die for yer insolence, or where's my reputation as a bloody, cruel, merciless monarch? Ye see this scrap of a useless boy? Slit his throat for me, and ye may live.

Long pause as ENID ARABELLA *looks in horror at the knife and at* TOM. *She even tries raising the knife as though to do it, making the crew gasp. But she lowers it again and hands back the knife, defeated.*

JOHNNY JOHNÉ: Ye won't?

ENID ARABELLA: I cannot, majesty. I guess I am not a bloodthirsty pirate after all. I cannot kill anyone. Do what you will.

JOHNÉ *feints at her viciously with the knife, than puts it away, laughing at her.*

JOHNNY JOHNÉ: HAR! Ye've passed the test, whelp! As wild and back-talking as ye are, I needed to know if ye'd stick a knife in my craw one dark night when me guard was down. But no, for all yer insolence, ye be just another weak, namby-pamby, mousey little coward of a girl, afraid to get her hands bloody. Oh, ye'll do, ye'll do. Ye can pull a rope like any other slaving wench and I need never fear ye. Is that not so?

ENID ARABELLA (*utterly humiliated*): Aye, your majesty.

Song: "Johné's Oath"

JOHNNY JOHNÉ: *But hark ye, fool*
   And mark me well
   If ye should find yer courage and cross me
   It will mean yer death
   Do ye hear me?

   I'll have ye know
   A Johné will never break his word
   Why, I once swore

To me darling brother Robert on his deathbed
That I will surrender our late great father's sword to
the one who defeats me
Fair
And square
And no one else
Though such a one there never shall be

But there
You see
The word of a Johné be sacred
I would not break an oath for all the jam . . .
In Jamaica!

So
I hereby swear
On me father's sword
To show ye no mercy
But cut ye down
Like a mad beast
If ye e'er defy me
Have ye heard me?

ENID ARABELLA (*spoken*): Aye, your majesty.

JOHNNY JOHNÉ: Aye. Welcome aboard!

PIRATE CREW: Welcome aboard!

JOHNNY JOHNÉ: Ye are now my subject and a member of the *Jolly Robert* pirate crew, FOREVER!

PIRATE CREW: Forever!

JOHNNY JOHNÉ: Ye'll have a penny share in every ten pounds of plunder, a cupful o' gruel every day, and a pint o' dark rum on Sundays!

PIRATE CREW: Rum on Sundays!

JOHNNY JOHNÉ: What say ye to that wench?

ENID ARABELLA: What can I say, your majesty? I am exactly as grateful as such a pledge is worth.

JOHNNY JOHNÉ: Har! Aye, ye may talk, there's no danger in ye, yer nothing but a harmless fool. And every king must have his fool. *(to* BEVIN*)* I be going for some shut-eye. Keep 'er steady, and call me if the wind changes.

BEVIN: Aye, aye, your majesty.

He goes below deck, and the crew slowly surrounds ENID ARABELLA.

MHINA: Well, you're a clever thing, aren't you? You think!

TOM: Yeah, that's what you think!

BEVIN: I'm sure you never meant any harm, but you mustn't make trouble.

MHINA: Who do you think you are, troublemaker?

BEVIN: You'd far better keep quiet and watch us, we know how to get along here.

TOM: Yeah, watch it!

MHINA: That's right, shut up and learn something!

AYANA: Yes, but maybe, Mhina?

MHINA: What?

AYANA: Maybe we shouldn't yell at her? She saved Tom.

MHINA: Saved him? She was just too scared to kill him.

BEVIN: Aye, she would have done it if she dared, poor Tom!

TOM: Yes! She's a weak namby-pamby coward of a girl afraid to get her hands bloody! Ha! That's what the captain said! He'd have killed me like that! *(He makes a violent gesture, gleefully.)* Ha! He's not afraid of anything!

MHINA: That's right. So face it, you've got a lot to learn, and you'd better learn fast.

The pirates have surrounded ENID ARABELLA, *beginning with rhythmic bangings and clappings, all hushed to avoid rousing* JOHNÉ.

Song: "We Know"

| MHINA: | *So listen up new girl* |
| PIRATE CREW: | *Hear what we say to you* |

BEVIN:	*Learn your place now*
PIRATE CREW:	*Do what we tell you to*
MHINA:	*Keep your mouth shut*
PIRATE CREW:	*When we tell you to*
AYANA:	*Keep your head down*
PIRATE CREW:	*When we tell you to*
	Chuh, chuh, chuh, chuh, chuh
	Chuh, chuh, chuh, chuh, chuh
	Chuh, chuh, chuh, chuh, chuh
	Chuh, chuh, chuh, chuh, chuh
TOM:	*Do as you're told*
PIRATE CREW:	*When we tell you*
BEVIN:	*Sleep in the hold*
PIRATE CREW:	*With the rats oh*
	Bake in summer
	Freeze in winter
	Cry yourself to sleep
	Chuh, chuh, chuh, chuh, chuh
	Chuh, chuh, chuh, chuh, chuh
	Chuh, chuh, chuh, chuh, chuh
	Chuh, chuh, chuh, chuh, chuh
BEVIN AND TITO ORLANDO:	*You'll pull a rope*
PIRATE CREW:	*Like we do*
MHINA AND AYANA:	*Swab down the deck*
PIRATE CREW:	*Like we do*
BEVIN AND TOM:	*Work your hands raw*
PIRATE CREW:	*Raw and bloody*
	Do as you're told
	Like we do
	And survive
	Like we do
	'Cause we know, we know
	How to get through
	We know, we know

> *Now you'll know too*
> *We know, we know*

BEVIN, TITO, MHINA, AYANA, AND TOM: *We're still alive*

PIRATE CREW: *We know we know*
> *How to survive*

JOHNNY JOHNÉ: Arr. Pipe down ye noisy curséd flounder . . . Oh, there's a mermaid . . . *(trailing off into sleepy sounds/snores)*

The song becomes ever more fast and aggressive, until the kids surrounded ENID ARABELLA, *driving her to her knees and hiding her from view. It ends abruptly, and the kids turn and move away. We see her again, crouched on the deck.*

ENID ARABELLA *(low)*: I will not give in. *(The kids turn back and look at her. She gets up, faces them.)* I will not live that way. I will escape, or I will fight, or . . . *(She falters.)*

MHINA: Or what? Shut up for a change?

AYANA: Oh, Mhina.

MHINA: Little sister, I am just trying to protect you.

BEVIN: Oh, well, Mhina, never mind her. She won't do anything, what can she do? And talk is cheap enough.

MHINA *(to* ENID ARABELLA*)*: That's true, you're all talk, anyhow.

TOM: Yes, you talk big, but that's all!

MHINA: The captain's new fool, isn't that what he said? You had your chance to stand up to him, and what happened? Nothing! You couldn't even kill little Tom!

TOM: You couldn't even kill me!

ENID ARABELLA: Perhaps I do not have the right sort of courage for killing a boy in cold blood! But perhaps that is not the sort of courage I wish to have. Perhaps it is not actually a very good reason to despise me. Perhaps you may have noticed that my so-called clever talk has so far saved my life, twice. So perhaps talk is something that could come in handy. And perhaps, perhaps, you all ought to consider letting me help you instead of telling me to be quiet, because I must tell you now, that is something I will never do! Nor will I ever submit to tyranny! I will fight for freedom, for me and for all of us!

MHINA: That's it, let's throw her over the side. *(slight pause—Is she serious?)* Get her!

She grabs ENID ARABELLA, *and some of the* PIRATE CHORUS *plus* TOM *rush in to grab her too.*

PIRATE CREW *(variously)*: YEAH! GET HER! GRAB HER! THROW HER! *(etc.)*

Shouting, they pick her up by her shoulders and legs and carry her toward the side of the ship.

BEVIN: Oh, good lord!

ENID ARABELLA: Stop, put me down!

MHINA: We'll put you down in the drink!

AYANA: Oh, no, Mhina, don't!

BEVIN: Everyone, stop!

MHINA: It's her or us!

TOM: It's her or us, throw her!

MHINA: On three! And a one—

BEVIN: For the love of heaven, Tito Orlando, do something!

MHINA *(to the others helping her, beginning to swing her)*: and a two—

TITO ORLANDO: Stop. *(Everyone stops and looks at him.* MHINA *and the others stop swinging but don't put her down yet.)* That's enough, put her down.

MHINA: Why should we?

AYANA: Please, Mhina, please don't throw her.

TITO ORLANDO: Has he brought us so low that we'll turn on each other like the dogs he says we are? Let her go.

Reluctantly, MHINA *and the others release her. She shakes them off, and she and* TITO ORLANDO *look at each other.*

ENID ARABELLA: Thank you.

TITO ORLANDO: You've got spirit. Got to give you that, I guess.

BEVIN: That's all very well, but what if it gets her killed?

MHINA: What if she gets us all killed!

AYANA: Yes, but, maybe?

MHINA: What, Ayana?

AYANA: Maybe we should listen to her? She is clever.

MHINA: So what?

AYANA: Well . . . it's bad, living the way we do.

MHINA: Better than not living at all.

TOM: No one will ever defeat the captain! He's the strongest man in the world! He'll kill you, like that! Ha! He's killed eight thousand people in cold blood! No one can beat him! He's the strongest! He'll kill you and kill you and kill you—

BEVIN: Hush, hush, hush; come here, Tom, calm down.

ENID ARABELLA: What do you think he would do if we attempted mutiny?

BEVIN: Oh, hush, don't say the word!

MHINA: It's not worth the risk. I won't let my little sister be murdered by Johnny Johné.

AYANA: I don't want that either.

BEVIN: We must protect the smaller ones, after all.

ENID ARABELLA: But what if we succeed? What if we defeat him and you are all made free? Surely you do not sail with him by your free will?

BEVIN: No! He captured all of us, one way or another, the devil.

AYANA: He stole us from our home when we were little.

SAYYIDA: He kidnapped me!

PAVEL: And me!

HARRIET AND ARTEMISIA: And me!

ALL: And me.

BEVIN: He fears mutiny, rightly enough, so he keeps a young crew.

AYANA: He thinks grown-up pirates would have overthrown him long ago.

BEVIN: And when we grow up—

AYANA: Don't tell her.

MHINA: She should know, maybe she'll finally pipe down.

ENID ARABELLA: What? When you grow up, what?

BEVIN: He'll murder us.

ENID ARABELLA: What? No.

BEVIN: Aye. It's the long, dark drink for a shipmate who dares to become a man, or a woman.

TITO ORLANDO (*looking at* BEVIN): And it's going to be soon for some of us.

SAYYIDA AND PAVEL: Aye.

BEVIN: You can't win against him. No one can.

ENID ARABELLA: That is horrible! You cannot let him get away with it!

AYANA: But what can we do?

ENID ARABELLA: I do not know. But oh! It makes me furious to think of him murdering and bullying you all. It is not right. It is not just.

TITO ORLANDO: You say that as if it's news. We've been on this ship for years, do you think no one but you has ever even tried to—(*He breaks off.*)

BEVIN: It's all right, Tito Orlando—

TITO ORLANDO: No, it is not. (*to* ENID ARABELLA) I tried to stand up to him. When I was no older than you. And he beat me down.

Pause. He is too upset so say more for a moment, and turns away. BEVIN *watches him sorrowfully.*

MHINA: You just walked onto this ship. And you think you know everything.

ENID ARABELLA: But do you not see, that is exactly my advantage, being new? I do not say I am better than you, or braver, or anything—but he has not yet had time to break my spirit, or not entirely. I must act quickly before I am too frightened. (TITO ORLANDO *turns back and looks at her.*) And I will. I promise you, I will stop him somehow! I just do not know how . . . I must think.

BEVIN: What'll we do? She won't be quiet.

MHINA: We've got to shut her up!

TITO ORLANDO: Wait. Let me see. *(He walks softly over and looks down the stairs. He returns.)* It's all right now. He finished his second bottle, a pistol shot wouldn't wake him. Let her talk.

ENID ARABELLA *(singing quietly, thinking)*:
> *What do you do with a wicked captain . . .*

MHINA: She thinks she's so smart.

ENID ARABELLA:
> *What do you do with a wicked captain . . .*

TOM: He'll kill you if you try anything, ha!

ENID ARABELLA:
> *What do you do with a wicked captain*
> *Early in the morning . . .*

The pirate band begins to play.

Song: "What If"

ENID ARABELLA:
> *What if . . .*
> *We all sneak up together*
> *When he's standing by the railing*
> *Then in a rush*
> *We give a push*
> *And send his highness sailing?*

PIRATE CREW:
> *Oh no*
> *Oh no*
> *Oh that would never do*
> *He'd see it coming*
> *And pull his sword*
> *And cut us all in two!*
> *Oh no*
> *Oh no*
> *Oh that would never do*

BEVIN: Give it up, girl.

ENID ARABELLA: Wait, wait, let me think.
> *What if . . .*
> *I creep up in the darkness*
> *And drop poison in his bottle*

                              Then when the bum
                              Knocks back his rum
                              We watch him slowly throttle?

PIRATE CREW: *Oh no*
                              Oh no
                              Oh that would never do
                              He guards his tipple
                              With a death-like grip
                              You'd never make it through
                              Oh no
                              Oh no
                              Oh that would never do!

TITO ORLANDO: You don't know what you're up against.

ENID ARABELLA: Just give me a chance!

                              What if . . .
                              We steer the ship toward landfall
                              Before he's even risen
                              Then once in port
                              We find a court
                              To throw him into prison?

PIRATE CREW: *Oh no*
                              Oh no
                              Oh that would never do

BEVIN AND TITO ORLANDO: *We'd be in trouble*

AYANA AND MHINA: *The same as him*

TOM: *For we are pirates too!*

PIRATE CREW: *Oh no*
                              Oh no
                              Oh that would never do!

ENID ARABELLA: *Oh this is quite a puzzle to unravel*
                              The captain won't be easy to derail
                              But still however far and wide we travel
                              I never will lose hope that we'll prevail

PIRATE CREW: *(with harmony)*
                              Oh this is not a puzzle to unravel

	The captain is impossible to derail
	No matter how so far and wide we travel
	We never will have hope that we'll prevail
ENID ARABELLA:	*(getting an exciting new idea)*
	Wait, wait . . .
	Perhaps we can't defeat him
	By violence or stealth
	But with some luck
	And daring pluck
	He might defeat himself!
PIRATE CREW:	*Oh—what?*

But before ENID ARABELLA *can explain,* JOHNÉ *comes back on deck, yawning and stretching. They all shrink away, as he looks out to sea.*

JOHNNY JOHNÉ: Steer away south-southwest, wench.

BEVIN: Aye, aye, your majesty, south-southwest it is.

ENID ARABELLA *has been staring at* JOHNÉ. *She looks at the others, and they all shake their heads at her furiously.*

TITO ORLANDO *(whispering)*: Don't try anything, Enid Arabella.

AYANA *(whispering)*: You'll only get yourself killed.

MHINA *(whispering)*: And us too.

ENID ARABELLA *(whispering)*: But I have an idea! He is over-confident, he thinks I am too afraid to do anything.

BEVIN *(whispering)*: You should be!

ENID ARABELLA *(whispering)*: Just get ready to set more sail when I give you the word!

BEVIN *(whispering)*: No! Wait!

JOHNNY JOHNÉ: What's this, what's this? What be ye whispering about, there!

Everyone freezes, terrified.

ENID ARABELLA: Oh! Oh, it was nothing, your majesty, nothing at all of interest to you.

JOHNNY JOHNÉ: Out with it, ye blasted chatterbox!

ENID ARABELLA: Oh, well, your majesty. We were just discussing . . . whether it would be possible for anyone—anyone at all—to swim all the way from the ship to that clump of seaweed way over there, and back again. It would be a stunning, heroic feat. The others did not think anyone in the world could accomplish it. But I said—

JOHNNY JOHNÉ: Aye, ye said I could do it, did ye not? You believe in me, my loyal little fool, even if my other wretched subjects do not! And so ye should! Why, I could swim right round this cursed globe and have breath enough left to beat ye senseless! Help me off with me gear, ye lowly worms, I'll show ye who can perform a heroic feat. *(He snaps his fingers at the crew, who help him off with his boots, hat, and coat.)* Come on, come on, hop to it! Ahoy, ye prisoners back there! Noodle out a tune while I do this. *(The orchestra plays some underscoring for this moment.)* Careful with me hat, it's worth three of ye. Pull, pull, put yer backs into it! *(He's ready to dive.)* Aye, now! Prepare to be dazzled by yer king's aquatic brilliance! *(He prepares to dive off the ship. Everyone leans forward, waiting to see what will happen.)* But now I bethink myself, be there not something strange and sudden in this challenge? Can it be ye think it some advantage to ye?

ENID ARABELLA: To me, your majesty?

JOHNNY JOHNÉ: Aye.

ENID ARABELLA: Your majesty, I am your loyal subject and your abject fool. You have proved it beyond contradiction. If you doubt it now, you only contradict yourself and that, as your loyal subject and fool, I cannot allow.

JOHNNY JOHNÉ *(laughs)*: Hah! Ye cannot allow! Aye, ye be a first-class fool, has ever a king had a greater one? Aye now, watch, ye faithless nonentities! Learn once more the unmatchable splendor of yer captain and yer king!

He prepares again to dive. Everyone leans forward in suspense again, but—

JOHNNY JOHNÉ: And yet, now I bethink myself, it be a year or more
   since I have bathed meself all over. The rare rich patina of me
   well-seasoned hide, and the rare rich well-steeped perfume
   of me body, I have painstakingly nurtured, to the glory and
   protection of me regal self. And shall I hazard it now?

ENID ARABELLA: Well, your majesty, as intensely seasoned and
   deeply fragrant as your majesty is, there is but one thing lacking.

JOHNNY JOHNÉ: Aye? And that be?

ENID ARABELLA: Salt, your majesty.

JOHNNY JOHNÉ: Hah! Very true! A splash o' salt water will be just
   the finishing touch to me aromatic splendor. Hark ye now, ye
   hopeless devils! Be ye witness to me Herculean prowess!

*He prepares again to dive, everyone leans forward in suspense again—and
are surprised when* ENID ARABELLA *speaks to stop him.*

ENID ARABELLA: Your majesty!

JOHNNY JOHNÉ: What, now?

ENID ARABELLA: May I have the honor of holding your sword for you,
   while you swim? *(He hesitates.)* It would be a shame if it were to
   hinder you.

JOHNNY JOHNÉ: Aye, that's so . . . *(His hand goes to his sword . . .)* But
   nay! Know ye not why I swore to me darlin' brother Robert on his
   deathbed that I will surrender our late great father's sword to the
   one who defeats me, fair and square, and no one else? Even if
   such a one there never shall be? But there you see,
>   THE WORD OF A JOHNÉ BE SACRED
>   I WOULD NOT BREAK AN OATH FOR ALL THE JAM . . .
>   IN JAMAICA!
   Nay, I shall swim with my sword at my side, and let the
      disadvantage only add to my glory!

ENID ARABELLA: Aye, your majesty.

JOHNNY JOHNÉ *(diving off the ship)*: HAH!

He hits the water with a tremendous splash. Instantly:

ENID ARABELLA: Quick! Set more sail! Steer away! NOW!!! PULL!!!

After a stunned hesitation, there's a tremendous flurry of activity as all the crew rushes around, the sails billow out, and they begin to sail away.

JOHNNY JOHNÉ *(off)*: What be ye doing? Curse ye, stop that ship!
TOM: Your majesty!
TITO ORLANDO: He's swimming after us!
MHINA: He's catching up!
BEVIN: We don't have enough wind!
AYANA: We're not going fast enough!
PIRATE CREW *(screaming)*: EEEEHHH!
ENID ARABELLA *(over the screams)*: Do not panic! Stand together!
    United we can fight him!

JOHNÉ *climbs back on board, dripping wet, and draws his sword. Everyone falls silent and cowers, horrified.*

JOHNNY JOHNÉ: Treachery. Base, low treachery. Oh, now ye've earned
    my wrath. D'ye think ye have suffered under me before? It be
    nothing to what comes now. Ye shall be sweated, hear me? Ye
    shall each of ye run up and down until ye faint, and when ye come
    to, ye'll do it again. Ye shall have no sleep nor food nor drink nor
    mercy till ye know in yer bones what it is to betray yer king.

They all groan miserably. MHINA *puts her arms around* AYANA. ENID ARABELLA *stands or steps forward.*

ENID ARABELLA: Leave them alone, you wicked man. They did
    nothing, it was I who tricked you.
JOHNNY JOHNÉ *(to* ENID ARABELLA*)*: Aye, ye be the leader of this
    mutiny, I make no doubt, and I do not forget ye. Ye shall be

KEELHAULED. (*All gasp in horror.*) But that will wait until morning. First, ye shall stand and watch as the rest of 'em suffer, knowing all the while that ye are the cause of it.

ENID ARABELLA (*realizing, appalled*): I am. I am the cause of it. (*looking at the crew*) What have I done?

JOHNNY JOHNÉ: What have ye done? Oh, ye shall see. (*to the crew*) UP! Up and prepare to sweat, ye rebel dogs, ARR! (*As he roars at them and waves his sword, they all rush to the bottoms of all the rope ladders and stairs on the ship, prepared to climb.*) Now climb! Climb, curse ye! Arr, run and sweat like the outlaw pigs ye are!

As he yells continuously, they all run up and down the stairs or climb up and down the ropes as fast as they can. A drumbeat joins JOHNÉ'S *orders, and beats faster and faster. It is not fun—it is hard and getting harder.* AYANA *slips and falls, and* MHINA *rushes to help her, but* JOHNÉ *stops her.*

JOHNNY JOHNÉ: Leave her be! Any one of ye that can't keep up will be thrown overboard! (AYANA *desperately scrambles up and keeps going as he roars.*) FASTER! D'ye think to take yer ease? Ye shall sweat until the last drop of rebellion is squeezed from yer tortured carcasses! ARRR!

ENID ARABELLA: STOP!

Instantly, the drum stops, and everyone stops and looks, panting and doubled over with exhaustion. ENID ARABELLA *has run and climbed up on the railing of the ship, as if she is going to jump off the ship.*

JOHNNY JOHNÉ: What be ye doing!

PIRATE CREW (*variously*): Gasp! No! Oh!

JOHNNY JOHNÉ: Nay! Ye'll not have such an easy death!

He sheathes his sword and leaps up onto the railing too. They face off.

ENID ARABELLA: I would rather die than know I was the cause of their suffering!

JOHNNY JOHNÉ: Now by the word of a Johné, now, ye'll come down and face yer shipmates' torment and yer own. Arr—(*He reaches for her but—*)

ENID ARABELLA: Now I've got you!

ENID ARABELLA leaps at him, and they both go flying off the side of the ship! The pirates rush to the side to look.

PIRATE CREW: OH!

TOM: What happened?

TITO ORLANDO: Where are they?

MHINA: I can't see them!

BEVIN: They've sunk!

AYANA: They're drowned!

Long pause, as everyone stares down into the water.

TITO ORLANDO: Wait, wait, look!

TOM: It's just her!

AYANA: It's Enid Arabella!

They lean down and help a dripping ENID ARABELLA *climb up over the side.*

BEVIN: Where's Johné?

ENID ARABELLA: Gone.

TOM: What?

MHINA: What do you mean?

ENID ARABELLA: He sank. I saw him sinking—I think he hit his head on the ship on the way down. (*pause*) He is gone.

Everyone is silent for a moment, staring at her and at each other.

TITO ORLANDO: He's really gone?

MHINA: I can't believe it.

AYANA: You did it, Enid Arabella.

ENID ARABELLA: I did. I did. I said I would defeat him, and I did. Now do you believe me?

AYANA (*giving her a pirate-like coat, too big for her*): You're shivering, here.

TITO ORLANDO: Bevin, she did it. Johné is dead. Bevin?

BEVIN *is looking at* TOM, *who has been as still as a stone since* ENID ARABELLA *said "Gone." He is dazed, looking at* ENID ARABELLA, *who becomes still too.*

TOM: You killed him? (*pause*)

ENID ARABELLA: I did. I had to. I am sorry.

BEVIN (*to* TOM): It's for the good now, Tom. We're free. (*to the pirate crew*) Everyone! Don't you realize?

MHINA: It's hard to believe. That he's really gone.

AYANA: But he is. He really is. We're free.

BEVIN: We're free, Tito Orlando.

TITO ORLANDO (*beginning to realize*): Free.

PIRATE CHORUS (*softly*): We're free.

BEVIN (*to* ENID ARABELLA): So don't you be sorry. I've been praying for this many a long year.

BEVIN *begins to sing, softly and tentatively. Maybe a fiddle plays a low soft vibrato.*

Song: "Now We Are Free"

BEVIN
> . . . Now we are free
> As free as the birds
> To fly where we will the world over
>
> Yes now we are free
> As free as the air
> And that's how we always will be

The musicians come in, and the song begins to pick up confidence. It builds until at the end it is a joyful hosanna.

BEVIN: Come, Come!

BEVIN	*Oh my name it is Bevin and Ireland*
	Was where I was raised by the sea
	One day my dear mother cried "Bevin,
	Will you run fetch some firewood for me?"
	Said I "Yes, dear mother" and ran to
	Gather driftwood that lay on the shore
	There the pirate king caught me and stole me
	And I never saw Ireland more
TITO ORLANDO	*I am Tito Orlando the pirate*
	But a nobleman's son once was I
	Though for all that our castles were ruins
	And sore hungry we often would lie
	One day when the fish looked like biting
	I sailed out in my little skiff red
	I meant to be homebound by nightfall
	But the pirate king took me instead
ALL (*except* ENID ARABELLA AND TOM):	*But now we are free*
	As free as the birds
	To fly where we will the world over
	Yes now we are free
	As free as the air
	And that's how we always will be
MHINA	*Oh Ayana do you still remember*
	Our home on South Africa's coast?
AYANA	*Where we lived with our father and mother*
MHINA	*And our grandmother deaf as a post*
AYANA	*Oh Mhina oh Mhina remember*
	How one day through the warm surf we swam
MHINA	*Then Johné came and happiness ended*
	Just as sure as your sister I am
BEVIN	*(to* TOM*) And you were a rich family's darling*

	When you fell off their yacht in the gloam
	The pirate king saved you but kept you
TOM	*(looking at* ENID ARABELLA*) And he never would let*
	me go home
BEGUM	*I was eight*
SAYYIDA	*I was ten*
LARS	*I was thirteen*
PIRATE CREW	*When a pirate he made me to be*
	While he lived I was frightened and homesick
	Now my future's at last up to me
ALL *(including* ENID ARABELLA*)*:	*For now we are free*
	As free as the birds
	To fly where we will the world over
	Yes now we are free
	As free as the air
	And that's how we always will be
	Yes, and that's how we always will be

The children (Roberto Sikaffy, Shefali Bijwadia, Brandon Brooks, Megan Fischer, Dot McDonald, Essence Stiggers, Emilee Hassanzadeh, Gabe Dale-Gau, Emily Scinto, and Haden Cadiz) are finally free of Captain Johnny Johné. Photograph by Dan Norman.

Music ends. By now night has fallen, and the ship is lit by a bright full moon.

PAVEL: Three cheers for Enid Arabella! Hip hip—

ALL PIRATES: Huzzah!

ARTEMISIA: Hip hip—

ALL PIRATES: HUZZAH!

SAYYIDA: Hip hip—

ALL PIRATES: HUZZAH!!!

TOM: Huzzah, huzzah, huzzah, huzzah, huzzah, for Captain Enid Arabella!

ENID ARABELLA: What?

MHINA: Captain! Who are you calling captain?

TOM: She killed the captain, she's our captain now!

BEVIN: Well, there's something in that, why not?

MHINA: Why not? Why not me, if we're going to have a new captain! I don't trust anyone else to protect my little sister.

BEVIN: None of us has ever stood up to Johné *(glancing at* TITO ORLANDO*)* and won. Enid Arabella has proven herself.

AYANA: That's true.

MHINA: Ayana, are you going to take her side against me?

AYANA: Oh, no, of course not!

BEVIN: Are we taking sides now?

MHINA: I guess we are!

BEVIN: Fine, let it be Enid Arabella and have an end on it.

TOM: Yes, Enid Arabella, the bravest and the fiercest!

MHINA: Bevin, I thought you were my friend!

BEVIN: Mhina, I love you, but you'd be no good at it. You've got too much of a temper.

MHINA: I do not! Take that back!

ENID ARABELLA: I do not even know that I wish to be captain.

MHINA: Fine, I do!

BEVIN: And that makes her more fit for it.

MHINA: What!

ENID ARABELLA: Though perhaps it is my glorious destiny after all. Mhina, let us discuss this reasonably—

MHINA: I don't think so! (*shouting out to all the pirates*) Who do you want for your captain? A new girl you hardly even know, or me, Mhina, tough and strong, your old shipmate and your loyal friend?

TOM: Enid Arabella!!!

A tumult breaks out, everyone shouting simultaneously, repeating and getting louder and louder.

HALF THE CREW (*shouting among the others*): Enid Arabella for captain! Enid Arabella defeated Johné! Enid Arabella is the bravest! I'm for Enid Arabella! (*etc.*)

OTHER HALF (*shouting among the others*): I'm for Mhina! Mhina should be captain! Mhina's tough enough! We know Mhina! Mhina for captain! (*etc.*)

MHINA AND AYANA (*shouting among the others*): Mhina! Mhina! Mhina for captain! Mhina! Mhina! Mhina for captain! (*etc.*)

BEVIN AND TOM (*shouting among the others*): Enid Arabella, Captain Enid Arabella! Enid Arabella, Captain Enid Arabella! (*etc.*)

TITO ORLANDO: NO! MORE! CAPTAINS!

Everyone stops and stares at him.

BEVIN: What's that, Tito Orlando?

TITO ORLANDO: I will have no more captains.

ENID ARABELLA: But surely we must have a leader.

BEVIN (*to* TITO ORLANDO): Perhaps it ought to be you.

TITO ORLANDO: No. (*pause*) I won't lead, nor follow anyone, ever again.

Pause. He has said this so firmly everyone is taken aback for a moment.

TOM (*bursting out*): Enid Arabella, huzzah!

BEVIN: Hush now, Tom, don't start it up again. Everyone, it's very late, and lord knows it's been a busy day. Shall we not sleep on it and see what the morning brings?

AYANA: Oh yes, please.

ALL (*suddenly yawning*): Aye.

TOM: Huzzah!

BEVIN: Hush, hush now, come on, let's get some sleep.

Tom chants in a near-whisper as he heads for his hammock.

TOM: Huzzah huzzah huzzah huzzah huzzah . . .

MHINA: All right. At least it's nice to know we won't be kicked awake
by Johné!

AYANA: That's right. Never again.

ENID ARABELLA: I will take the first watch.

TITO ORLANDO: Wake me for the second watch. Good night, Bevin.

BEVIN: 'night.

*One or two of the musicians plays quietly as hammocks appear all over the
ship and rigging, and soon everyone is lying in one, rocking gently with
the ship's motion and fast asleep, except for ENID ARABELLA at the wheel.*

ENID ARABELLA: Whatever happens, at least we shall never see that
wicked old Johnny Johné again.

*The ship drifts across the stage and off, with the sounds of water lapping
against it. After a pause, we see a small rowboat inching along, with
ENID ARABELLA'S MOTHER rowing, and her FATHER in the prow peering
through the dark.*

MOTHER: Can you see anything?

FATHER: No . . . I thought for a moment . . .

MOTHER: Well, did you or did you not?

FATHER: I said, I thought I did, I am not sure.

MOTHER: Well, what did you think you saw?

FATHER: A light. Perhaps. I think. It might be helpful, my dear, if
you could just row a little steadier—

MOTHER: Oh, yes, that reminds me, may I hope it will be your turn to
row sometime soon?

FATHER: Oh, my dear, you know, my rheumatism . . . Anyhow, I have got better eyesight, you know.

MOTHER: And I have got better hearing!

FATHER: Oh, yes . . .

MOTHER: I have! I know I heard Enid Arabella's voice! And—

FATHER: And singing?

MOTHER: Yes, and singing!

FATHER: Oh yes, our little girl is kidnapped by pirates and what does she do? She sings! And no doubt she also danced a jig!

MOTHER: Oh, never mind. All that matters is that we rescue Enid Arabella.

FATHER: Hear, hear; well said.

Mother (Autumn Ness) and Father (Reed Sigmund) look for their daughter, Enid Arabella (Megan Fischer). Photograph by Dan Norman.

MOTHER: Now do you see anything?

FATHER: No . . . no . . . Kindly row more smoothly, my dear.

MOTHER (*murmuring*): Kindly have your eyes checked, my dear.

FATHER: I beg your pardon?

MOTHER: Never mind, never mind.

They have rowed out of sight . . . and JOHNNY JOHNÉ *enters, swimming stealthily after them. He crosses the stage—and the moment after he disappears, we hear a bloodcurdling SCREAM off from* MOTHER *and* FATHER.

ACT TWO

The ship the next morning is a scene of chaos and anarchy. The skull on the flag now looks anxious. The sky is overcast. The sails are fluttering and gusting, and the wheel is loose and unattended. As the lights come up, all the pirates except ENID ARABELLA *are on deck, SHRIEKING and ROARING with laughter. Many of them are wearing bits and pieces of fancy garb from* JOHNÉ'S *collection, which they've looted, or brandishing his various belongings.* HARRIET *is sitting on* PAVEL'S *shoulders (or is piggyback on him). She is wearing* JOHNÉ'S *hat and his coat, which hang down over* PAVEL *so it looks like they are one towering figure, though we can still see* PAVEL'S *face.* PAVEL *is clomping in* JOHNÉ'S *too-big boots. Together they are strutting up and down in mockery of him while the others howl with jeering laughter.* HARRIET *scowls horribly and shakes her fist and shouts "Arrr" at will, while* PAVEL *speaks in a rough imitation of* JOHNÉ *but with his Russian accent.*

PAVEL: How dare you to laugh! I am great, wicked, terrible pirate king! ARRR!

MHINA: You're the great, wicked, terrible STINKY pirate king!

PIRATE CREW *all scream with laughter.*

PIRATE CREW (*chanting, then laughter*): STINKY STINKY STINKY STINKY, ARR, HA HA!

PAVEL: Silence! Don't you know I am great Johnny Johné? Look on my magnificence and tremble, you worms! Snakes! Jackals! Nasty . . . things!

TOM: You're nasty—nasty, stinky, and dead dead dead!

PIRATE CREW *(chanting, then laughter)*: DEAD DEAD DEAD DEAD DEAD ARR HA HA!

Another roar of laughter, during which ENID ARABELLA *comes up from below deck, now dressed in dashing pirate clothes her own size. She stares, startled at the noise.*

PAVEL: I tell you, you are dogs!

BEGUM *(breaking into a dog howl)*: Dogs? We're dogs! Ahhh ooooh!

AYANA AND BEGUM: Ahhh ooooh!

BEGUM, AYANA, AND OTHERS AT WILL *(barking and howling)*: ARF ARF ARF AHHH-OOOH-WOO-WOO!

ENID ARABELLA: What is this? Why is no one at the wheel?

No one pays any attention to her.

PAVEL *(to the others, ignoring* ENID ARABELLA*)*: Address me as your majesty, dogs!

ARTEMISIA *(very rudely)*: Address me as your mother!

PIRATE CREW *(laughter)*: HAHAHAHAHAHA!

ENID ARABELLA: Why is no one on lookout? *(hugely alarmed!)* Oh dear lord, those—those are storm clouds!

BEGUM: It's my turn to be the wicked pirate king!

HARRIET: I'm not done yet!

BEGUM: No, it's my turn, give me the coat!

PAVEL *(not as* JOHNÉ*)*: Hey, careful!

ARTEMISIA: Well, I want to wear the hat!

*A chaotic melee—*BEGUM *and* ARTEMISIA *drag* HARRIET *off* PAVEL, ARTEMISIA *grabs the hat, and* PAVEL *tries to stop her,* HARRIET *and* BEGUM *have a tug-of-war with the coat, while* TITO ORLANDO, BEVEN,

MHINA, *and* AYANA *shout and try to break it up, and* ENID ARABELLA *tries to shout over them, pointing desperately at the approaching storm!*

HARRIET AND BEGUM *(shouting among the others)*: Let go, give it, it's my turn, it isn't, it's mine, no it's mine now *(etc.)*.

PAVEL AND ARTEMISIA *(shouting among the others)*: Give it back, no I won't, you'll ruin it, I'll wear it if I want to *(etc.)*.

TITO ORLANDO, BEVIN, MHINA, AND AYANA *(shouting among the others)*: You're ruining the trial, I'll be Johné now, stop fighting, this is stupid *(etc.)*.

ENID ARABELLA *(shouting among the others)*: Those are storm clouds! We must take in the sails and batten down the hatches! Listen to me! Don't you see? A storm is coming!

HARRIET *and* BEGUM *rip the coat in two! Everyone gasps! Then* HARRIET *and* BEGUM *each put on one of the fragments, as* ARTEMISIA *puts on the hat, and they all three strike poses as* JOHNÉ.

ARTEMISIA: We are all Johnny now, arrr!

PIRATE CREW *(laughter)*: HAHAHAHAHAHA!

Now ENID ARABELLA *finally cuts through—the laughter fades, and we hear her clearly.*

ENID ARABELLA: Look! LOOK! Storm clouds! Those are storm clouds! And we are heading straight for them! We are in terrible danger!

MHINA *comes out of the cabin with a huge framed portrait of* JOHNÉ.

MHINA: Hey! Look! *(She smashes her head through the back of the portrait, so her face is now where his was.)* Now I'm Johnny Johné!

PIRATE CREW *(laughter)*: HAHAHAHAHAHA!

A terrifically loud CRACK of thunder and the storm hits. The ship rocks wildly! Some are knocked down, some grab ropes and hold on for dear life—

PIRATE CREW (*screaming variously*): AHHH! HELP!!! OH NO!

—*and* AYANA, *who is standing near the rail, is knocked over it and barely hanging on!* MHINA *is on the opposite side of the deck and can't reach her.*

MHINA: AYANA!

AYANA: MHINA! HELP!

MHINA *struggles to reach her but is physically unable.*

MHINA: Hold on, Ayana!

AYANA (*screaming*): Ahh!

ENID ARABELLA: Hold on, Ayana! Hold tight!

As everyone else screams and the ship rocks violently, ENID ARABELLA *struggles to* AYANA, *and maybe with* MHINA'S *help pulls her back onto the deck, where the sisters hug.*

MHINA: Oh, Ayana!

There is a terrific noise of wind and thunder, and the ship continues to rock.

TITO ORLANDO (*shouting*): Bevin, are you all right?

BEVIN: The ship will sink!

Everyone is rushing to obey the orders. ENID ARABELLA *is working too. The musicians begin to play an upbeat work song, and everyone works to its rhythm.*

Song: "Pull and Go"

ENID ARABELLA:	*It's through the storm we've got to sail*
TITO ORLANDO AND ENID ARABELLA:	*Way hey, pull and go*
ENID ARABELLA:	*For we've a demon by the tail*
PIRATE CREW:	*Way hey, haul away*
ENID ARABELLA:	*The foam may fly, the wind may roar*
PIRATE CREW:	*Way hey, pull and go*
ENID ARABELLA:	*But we will sail it round once more*

PIRATE CREW:	*Way hey, haul away*
ENID ARABELLA:	*Storms may do their best to sink us*
PIRATE CREW:	*Way hey, pull and go*
ENID ARABELLA:	*Old devil sea will never drink us*
PIRATE CREW:	*Way hey, haul away*
ENID ARABELLA:	*We fly like sea birds through the spray*
PIRATE CREW:	*Way hey, pull and go*
ENID ARABELLA:	*And live to sail another day*
PIRATE CREW:	*Way hey, haul away Joe*

The ship is riding more steadily but the storm continues, loud and furious.

TITO ORLANDO:	*If we don't get through the storm soon the ship won't make it!*
BEVIN:	*Her timbers are straining! We'll spring a leak!*
ENID ARABELLA:	*We are almost through, hold on, hold on!*
	Work, friends, work, though day is dark
PIRATE CREW:	*Way hey, pull and go*
ENID ARABELLA:	*I wasn't born to feed a shark*
PIRATE CREW:	*Way hey, haul away*
BEVIN:	*The clouds will break, the sun will shine*
PIRATE CREW:	*Way hey, pull and go*
TITO ORLANDO:	*I'll live to ask, will you be mine*
PIRATE CREW:	*Way hey, haul away*
AYANA:	*Mermaids sing, oh have no fear*
PIRATE CREW:	*Way hey, pull and go*
MHINA:	*Our dying day is not yet here*
ENID ARABELLA AND ALL:	*Way hey, haul away*
	Way hey, haul away
	Way hey, haul away Joe
TOM:	Away, away, away, away, Joe!

They have sailed out of the storm, the storm noise fades away, the sun comes out and shines brilliantly on the ship as the music ends. Some half collapse in exhaustion and relief, and all stare at the sky and at each other, dazed.

BEVIN: Well, that was a near thing.

TITO ORLANDO: But we made it through, we're alive.

TOM: Alive, alive, alive!

MHINA: Thanks to Enid Arabella. *(Everyone looks at her.)* It's true. Didn't you see, she saved my sister's life?

AYANA: You did, you saved my life! She saved my life!

TITO ORLANDO: She saved all our lives.

MHINA: Oh, this changes everything! *(to* ENID ARABELLA*)* It doesn't mean I'll follow you blindly. You can count on me to tell you when you're wrong. But you've earned a chance.

BEVIN: Aye. You've proven yourself yet again.

AYANA: Be our captain, Enid Arabella.

TOM: Yes, yes, yes!

PIRATE CHORUS: Enid Arabella for captain!

MHINA: Well?

ENID ARABELLA: Well . . . I am not sure. *(to* TITO ORLANDO*)* You said before, you did not want a captain anymore. Why?

TITO ORLANDO: Power is a dangerous thing in one person's hands. It corrupts. Who knows, perhaps Johnny Johné was not always a bad man, until he had too much power over people.

MHINA: Look, we need someone in charge.

BEVIN: Just not too much in charge.

AYANA: Oh! What if we made being the captain temporary?

MHINA: What, take turns?

ENID ARABELLA: Wait, Wait! Now, there is a thought. We could have a vote!

BEVIN: Yes, we could vote a captain in, and keep the right to vote them out again.

TOM: Yes, let's vote for Enid Arabella, vote-vote-vote!

BEVIN *(to* TITO ORLANDO*)*: What do you think?

TITO ORLANDO: Maybe that could work, if we paid attention. We'd have to remember that we give the captain power—and we can take it away.

BEVIN: Yes, indeed. We must remember that.

MHINA: And then we would never be under the boot of a Johné again.

BEVIN: Everyone? Shall we take a vote for our first freely elected captain?

PIRATE CREW: Aye!

BEVIN: All in favor of Enid Arabella?

TOM: Yes!!

PIRATE CREW: AYE!

BEVIN: All opposed?

TOM: No!!!

BEVIN: There! It's unanimous. *(Everyone cheers.)*

ENID ARABELLA: Very well. I am honored to accept.

TOM: Three cheers for Captain Enid Arabella! Hip hip—

ENID ARABELLA: Oh, no, no more cheering.

TOM *(under his breath)*: Hip, hip, hip, hip, hip . . .

ENID ARABELLA: I would just like to promise I will do my best to keep us all safe and free. And never to become conceited and start pushing people around.

AYANA: Well, you've shown us what to do if you do.

MHINA: Push you overboard!

Everyone including ENID ARABELLA *laughs.*

ENID ARABELLA: I swear, it will never come to that! And may I propose Mhina for second-in-command and first mate?

PIRATE CREW: Aye! Mhina for first mate!

ENID ARABELLA: Do you accept?

MHINA: I do. And maybe I'll start getting ready for the next election.

ENID ARABELLA: You'll have my vote.

They shake on it, as BEVIN *speaks.*

BEVIN: Well, now, Captain Enid Arabella. What next?

ENID ARABELLA: I believe that is for you to tell me. Let us parlay.

PIRATE CREW: Aye, Captain!

They gather around, some looking down from the rigging.

ENID ARABELLA: Now, for long years you have sailed under a tyrannical king, never having a say in where you went or what you did. So I think it is time someone asked you what you would like to do. We have the whole world to roam, we can do anything. What do you think? *(brief pause.* TOM *starts thinking and doesn't join in until his next solo line.)* Anyone?

SAYYIDA: I think we should sail around looking for shipwrecked sailors, and rescue them.

PIRATE CREW *(very interesting idea)*: Mmm, ahhh.

PAVEL: Sea monsters! We should battle sea monsters!

PIRATE CREW *(exciting maybe scary idea)*: Yeee!

ARTEMISIA: No, we should tame a sea monster and keep it as a pet!

PIRATE CREW *(best idea yet!)*: YEAHHH!

PAVEL: Battle!

ARTEMISIA: Tame!!

PAVEL: BATTLE!

ARTEMISIA: TAME!!

TOM *(quietly)*: Could I go home?

BEVIN: What's that, Tom?

TOM: I think . . . I want to go home. *(slight pause)*

BEVIN: Does anyone else want to go home?

SAYYIDA: Maybe . . .

HARRIET: Not me, no thanks.

ARTEMISIA: It's been so long.

BEGUM: What if they've forgotten me?

PAVEL: What if I don't remember how to get there?

ENRIQUE: What if they moved?

SAYYIDA *(deciding)*: But yes. Yes, I do want to go home.

PAVEL: I would like to go look for it, at least!

ENID ARABELLA: But . . . do you all want to look for your homes, truly? Instead of having adventures?

PIRATE CREW: Yes.

BEVIN: Well, Captain. I wouldn't want you to get the wrong idea. To sail with you throughout all the adventures of the world to the four corners of it and back again, that's the life for me, sure. But now

I think of it, if I were to confess my heart's desire, I would dearly love to just see Ireland again, and tell my mother I'm all right.

TITO ORLANDO: I must admit I have often thought I would like to visit my home again. And bring them my share of our plunder, so they need never go to sleep hungry again.

MHINA: Do you want to go home, Ayana?

AYANA: Grandmother's fish stew!

MHINA AND AYANA: Yeah!

TOM: I want to go home and see my mother!

The crew all burst out, overlapping each other.

SAYYIDA: I promised I'd be back.

ARTEMISIA: I miss my papa!

HARRIET *(to ARTEMISIA)*: Can I go home with you?

ARTEMISIA: Of course!

BEGUM: I want to see my brothers.

PAVEL: I want to show off my tattoos!

LARS: I bet they've been worried.

TOM *(in the clear)*: And my dog!

MHINA: What do you say, Captain?

ENID ARABELLA: I say, yes, of course. We shall bring everyone home, everyone who wants to.

BEVIN: But not to stay, surely? We cannot abandon you, after you've saved us.

ENID ARABELLA: Oh, well, that . . . that is entirely up to you. I shall stay on the ship. But you of course will be perfectly free to stay at home, or return to the ship and sail on with me.

TITO ORLANDO: But what about you? Don't you want to go home?

BEVIN: Are you not homesick?

AYANA: Don't you think your parents are worried about you?

ENID ARABELLA: Oh, no. I do not suppose they still even think of me. I am sure they are relieved I am gone.

MHINA: Well, then, they are idiots!

BEVIN: Aye, you don't need them. We are your family now.

PIRATE CREW: AYE!

ENID ARABELLA: Oh. Yes, that is true. You are. Thank you. Ahem. *(She clears her throat, trying to hide that she is moved.)* Well, well. I must plot our course. Gather round, if you will, and show me where your homes were.

The musicians play an instrumental version of "We Will Go Home." The crew all gather around ENID ARABELLA; *she draws on a sea chart as they each point out where they are from. Finally* ENID ARABELLA *holds up the chart, densely covered in squiggly lines.*

ENID ARABELLA: Well, it is going to take quite some time. Perhaps years. But we have our course. Prepare to set sail, pirates!

PIRATE CREW: Aye, aye, captain!

ENID ARABELLA: Oh, wait!

BEVIN: What's wrong?

ENID ARABELLA: Well, it occurs to me, perhaps we ought not to be pirates any longer. Perhaps we ought to consider ourselves buccaneers.

TITO ORLANDO: What's the difference?

MHINA: It's only words.

ENID ARABELLA: Well, but words have power, you know. I mean, we all know pirates are terrible violent criminals. Just look at Johnny Johné. He was a pirate. He was vain and selfish and mean and bullying and rotten to the core. We do not want to be like him, do we?

PIRATE CREW: No!

ENID ARABELLA: But buccaneers just want to live freely and do no harm to anyone. Would we not rather be buccaneers?

PIRATE CREW: Aye!

ENID ARABELLA: Then let us prepare to set sail, buccaneers!

ALL: Aye, Captain!

MHINA: Let's go home!

All cheer and whoop, and the music quickens. AYANA *and* MHINA *start an African-inspired beat, clapping or stamping, and the others join in.*

Song: *"We Will Go Home"*

AYANA: *We'll ride the Gulf Stream current*

MHINA: *Catch the north Atlantic drift and*

AYANA: *Sail down Canary sea road*

MHINA: *To the coast of Africa and*

AYANA: *Glide south on leeward breezes*

MHINA: *Past Dakar, Bissau, Conakry*

AYANA: *Past Abidjan and Lomé,*

MHINA: *Libreville, and Brazzaville and*

AYANA AND MHINA: *Soon we will find our village*
                   On the coast of Africa and
                   We will be home at last and
                   All the world's winds, blew us there and

ALL: *Oh we will go home*
                   Oh winds of the world
                   Oh will take us home
                   Oh the ocean waves
                   Oh will take us home
                   Oh we'll ride the streams
                   Oh we'll ride the winds
                   Oh we will go home

TITO ORLANDO: *We'll coast the south equator*

BEVIN: *Skirt the calms of Capricorn and*

TITO ORLANDO: *Glide up the Caribbean*

BEVIN: *Fill our sails with northeast trade winds*

TITO ORLANDO: *Shoot past the fogbound whalers*

BEVIN: *Till the lights of Portmagee shine*

TITO ORLANDO: *Onto the dingle shore you'll leap*

BEVIN: *And past Slea Head you'll sail on and*

TITO ORLANDO AND BEVIN: *Quick southward brave the headwind*
                   Past Bordeaux and Bay of Biscay
                   Take in the sails for then my home
                   La Coruña, lies alee and

ALL: *Oh we will go home*

Oh winds of the world
Oh will take us home
Oh the ocean waves
Oh will take us home
Oh we'll ride the streams
Oh we'll ride the winds
Oh we will go home

Oh we will go home
Oh winds of the world
Oh will take us home
Oh the ocean waves
Oh will take us home
Oh we'll ride the streams
Oh we'll ride the winds
Oh we will go home

ALL *(a cappella)*:   *We will go home*
We will go home
We will go home
We will go—

JOHNNY JOHNÉ *(shouting)*: STOP THAT SONG!

Everyone gasps and freezes where they are. Over the side comes JOHNNY
JOHNÉ, *who draws his sword. He is much the worse for his long swim,
bedraggled and damp, covered in seaweed, with clams and crabs clinging
to him.*

JOHNNY JOHNÉ: Aye. It's me. Ye thought ye could get rid of me, did ye,
    captain? Ye thought ye could trick me and sink me in the briny
    deep. But now ye see, Johnny Johné be not so easy to escape.
ENID ARABELLA: You are not king here anymore, Johné. We will
    never let you bully us again.
JOHNNY JOHNÉ: Oh, ye won't, won't ye? Not even if I have something
    ye might find mighty precious?
ENID ARABELLA: There is nothing you could have that would
    tempt me.

JOHNNY JOHNÉ: Oh, no? Not even . . . this?

He hauls on a rope, and ENID ARABELLA'S parents come up over the side. They see ENID ARABELLA and try to speak and rush to her, but they are still gagged and tied.

JOHNNY JOHNÉ: Har! That's a sad sight and no mistake!

ENID ARABELLA: What! Where did you find them?

JOHNNY JOHNÉ: Where? Why, they was rowing across the sea to rescue you, wee rat girl! But now who will rescue them?

ENID ARABELLA (*amazed, to parents*): Did you truly come to find me? (*They nod emphatically. To* JOHNÉ) Let them go at once!

JOHNNY JOHNÉ: Oh, now, I don't think I will. Ye see, I be a pirate. I be . . . what was it now? Oh aye. I be vain and selfish and mean and bullyin' and rotten to the core. Am I not? So I be thinking, ye'll want to do what I say. Or it's over the side with the two of them!

He pokes at the parents with his sword until they are on the very edge of the railing, squeaking behind their gags with alarm.

ENID ARABELLA: Stop!

JOHNNY JOHNÉ: Well, maybe I will. Maybe if ye beg for mercy, I'll let them live. Maybe if ye surrender unconditionally and swear to be my crawling slave to the end of yer days, I'll set yer poor parents free.

BEVIN: No, Enid Arabella.

AYANA: Don't surrender.

MHINA: You're our captain now, not him.

ENID ARABELLA: But he has my parents!

JOHNNY JOHNÉ: Aye. Ye've not a choice in the world if ye won't see yer mother and father drowned before yer eyes. Ye defeated me once when ye took me by surprise and knocked me boots over periwig into the drink. But ye'll never defeat me again.

ENID ARABELLA: It is true. It is true. I cannot let him kill them.

JOHNNY JOHNÉ (*a roar of triumph*): ARRR! Behold another triumph for the great and grim Captain King Johnny Johné!

MHINA: No.

TITO ORLANDO: No.

PIRATE CREW: NO.

TITO ORLANDO: We can't go back. We can't be his dogs again.

ENID ARABELLA: What else can I do?

TITO ORLANDO: Enid Arabella, this is not your decision to make.

BEVIN: Will you save your parents by betraying us?

TOM: You said you'd take us home.

ENID ARABELLA: I have no choice!

BEVIN (*to* JOHNÉ): She may not. But we do!

Captain Johnny Johné (Bradley Greenwald) has a final confrontation with Enid Arabella (Megan Fischer) at the peril of Mother (Autumn Ness), Father (Reed Sigmund), and fellow buccaneers (Brandon Brooks, Shefali Bijwadia, Roberto Sikaffy, Nicole Akingbasote, Emilee Hassanzadeh, and Gabe Dale-Gau). Photograph by Dan Norman.

MHINA: That's right, Johné! We will not surrender!

TITO ORLANDO: Aye!

PIRATE CREW: AYE!

TITO ORLANDO: Do you hear that, Johné? We know what it is to be free now. You can kill every last one of us, but we will never yield to you again.

JOHNNY JOHNÉ: And d' y' think killing every last one of ye presents a dilemma for me?

AYANA *(who has been thinking)*: Wait a minute. What was that you said?

JOHNNY JOHNÉ: Eh? I be saying, d' y' think killing every last one of ye—

AYANA: No, no, not that, before. You said that Enid Arabella defeated you once.

JOHNNY JOHNÉ: She defeated me once, aye, what of it? I'll admit that when she knocked me overboard, she bested me fair and square, what's that to—

He hears himself and stops short. ENID ARABELLA *perks up and stiffens her spine.*

AYANA: Does that ring a bell, captain?

MHINA: Oh, Ayana. You're brilliant.

ENID ARABELLA: Thank you, Ayana. *(to all)* Buccaneers, do you recall a story Johnny Johné has often told, of a certain oath?

PIRATE CREW: Aye, Captain.

ENID ARABELLA: What were his words exactly?

AYANA *(singing)*:   *Why he once swore to his darlin' brother Robert*

BEVIN *(singing)*:   *On his deathbed*

MHINA *(spoken)*: Never mind that he put him there!

TITO ORLANDO: *That he will surrender their late great father's sword*

BEVIN: *To the one who defeats him*

PIRATE CREW: *Fair and square*

ENID ARABELLA: And do all here witness that Johnny Johné has admitted that I defeated him, fair and square?

PIRATE CREW: Aye, Captain!

TOM (*belatedly getting it*): Oh . . . !

ENID ARABELLA (*to* JOHNÉ): Well? (*He stares at her. She sing-quotes his earlier words to him.*) The word of a Johné be sacred

JOHNNY JOHNÉ: Aye, that it is.

ENID ARABELLA (*at the same time as* JOHNNY JOHNÉ):

You would not break an oath for all the jam . . .

in Jamaica!

JOHNNY JOHNÉ (*at the same time as* ENID ARABELLA):

I would not break an oath for all the jam . . .

in Jamaica!

JOHNNY JOHNÉ: That is so, that is so . . . But no! I won't be vanquished by a loophole, a low cunning sea-lawyer's trick!

ENID ARABELLA: You have vanquished yourself. And now it is you that has a choice to make.

JOHNNY JOHNÉ: No. No. No!

ENID ARABELLA: Yes. Yes. Yes! Will you stand here in front of all these witnesses and profane your sacred oath, betray your darling brother Robert's memory and your late great father's sword, and shame the name of Johné for all time? Or will you keep your word, and yield like the man of honor you have proclaimed yourself.

He hesitates another moment. Then roars with impotent rage.

JOHNNY JOHNÉ: ARRR. (*He kneels and offers* ENID ARABELLA *the hilt of his sword.*) Here, curse yer name to the end of days, take it, I am done.

She takes his sword and points it at his chest.

ENID ARABELLA (*without taking her eyes off* JOHNÉ): Buccaneers, will you be so kind as to release my parents?

BEVIN, TITO ORLANDO, TOM, *and the sisters pull the parents aside and untie them, as* ENID ARABELLA *continues to hold* JOHNÉ *in a steely regard.*

MOTHER: Oh, Enid Arabella—

BEVIN (*low, to* MOTHER): Wait a bit now, Missus.

ENID ARABELLA: Well, Johné, what shall I do with you now? It is no good tossing you overboard, you really are a champion swimmer. Most probably I should do all of us a favor—and run you through. Should I not? (*pause. Everyone is still, watching.* ENID ARABELLA *is deadly serious.*) You once dared me to kill an innocent boy, to save my own life. I could not. But kill a monster, to save my whole crew? That is a very. Different. Matter.

JOHNNY JOHNÉ: Enid Arabella, ye have defeated me, I cannot deny it. But ye need not kill me. It has just now been proven beyond any doubt that I will never be an oath-breaker. So if I here swear that I will be yer loyal, humble servant, and never do ye harm again, ye may believe it.

ENID ARABELLA: Well, buccaneers. Can we trust him to keep his word?

BEVIN: Well, strange to say, Captain, the one thing the villain never was, was a liar.

AYANA: He's an exaggerator,

MHINA: A boaster and a braggart,

TITO ORLANDO: A vile manipulative scoundrel,

TOM: And a bad, bad man!

BEVIN: But if he swears to a thing, you may rely upon it.

ENID ARABELLA: Well, then. Perhaps I will let you live. But if I do, what good are you? What can you do for me and my ship and my brave crew to make up for all the harm you've done? What do you have to offer?

JOHNNY JOHNÉ: Nothing in the world. I was born to be a wicked pirate king. Now I'll be nothing, and the king of nothingness. Do what you will.

TITO ORLANDO (*here comes* TITO ORLANDO'S *revenge*): That's not quite true.

JOHNNY JOHNÉ: Eh?

TITO ORLANDO: There is a story among us, the mere whisper of a legend . . .

JOHNNY JOHNÉ: What's that?

TITO ORLANDO: The story is that before Johné took over the *Jolly Robert,* he was famous for his—

JOHNNY JOHNÉ: Don't ye dare say it—

TITO ORLANDO: Dancing.

Everyone looks at JOHNÉ.

ENID ARABELLA: I beg your pardon?

JOHNNY JOHNÉ: Don't listen to the boy, he's always been a bit simple.

TITO ORLANDO: They say he was the finest dancer the pirate kingdom had ever seen. For skill, power, and grace, he had no equal, they say.

ENID ARABELLA: Well, Johné? I think we would all like to see this famous dancing.

JOHNNY JOHNÉ: Nay. I won't dance, don't ask me.

ENID ARABELLA: I am not asking. *(He looks at her.)* What would you do to a crew member who refused an order? Kill them slowly and terribly? Or quickly and terribly? Look in my eyes, Johné. Do you really think I will show you more mercy than you have ever shown anyone? *(ENID ARABELLA gestures to the musicians.)* Play a tune, if you will. Let us see this wonderful dancing!

Song: "Johné's Dance" (instrumental)

The musicians play, and JOHNNY JOHNÉ *begins to dances a hornpipe-inspired dance, reluctantly at first, and then getting caught up in it. It really is excellent, amazingly graceful and athletic. Perhaps at one point* JOHNÉ *sweeps* ENID ARABELLA'S *mother off to dance with for a moment. When the music ends and* JOHNÉ *finishes with a big flourish, they can't help but applaud him.*

ENID ARABELLA: Well, Johnny Johné, it is true. You are without a doubt the finest dancer in all the pirate kingdom. How did you come to abandon such a wondrous gift and turn into the vile man we knew?

JOHNNY JOHNÉ: Oh, ar, now it's out, I'll admit it. In me youth, I loved nothing better than to dance. But we Johnés have always been wicked, powerful pirate kings, lords of the seven seas. Me own father would have ripped out my still-beating heart and roasted it on a spit if I'd defied him. I did what I had to for the family honor. But now I've felt the boards beneath me feet again, I say to the devil with tradition, I'll pirate-king it no more. Captain Enid Arabella, let me stay on the ship, let me dance, and I'll be your faithful servant to the end of me days.

ENID ARABELLA: I know something myself about defying family expectations. *(to the buccaneers)* What say you all? Can you accept him as crew member, and take no more revenge for his wickedness and cruelty? Can you grant him amnesty for his past, in the hopes of a peaceful future?

BEVIN: Aye. If he behaves himself.

TITO ORLANDO: For a peaceful future, aye. I say, let him prove himself loyal and true, and I'll forget the past.

AYANA, MHINA, AND TOM: Aye.

PIRATE CREW: AYE.

ENID ARABELLA: Very well. Johnny Johné. Do you now swear a solemn oath to be a worthy mariner and a credit to the ship, to be loyal and true, and never ever to do harm to me, to the ship, or to anyone who sails in her?

JOHNNY JOHNÉ: Aye. I do so swear.

ENID ARABELLA: There, then. That is settled. *(She puts the sword through her belt or sash, as* TITO ORLANDO *hands* JOHNÉ *a swab bucket.* JOHNÉ *takes it and humbly leaves center stage.)* Now, my buccaneers. Would you lose all respect for me if I were to embrace my parents?

PIRATE CREW: No!

BEVIN: Never in life, dear Captain.

AYANA: Any of us would do the same.

ENID ARABELLA: Thank you. *(She goes to her parents, and they all embrace. She steps back and looks at them.)* Did you really come all this way and put yourself in terrible danger all to find me?

MOTHER: Oh, Enid Arabella, of course we did.

FATHER: You are the dearest thing in the world to us. Did you not know that?

ENID ARABELLA: No, I did not. After all, you were about to send me away.

MOTHER: Oh, dearest, we are so sorry.

FATHER: We should never have considered such an extreme step, Though we meant it for the best.

MOTHER: Oh, Enid Arabella. I am ashamed to say I hardly knew you. I had no idea you were so brave and resourceful and clever—and strong!

FATHER: Enid Arabella, I have something to say to you. You are not the girl I wanted you to be. You are a thousand times more admirable, and I was wrong to wish you anything other than you are.

MOTHER: Can you forgive us for underestimating you so dreadfully, and for treating you so shamefully?

ENID ARABELLA: Yes. Yes, of course I forgive you.

MOTHER: Thank you, dearest. And as soon as you are safe at home once more—(They stop, as ENID ARABELLA takes a step away from them.) Dearest?

FATHER: Enid Arabella?

ENID ARABELLA: I cannot go back. Not yet. My shipmates elected me their captain, and I promised I would take them all home. That is what I must do.

FATHER: But, my dear. Enid Arabella, do you not wish to come home?

MOTHER: Do you not want to come home with us, Enid Arabella?

ENID ARABELLA: Well, to be perfectly honest . . . I would not have, before. Now I think it would be different, and a part of me would like to go home. And just that—just knowing I have a home to go back to—that means a great deal. (They beam at each other.) But at the same time—I believe my adventures are only beginning. I really cannot wait to see what will happen next! And anyhow, you know, I made a promise to my crew. We will begin our journey by taking you home. Oh, and when we get there, I will show you where some pirate treasure is buried.

JOHNNY JOHNÉ: What!

ENID ARABELLA *(warningly)*: What is that, Johné?

JOHNNY JOHNÉ *(surrendering)*: Oh, nothing, nothing, never mind, Captain.

ENID ARABELLA: That is better. *(to her parents.)* After my crew's rightful share, it shall all be yours. You need never worry about money again.

MOTHER AND FATHER: Oh! Thank you, dear!

MOTHER: You will come home when you can? To visit?

ENID ARABELLA: Oh, certainly! *(ENID ARABELLA turns back to the crew.)* Well, buccaneers. Are you ready for a voyage worthy of your spirit?

PIRATE CREW: Aye!

ENID ARABELLA: Are you ready for adventures unimaginable?

PIRATE CREW: Aye!

ENID ARABELLA: And dangers stupendous!

PIRATE CREW AND MOTHER: Aye!

ENID ARABELLA: And freedom everlasting!

PIRATE CREW, MOTHER, AND FATHER: Aye!

ENID ARABELLA: Then prepare to set sail!

PIRATE CREW, MOTHER, FATHER, AND JOHNNY JOHNÉ: Aye, Captain, huzzah!

As the music begins, the buccaneers haul on ropes, and the sails billow out beautifully. The pirate flag looks very happy. Throughout the song there is a sense of a journey beginning, and the ship surging forward.

Song: "Into the Blue"

ALL:
    Set the sails now
    Pull together
    Turn her head round
    Into the weather
    Trim and true now
    Me and you now

Sailing onward
Into the blue
BEVIN: *We were lost once*
Tempest tossed once
TITO ORLANDO: *Never knowing*
How we'd get by
AYANA: *Now the sky's clear*
And we have no fear
MHINA: *Through the calm waters*
We will fly
ENID ARABELLA: *I was lost once*
Tempest tossed once
Never knowing
How I'd survive
But together
We can weather
All and whatever
Storms may arrive
ALL: *Set the sails now*
Pull together
Turn her head round
Into the weather
Trim and true now
Me and you now
Sailing onward
Into the blue
Sailing homeward
Into the blue
Sailing homeward
Into the blue

THE END

A Year with Frog and Toad

Book and lyrics by Willie Reale
Based on the books by Arnold Lobel
Music by Robert Reale

Directed by David Petrarca

The North American premiere of *A Year with Frog and Toad* opened on August 23, 2002, at Children's Theatre Company, Minneapolis, Minnesota.

CREATIVE TEAM
Choreography by Daniel Pelzig
Music direction by Wendy Bobbitt Cavett
Scenic design by Adrianne Lobel
Costume design by Martin Pakledinaz
Lighting design by James F. Ingalls
Orchestration by Irwin Fisch
Sound design by Rob Milburn and Michael Bodeen
Stage management by Stacy McIntosh
Assistant stage management by Erin Tatge
Assistant direction by Leland Patton
Casting by Cindy Tolan

ORIGINAL CAST

FROG	Jay Goede
TOAD	Mark Linn-Baker
BIRD, MOTHER FROG, TURTLE, SQUIRREL, MOLE	Danielle Ferland
BIRD, YOUNG FROG, MOUSE, SQUIRREL, MOLE	Kate Reinders
BIRD, FATHER FROG, SNAIL, LIZARD, MOLE	Frank Vlastnik

ORCHESTRA

woodwinds 1	Brian Grivna
woodwinds 2	Mark Henderson
trumpet	Gus Lindquist
trombone	Wade Clark
acoustic bass and tuba	Bruce Heine
guitar and banjo	Kent Saunders
percussion	Jay Johnson
keyboard and conduction	Wendy Bobbitt Cavett

CHARACTERS IN ORDER OF APPEARANCE

MAN BIRD

LADY BIRD 2

LADY BIRD 1

FROG

TOAD

MOUSE

SNAIL

TURTLE

LIZARD

SQUIRREL 1

SQUIRREL 2

YOUNG FROG

FATHER FROG

MOTHER FROG

LARGE AND TERRIBLE FROG

MOLE 1

MOLE 2

ACT ONE

Stage right is TOAD's *house, stage left is* FROG's *house.* FROG *and* TOAD *are asleep in their respective beds.*

   Three BIRDS *enter.*

Song: *"A Year with Frog and Toad"*

THREE BIRDS: *We flew south for the winter*
                South for the winter
                Ev'ry fall we pack our things and go

                We know just how to time it
                To find the proper climate
                One that doesn't feature any snow

                Cause when it snows you shiver
                And it's difficult to fly
                There isn't any food
                Which is another reason why

                We go south for the winter
                South for the winter
                But we're back it's almost spring
                In spring the weather's lovely
                It elevates the mood
                But even more important
                There's a plentitude of food

                So if you're feeling peckish
                You can go for seconds
                Even thirds
MAN BIRD: *Winter's for the birds*
LADY BIRD 2: No it isn't.
MAN BIRD: It's an expression.
LADY BIRD 2: Oh.
THREE BIRDS: *Winter now is over*
                The snow has all been snowed
                Spring is near
                Which starts a year
                With frog and toad

Three Birds (Frank Vlastnik, Kate Reinders, and Danielle Ferland) have come back for spring in the world premiere of *A Year with Frog and Toad*. Photograph by Rob Levine.

MAN BIRD: Well, it's true, folks. Spring is almost here. The sun will be shining. The flowers will be growing, and the birds will be chirping.

LADY BIRD: Chirp chirpitty chirp.

MAN BIRD: Over here we have Frog. And over here we have Toad. They are both at the end of a winter-long hibernation. Let's take a peek in and see what they're dreaming about.

FROG *pops up from his bed in full dress.*

FROG:
I'd like to sing a little ode
About my good friend Toad
Toad with whom I frequently take tea
He's not so good at sports
And of course he's got those warts
But Toad has been a lovely friend to me

Toad, I feel, is vastly underrated
And furthermore, I think, misunderstood
And in conclusion I will add
He is the finest friend
Of all the critters in the neighborhood

TOAD *pops up from his bed.*

TOAD: *I love a lively dialogue*
                With my good friend Frog
                Chatting over cozy cups of tea
                He knows just the thing to say
                That will brighten up my day
                Oh Frog has been a lovely friend to me

                Frog is very kindly in his nature
                Magnanimous whenever playing host
                Of all the creatures in my sphere
                Of influence
                I'm fondest of the frog the most
TOAD: *There is a frog*
FROG: *There is a toad*
FROG AND TOAD: *And he lives just down the road*
TOAD: *There could be no better friend for me*
FROG: *Or me*
FROG AND TOAD: *It seems*
TOAD: *Frog is the frog*
FROG: *Toad is the toad*
FROG AND TOAD: *Of my dreams*

FROG: Hello, Toad.

TOAD: Hello, Frog.

FROG: What are you doing in my dream?

TOAD: Funny, I was about to ask you the same thing.

FROG: Oh, well it's certainly nice to see you.

TOAD: I feel the same way. How has your winter been?

FROG: Well, I'm hibernating, so there isn't much to report.

TOAD: It's about the same for me. This is a very nice dream though.

FROG: Yes, it is. Well, I'm getting ready to wake up so you better get back to your own dream. I'll see you when you wake up.

TOAD: Yes, I'd better get back to hibernating. Spring is just around the corner.

FROG: Oh, I think it's just around the corner. Birds?

THREE BIRDS: *The sun is out*
                      The sky is clear we came back
                      Spring's almost here
                      So let's begin another year
FROG, TOAD, AND THE BIRDS: *A year with Frog and Toad*
                      A year with Frog and Toad

FROG *wakes up and crosses to* TOAD'S *house.*

Song: "It's Spring"

FROG: *Tooooooooooad*
TOAD: Blah.
FROG: *Tooooooooooad*
TOAD: Blah.
FROG: *Hibernation's over*
TOAD: No it isn't.
FROG: *Oh but it is so, Toad*
                      Flowers grow, Toad
                      Sprouting through the clover
TOAD: Blah. *(disdain, muttered)* Clover.

FROG *takes* TOAD'S *alarm clock and winds it. The alarm bell rings.*

FROG: Toad.
TOAD: Blah.
FROG: Toad, your alarm clock is ringing. It's spring.
TOAD: It's spring?
FROG: Yes.
TOAD: *Ding ding a ling ding a ling*
                      Is it spring?
                      Is it true?
FROG: Yes.
TOAD: *Frog would you please be so kind*
                      As to hand me my shoe?

FROG (*handing over a shoe*): Why of course, Toad.

TOAD: Thank you, Frog. (TOAD *bashes the alarm clock with his shoe. The bell stops ringing.*) Good night. (TOAD *pulls the covers back over his head.*) Clover.

FROG: But Toad, it's April.

TOAD: Oh, is it April?

FROG: Yes.

TOAD: Good. (*turning*) Wake me up in May!

TOAD *pulls the covers back over his head.*

FROG: But Toad, I will be lonely without you.

TOAD (*from under the covers*): Blah.

FROG:
> *I love the spring*
> *It's an excellent season*
> *Wonderful things*
> *To see and to do*
>
> *And yet I am sad*
> *For an excellent reason spring*
> *Isn't ... springy*
> *No not without you*

FROG *takes* TOAD'S *calendar from the wall. He tears off the pages.*

FROG: It is a long time until May. Well, January's over. February's over. March is over. April's almost over. (FROG *gets an idea and rips the April page off the calendar.*) Ooops, I guess April is over. Toad, it's May.

TOAD (TOAD *bolts upright in bed.*): It's May?

FROG (FROG *shows* TOAD *the calendar.*): According to this.

TOAD: Oh my. There is so much to do. I've got to clean the house, I've got to mulch the yard, and I've got to have some breakfast. I haven't eaten since January. *Frooooooooooooog.* (TOAD *gets dressed.*)

FROG: Yes, Toad?

TOAD: *Frooooooooooooog*

FROG: What is it?

TOAD: You know, I was just thinking; that extra month of sleep really
    makes a difference.

FROG *opens the door, and he and* TOAD *step outside.*

FROG: *Smell the flowers*
TOAD: *See the plants*
FROG AND TOAD: *Hear the marching of the ants*
                   Feel the sunshine
                   Feel the breeze
TOAD: *Look out, Frog*
                   Here come some bees

FROG *and* TOAD *duck giant bees.*

FROG AND TOAD: *Listen to the birdies sing*
BIRDS: *Tweet tweet tweet*
                   Let's greet the spring
ALL: *Let's greet the spring*
                   It's spring
                   Spring

FROG *and* TOAD *are in their respective yards.*

TOAD: Frog, I think that this year I would like to plant a garden.
FROG: You would?
TOAD: Yes, I would.
FROG: A garden can be hard work.
TOAD: I'm not afraid of hard work.
FROG: Well, it just so happens that I have some flower seeds here in
    my pocket. Plant the seeds in the ground and water them. And
    soon you will have a garden.
TOAD: How soon?
FROG: Quite soon.

TOAD *goes to his house. He plants the seeds, pressing them down one at time with his finger.*

TOAD: All right, now I will plant the seeds. There's one, two three four five . . . (TOAD *dumps the remainder of the seeds on to the stage and presses them down very quickly.*) Sixseveneightnine-tenelevenlalalalafifty. Seeds, you have been planted. And now some water. (TOAD *pours water on the seeds.*) All right. Start growing . . . I said start growing! (TOAD *bends to the ground.*) GROW!

FROG *comes over to investigate.*

FROG: Toad, what is the matter?

TOAD: My seeds are not growing.

FROG: You're shouting. Those seeds are afraid to grow.

TOAD: Really?

FROG: Of course. Leave them alone for a while.

TOAD: I'm afraid that would be impossible.

FROG: Why is that?

TOAD: My clock is broken.

FROG: I wonder how that happened.

TOAD: I have no idea. But with a broken clock, how will I ever know when a while is over?

FROG: You'll know, because the seeds will have grown.

TOAD: Yes, but when will that be?

FROG: Soon.

TOAD: But when is soon?

FROG: Somewhere between now and later.

TOAD: You're not helping, Frog.

FROG: Just be patient, Toad.

FROG *exits, leaving* TOAD *alone.* TOAD *sits down and stares at the seeds for a long beat. Night falls. There is a sound of crickets.*

TOAD: Frog said the seeds would grow soon. But soon was over a long time ago. Yes, I'm quite sure that soon is over and now it is later. Much later. This is all my fault. I must have frightened them very badly. Oh seeds, I am very sorry, I did not mean to raise my voice at you.

TOAD *settles in to watch his seeds. Night falls.*

Song: "Seeds"

TOAD: *Don't be afraid*
              Go on and grow
              Are you afraid
              Or are you slow?

              I am your gardener
              You are my seeds
              I will attend
              To all of your needs

              Come on come on
              Up out of the dirt
              It's safe out here
              You won't get hurt

              It's safe out here
              You have my word
              You don't believe
              Me, let's ask a bird
              Hey bird!
LADY BIRD 2: What is it, Toad?
TOAD: I have some seeds planted in the ground.
LADY BIRD 2: Seeds? Terrific. I love seeds.
TOAD: You see, seeds, you are loved here.
LADY BIRD 2: Where are they? I want to eat 'em.
TOAD: Bird!

LADY BIRD 2: What?

TOAD: Go away! They will hear you!

LADY BIRD 2: Seeds can't hear.

TOAD: They hear everything.

LADY BIRD 2: Oh brother.

TOAD: Shhhhh.

> *No one will harm you*
> *No one will dare*
> *If anyone tries*
> *I'll be there*
>
> *I will be watching*
> *Ev'ry minute*
> *Ev'ry hour*
> *Til you grow up*
> *To be a flower*
>
> *Don't be afraid*
> *Go on and grow*
> *Are you afraid*
> *Or are you slow?*
>
> *I am your gardener*
> *You are my seeds*
> *I will attend*
> *To all of your needs*

TOAD: Seeds, I will recite for you a poem.

> *Roses are red*
> *Violets are blue*
> *They are flowers*
> *Just like you*

TOAD: Seeds, I will do an interpretive dance for you.

TOAD *performs an interpretive dance. He dances into the house and emerges with a tuba.*

TOAD: Seeds, I will play the tuba for you.

TOAD *plays the tuba.*

TOAD: Seeds, I gotta rest. But I will be right here, if you need me.

TOAD *falls asleep. We hear crickets. Morning breaks.* FROG *comes along.*

FROG: Toad, wake up.
TOAD: Oh Frog, I was up half the night. I think I must have frightened my seeds very badly.
FROG: Well, you couldn't have frightened them too badly, Toad. They are growing.
TOAD: They are?
FROG: Look.
TOAD: I don't see.
FROG: Look more closely.
TOAD: Oh my. You're right, Frog. They are growing. *(beat)* They're awfully small.
FROG: They will grow bigger.
TOAD: When?
FROG: Soon, Toad, soon.

The lights change, and the flowers grow. TOAD *reclines in his yard.* FROG *goes to his mailbox.*

TOAD: Gardening is hard work.
FROG: Yes, but doesn't it make you happy?
TOAD: Well, yes, it does. What time is it, Frog?
FROG: It's around ten o'clock.
TOAD: I am no longer happy.
FROG: Why?
TOAD: Ten o'clock is my sad time of day.
FROG: Why is that?
TOAD: Because it's the time when the mail should come.

FROG: And?

TOAD: It never does. I never get any letters. I have never ever gotten a letter.

FROG: Never?

TOAD: Never ever.

FROG: Will you please excuse me, Toad? There is something I must do.

TOAD: Sure, go ahead, Frog.

FROG crosses to his own house. MOUSE *crosses the stage.*

MOUSE: Hello, Frog.

FROG: Hello, Mouse.

FROG sits at a table to write. SNAIL *approaches.*

FROG: Hello, Snail.

SNAIL: Hello, Frog. What are you doing, Frog?

FROG: I have just finished writing a very important letter to Toad.

SNAIL: An important letter. Wow.

FROG seals the letter.

FROG: Snail?

SNAIL: Yes, Frog?

FROG: Will you do me a favor?

SNAIL: Why, of course I will.

FROG: Will you deliver this letter to Toad for me?

SNAIL: Me? You want me to deliver a letter?

FROG: Yes. Would you?

SNAIL: Why, absolutely. And I am flattered that you are putting your trust in me. I will deliver your letter, Frog. You can count on me.

FROG gives the letter to SNAIL *and exits.* SNAIL *is alone. He begins a trek across the stage.*

Song: "The Letter"

SNAIL: *I'm carrying a letter*
          A most important letter
          A letter Frog has written to Toad
          I'd love to stay and chat
          Stick around and chew the fat
          But duty calls and I must hit the road

          I'm the snail with the mail
          I'll deliver without fail
          In the rain or sleet or snow

          No snail has feet more fleeta
          Why I'm practically a cheetah
          I put the go in escargot

FROG *and* TOAD *are near the riverbank.* TOAD *wears a robe.* FROG *is in his bathing suit. He carries a towel.*

FROG: Oh Toad, I meant to ask, did you get any mail today?
TOAD: No, I did not, Frog.
FROG: Oh well. It certainly is a lovely day for a swim.
TOAD: Yes, it is. Frog, I have to ask you a favor.
FROG: What is it?
TOAD: I want you to turn away until I get into the water.
FROG: Why is that?
TOAD: Well because . . .

Song: "Getta Load of Toad"

TOAD: *I look funny in a bathing suit*
          I look funny in a bathing suit
          It's a fact you can't dispute
          I look funny in a bathing suit

FROG: You do?

TOAD: Yes I do.

FROG: But . . .

TOAD: Trust me.

FROG: Very well.

TOAD *edges to the water.*

TOAD: No peeking.

FROG: I won't peek.

TOAD *slips into the water.*

TOAD: All right. It's safe to look now. I'm in the water.

FROG: How is the water?

TOAD: It's cold.

FROG *jumps into the water.*

FROG: But isn't it refreshing?

TOAD: It's more cold than refreshing if you ask me.

FROG: Swim a little.

TOAD: I am swimming.

FROG: You swim slowly.

TOAD: I swim as fast as toads are meant to swim.

FROG: I'm sure that's true.

TURTLE *enters and stands along the riverbank.*

TOAD: Oh no.

FROG: What's the matter?

TOAD: Turtle.

FROG: What's wrong with Turtle?

TOAD: When I come out of the water, she will see me in my bathing
suit and I . . .

FROG: I know. I know. You look funny in a bathing suit.

TOAD: Would you ask her to leave?

FROG: All right, Toad. (FROG *goes over to* TURTLE.) Turtle?

TURTLE: Yes, Frog?

FROG: I'm afraid you will have to go away.

TURTLE: Why should I?

FROG: Well apparently . . .

> *Toad looks funny in a bathing suit*

TURTLE: Toad looks funny in a bathing suit?

> *Gee that oughta be a hoot*
>
> Hey everybody!
>
> *Toad looks funny in a bathing suit*

FROG: Now see here, Turtle . . .

MOUSE *approaches.*

TURTLE: Hiya, Mouse.

MOUSE: What's all the hubbub?

FROG: I want Turtle to leave, and she won't leave.

MOUSE: How come you won't leave?

TURTLE: Because I'm waiting for something.

MOUSE: What are you waiting for?

TURTLE: I'm waitin' to . . .

> *Getta loada Toad*
> *Getta loada Toad*
> *Getta loada Toad*
>
> *I'm here to*
> *Getta loada Toad*
> *Getta loada Toad*
> *Getta loada Toad*
>
> *Can't wait to*
> *Getta loada Toad*
> *Getta loada Toad*
> *Getta loada Toad*

MOUSE: *Please tell me why*

TURTLE: *I'll tell you why*

                                          Toad looks funny in a bathing suit

MOUSE: Toad looks funny in a bathing suit?

TURTLE: *It's a riot*

                                          It's a hoot

                                          Toad looks funny in a bathing suit

MOUSE: Are you sure?

TURTLE: Sure I'm sure. It's a fact. It's indisputable. You know where bamboo comes from dontcha?

MOUSE: A bamboo shoot.

TURTLE: *Two things you cannot dispute*

                                          Bamboo comes from the bamboo shoot

                                          And Toad looks funny in a bathing suit

LIZARD *enters.*

LIZARD: What's everybody standing around for?

TOAD: Oh no.

TURTLE: *We're here to*

TURTLE AND MOUSE: *Getta loada Toad*

                                          Getta loada Toad

                                          Getta loada Toad

                                          He's funny

                                          Getta loada Toad

                                          Getta loada Toad

                                          Getta loada Toad

                                          So funny

                                          Getta loada Toad

                                          Getta loada Toad

                                          Getta loada Toad

                                          He's hilarious

LIZARD: What's so funny about Toad?

MOUSE: Tell Lizard.

TURTLE: *Toad looks funny in a bathing suit*

LIZARD: Toad looks funny in a bathing suit?

TURTLE AND MOUSE: *It's a riot*
It's a hoot
Toad looks funny in a bathing suit

LIZARD: Are you sure?

TURTLE: Sure I'm sure. It's a fact. It's indisputable. You know where rutabaga come from dontcha?

FROG: Rutabaga root.

TOAD: Frog!

TURTLE AND MOUSE: *Three things you cannot dispute*
Bamboo comes from the bamboo shoot
Rutabaga comes from the rutabaga root
And Toad looks funny in a . . .

TOAD: Frog, I am freezing.

TURTLE: So come on out.

TURTLE, LIZARD, AND MOUSE: We can't wait to . . .
Getta loada Toad
Getta loada Toad
Getta loada Toad
He's funny

Getta loada Toad
Getta loada Toad
Getta loada Toad
So funny

Getta loada Toad
Getta loada Toad
Getta loada Toad
He's hilarious

FROG: What's so funny about Toad?

TURTLE, LIZARD, AND MOUSE: What's so funny about Toad?
Toad looks funny in a bathing suit
Toad looks funny in a bathing suit

It's a riot

It's a hoot

Toad looks funny in a bathing suit

TOAD: I don't see what's so funny.

TURTLE: That's because you don't know from funny. I bet you don't even know what the funniest fruit is, do you?

TOAD: I'm sure I don't.

TURTLE: Tell him.

LIZARD AND MOUSE: Bananas.

TURTLE, LIZARD, AND MOUSE: *Four things you cannot dispute*

Bamboo comes from the bamboo shoot

Rutabaga comes from the rutabaga root

Bananas are the funniest fruit

And Toad looks funny in a bathing suit

TOAD: That's it. I've had it. I'm turning blue. I'm getting out of the water.

Frog (Jay Goede) and Turtle (Danielle Ferland) agree that Toad (Mark Linn-Baker) looks funny in a bathing suit. Photograph by Rob Levine.

TURTLE, LIZARD, AND MOUSE: *Getta loada Toad*
He's funny
Getta loada Toad
So funny getta
Getta loada
Getta loada Toad
He's hilarious

TURTLE: Ain't it the troot?

TURTLE, LIZARD, AND MOUSE: *Five things you cannot dispute*
Turtle always tells the troot
Bamboo comes from the bamboo shoot
Rutabaga comes from the rutabaga root
Bananas are the funniest fruit
And Toad looks funny toad looks funny

FROG: It's true, Toad. You do look funny.

TOAD: I know.

ALL BUT TOAD: *Toad looks funny in a bathing suit*

Song: "Underwater Ballet"

TURTLE *does a dance underwater.*

The scene shifts. **TOAD** *goes to* **FROG'S** *house. He carries a basket of sandwiches and iced tea. There is a note pinned to the door, which* **TOAD** *does not notice at first.* **TOAD** *knocks on the door.*

TOAD: Frog? Frog? I have come to surprise you with a fine lunch of iced tea and sandwiches. Oh look, there is a note. *(reading)* "Dear Toad, I am not at home, I went to the island in the lake to be alone." He wants to be alone? He has me for a friend. Why does he want to be alone? He must be very sad. What can I do? I should bring him a surprise to cheer him up. What can I bring? I know, lunch. I will bring him this fine lunch of sandwiches and iced tea.

TOAD *crosses the stage, and the lights come up on* **FROG'S** *back way up stage, sitting on a tiny island.* **TOAD** *sees him.*

TOAD: Oh poor Frog sitting out there all alone. Frog! Frog!! It's me, your best friend Toad. *(no response from* FROG*)* I must get to that island!

TOAD *and* TURTLE *float in on a log.*

TURTLE: Watch it. This thing's wobbly.
TOAD: I have to get to the island. Frog wants to be alone.
TURTLE: If he wants to be alone, maybe you should leave him alone.
TOAD: Maybe you're right. Maybe he does not want to be my friend anymore.
TURTLE: Maybe.
TOAD: Frog! I'm sorry for all the silly things I say and do. Please be my friend again.

TOAD *sits up, waves to* FROG *and falls off the log with a great splash. The commotion gets* FROG'S *attention.* TURTLE *floats away.*

TURTLE: Told you it was wobbly.
FROG: Toad, is that you?
TOAD: Yes, it is me. Help me.
FROG: Here give me your hand.

FROG *lifts* TOAD *onto the island.*

TOAD: Oh look, the iced tea is gone. And the sandwiches are all wet. I made lunch for you so that you would be happy.
FROG: But Toad, I am happy.
TOAD: You are?
FROG: Yes, I am very happy.
TOAD: But why did you want to be alone?

Song: "Alone"

FROG: *Sometimes the days*
                        They can be very busy

So I like to stop
And think now and then

I think of the reasons
I have to be happy
And that makes me happy
All over again
What made you think that I was unhappy?
What were you thinking was making me blue?

I only come out here
To sit and remember
I love being a frog
In the warm sunny summer
On days such as this one
That's what I do

This morning I woke up
And thought I am happy
It's been since April
Since I have been sad

I'll go be alone to think
How I'm happy
For all that I have
And all that I've had

What made you think that I was unhappy?
What were you thinking was making me blue?

I only came out here
To think how I'm happy
I love being a frog
In the warm sunny summer
But mostly I'm happy
Because I have you

TOAD: Oh. That is a very good reason for wanting to be alone.

FROG: Yes indeed. But now, I will be glad not to be alone. Let's eat lunch.

TOAD: The iced tea spilled.

FROG: I know, Toad.

TOAD: The sandwiches are wet.

FROG: I know, Toad.

Lights come down and back up on SNAIL.

Song: "The Letter" (reprise)

SNAIL:
I'm carrying a letter
A most important letter
A letter that was written by Frog
I'm traveling so fast
I'm assuming you're aghast
Or at the very least you are agog

I'm the snail with the mail
I'll deliver without fail
Pardon the cloud of dust

I'm speeding with an envelope
As fast as any antelope
Forward and onward I thrust

FROG *and* TOAD *are in* TOAD'S *kitchen.*

FROG: Toad?

TOAD: Yes, Frog?

FROG: I'm just curious. Did you happen to get any mail today?

TOAD: No, I did not.

FROG: Oh.

TOAD: Frog, I never . . . never mind. I am putting the cookies into the oven, and tonight after dinner we shall have cookies for dessert.

FROG: Oh good.

TOAD: Now in seven to eight minutes they will be done. What time do you have?

FROG: Oh, I didn't wind my watch today.

TOAD: You didn't?

FROG: No.

TOAD: But my clock is broken.

FROG: You don't say?

TOAD: How will we know when it's time to take the cookies out?

MOUSE *enters.*

MOUSE: Hiya, Toad.

TOAD: Oh hello, Mouse.

MOUSE: Is something wrong?

TOAD: Yes. I'm making cookies.

MOUSE: And?

TOAD: Well, I made the cookie dough precisely according to the recipe. But now the recipe says, "Put the cookies in the oven to bake them for seven to eight minutes until they are golden brown."

MOUSE: And?

TOAD: My clock is broken.

MOUSE: And?

TOAD: The cookies are in the oven.

MOUSE: And?

TOAD: I don't know when to take them out.

MOUSE: Well, how long ago did you put them in?

TOAD: I don't know. My clock is broken.

MOUSE: Well, are they golden brown?

TOAD: I don't know. My clock is broken.

MOUSE: But Toad, you could just check to see if the cookies are golden brown.

TOAD: Quiet, Mouse. I'm getting an idea. I could just check to see if the cookies are golden brown.

MOUSE: Good idea, Toad. (TOAD *peers into the oven.*) Well?

TOAD: They are golden brown.

MOUSE: Take them out.

TOAD: Quiet, Mouse, I'm thinking. *(beat)* I'm going to take them out.

TOAD *removes the cookies from the oven.*

MOUSE: Well?

TOAD: They look perfect. How about a cookie?

MOUSE: No thanks, Toad. I don't want to spoil my appetite. I'm having lunch at twelve o'clock.

TOAD: Oh.

MOUSE: What time is it now?

TOAD: I don't know, my . . . Frog?

FROG: His clock is broken.

MOUSE: Right. Well, I better get going.

TOAD: I'm going to put another batch in the oven.

FROG: Goodbye, Mouse.

MOUSE: See you, Frog. *(MOUSE exits.)*

TOAD: Try a cookie, Frog.

FROG: But I thought these were for after dinner.

TOAD: Well, they are, Frog. We are merely tasting one to see how they came out. *(FROG tastes a cookie.)* Well?

Song: "Cookies"

FROG:	*This is a marvelous cookie*
	Sweet with an excellent crunch
	Perfect to follow a dinner
TOAD:	*Or just after breakfast*
FROG AND TOAD:	*And prior to lunch*
FROG:	*Crisp but not overly brittle*
	Just a scintilla of spice
	Cunningly soft in the middle
TOAD:	*Let's have another*
FROG AND TOAD:	*These cookies are nice*

> *Eating cookies eating cookies*
> *We're so happy eating*
> *Cookies cookies cookies cookies we adore*
> *Cookies cookies cookies cookies*
> *We go kooky eating cookies*

FROG: *Maybe we should stop . . .*

TOAD: *Let's have more*

FROG *(eating cookies)*: Toad, we must stop eating these cookies. I know, get me a box and some string.

TOAD *complies, eating cookies the whole time.*

TOAD *Eating cookies eating cookies*
I'm so happy eating cookies

Toad (Mark Linn-Baker) and Frog (Jay Goede) enjoy cookies. Photograph by Rob Levine.

	Cookies cookies cookies I adore
	Cookies cookies cookies cookies
	I go kooky eating cookies
FROG:	*Maybe you should stop . . .*
TOAD:	*Just one more*

FROG: Now I will put these cookies in the box and will tie it up with string. Then we shall eat no more cookies.

TOAD: What an excellent plan. However . . .

	There is a problem with the plan

FROG: What plan?

TOAD:	*The no more eating cookies plan*

FROG: What is it?

TOAD:	*The problem with the plan*
FROG:	*The no more eating cookies plan*
TOAD:	*Is if we want to eat more cookies*
	Then in fact we can
	We could untie the string and open it
FROG:	*That's true*

TOAD: How 'bout a cookie?

FROG: Don't mind if I do.

FROG AND TOAD:	*Eating cookies*
	Eating cookies
	We're so happy eating cookies
	Cookies cookies cookies we adore
	Cookies cookies cookies cookies
	We go kooky eating cookies
	Maybe we should stop . . .
TOAD:	*Let's have more*

FROG: Toad, we have to do something!

TOAD: You're right! I'll get some milk.

FROG: No no no. We must stop eating these cookies. I know! We'll give them to the birds. Hey birds!

The BIRDS *appear.*

BIRDS: What?

FROG: Do you want some cookies?

MAN BIRD: Sure, bring 'em on.

LADY BIRD: Wait.

> *Should we be eating these cookies*
> *Or should we rather have worms*
> *Worms are a product of nature*
> *Toad did the baking*
> *Think of the germs*

TOAD: Well, I never.

MAN BIRD:
> *Toad makes the tastiest cookies*
> *Go on and try one*

LADY BIRD:
> *They're great*

MAN BIRD:
> *If you eat one of these cookies*
> *I'm here to tell you*
> *You're gonna eat eight*

LADY BIRDS:
> *Eating cookies eating cookies*
> *We're so happy eating cookies*

THREE BIRDS:
> *Cookies cookies cookies we adore*
> *Cookies cookies cookies cookies*
> *We go kooky eating cookies*

BIRDS AND FROG:
> *Empty out the box*
> *And let's have more*

ALL:
> *Eating cookies eating cookies*
> *We're so happy eating cookies*
> *Cookies cookies cookies we adore*
> *Cookies cookies cookies cookies*
> *We go kooky eating cookies*

FROG AND TOAD (*with* BIRDS): *We will never stop*

THREE BIRDS (*with* FROG *and* TOAD): *Cookies cookies*
> *Cookies cookies*
> *Cookies*

FROG, TOAD, AND MAN BIRD (*with* LADY BIRDS): *Let's have more*

LADY BIRDS (*with the guys*): *Cookie cookie cookie cookie*
> *Cookie cookie cookie cookie*

ALL:
> Cookie cookie cookie cookie
> Cookies cookie cookie
> More—Cookies!

Curtain

ACT TWO

FROG *and* TOAD *enter.* FROG *carries a kite.*

FROG: Toad?

TOAD: Yes, Frog?

FROG: We are in luck. There is a nice breeze today. Our kite will fly
up and up into the sky.

TOAD: Really, Frog? Do you think so?

FROG: I'm sure of it. Now, I will hold on to the string, and you hold
the kite and run and run.

TOAD: All right. Here I go.

TOAD *runs across the stage with the kite over his head. He lets go, and
the kite falls to the ground with a thud. Three* BIRDS *sitting in the bushes
laugh at* TOAD.

TOAD: What is so funny?

LADY BIRD 1: That kite won't fly.

LADY BIRD 2: Not in a million years.

MAN BIRD: You might as well give up.

TOAD: This kite will fly, way up into the air.

TOAD *tries again and fails. The* BIRDS *laugh.*

Song: "The Kite"

BIRDS:
> *Look up there*
> *In the air*

I don't see it anywhere
I guess it must be on the ground

Woo woo woo
In the blue
I don't see a kite do you?
I wonder where it could be found

The weather is lovely
Sunny and bright
An absolutely perfect day
To go outdoors and drag a kite

Way up high
In the sky
That piece of junk will never fly
You'll never get it off the ground

TOAD *returns to* FROG.

TOAD: Frog, I give up. This kite will not fly.
FROG: This kite will fly.

By and by it'll fly
We must make another try
No matter what those birds have said

This time though
When you go
Here's a trick you need to know
Keep the kite above your head

TOAD:
Way up high
In the sky
Now this kite is gonna fly
I'm gonna get it off the ground

FROG: That's right.

TOAD: I will run and hold the kite above my head, and then you birds will see some real flying.

LADY BIRD 1: Oh, we believe you, Toad.

LADY BIRD 2: We can't wait to see some real flying.

The BIRDS *laugh.* TOAD *makes a second run, this time holding the kite above his head. The kite falls to the ground as does* TOAD, *tangled in the string. The* BIRDS *laugh harder.*

THREE BIRDS:
Holy smokes
Holy cow
That kite is really flyin' now
We thought it might have been a dud

We were wrong, you were right
That's a mighty kind 'a kite
It's difficult to fly through mud

Ha ha ha ha ...
BAH BAH BAH
BAH BAH BAH
BAH BAH BAH BAH BAH BAH BAH

TOAD: Frog, this kite is a piece of junk.

FROG: It is not a piece of junk.

THREE BIRDS:
You'll never get it off the ground

TOAD *again returns to* FROG.

FROG:
Our kite is a dandy
Superior string
You ran fast and held it high
But there is just one other thing

TOAD: What's that?

FROG: While you are running and holding it high, you must jump and wave your arms.

TOAD: Very well, Frog, but I'm warning you . . .

> *This is my*
> *Final try*
> *This time if it doesn't fly*
> *I'm gonna leave it on the ground*

LADY BIRD 2: Yeah, Toad, wave your arms. That'll make all the difference.

MAN BIRD: I can't believe he's gonna try it again.

LADY BIRD 1: Toad never learns.

LADY BIRD 2: Hey, wait a minute, look at that!

THREE BIRDS:
> *Could it be*
> *Yup yup yup*
> *It looks like it's goin' up*
>
> *Holy smokes*
> *Holy cow*
> *He's really got it flying now*
>
> *Oh my gosh*
> *Golly gee*
> *That looks mighty high to me*
> *That kite is really flyin'*

FROG AND TOAD: *Our kite is really flyin'*

ALL: *Our/that kite is really off the ground*

The BIRDS take center stage. They carry suitcases. Leaves fall all around them.

Song: "A Year with Frog and Toad" (reprise)

MAN BIRD:
> *The summer has ended*
> *The summer has ended*

LADY BIRD: *Notice if you will the swirling leaves*

BIRDS:
> *And as they swirling*
> *Squirrels they are squirreling*
> *Nuts and other goodies up their sleeves*

MAN BIRD: *Soon it will be cold*
And we will bid you all adieu

BIRDS: *Cause when you are a bird*
It's either fly or get the flu
So we'll go south for the winter
South for the winter
And we'll come back in the spring

Under music, leaves fall covering the stage. FROG *and* TOAD *simultaneously come out of their houses.*

FROG: Look at all these leaves.

TOAD: Look at all these leaves.

FROG: I know, I will go and rake Toad's yard, and he will have a wonderful surprise.

TOAD: I know, I will go and rake Frog's yard, and he will have a wonderful surprise.

They each take rakes and cross to the other's yard. They meet center, hiding the rakes behind their backs.

FROG: Hello, Toad.

TOAD: Hello, Frog.

FROG: It's a lovely autumn day.

TOAD: Yes, it is, and that is why I am taking a walk—yes, that's right, I'm going out for a walk.

FROG: It's a perfect day for a walk.

TOAD: And where are you going, Frog?

FROG: Me?

TOAD: Yes.

FROG: I'm off on a stroll. Yes, a leisurely stroll, which is a little slower than a walk or I'd join you.

TOAD: Ah yes, well, a stroll would be a little slow for me, because I'm out for a walk. A brisk walk.

FROG: Well, OK then. Enjoy your walk, Toad.

TOAD: I will. And you enjoy your stroll, Frog.

FROG: I will.

TOAD: Oh boy, this plan is working perfectly. Frog will never know who raked his yard.

FROG: This plan is working perfectly. Toad will never know who raked his yard.

Song: "He'll Never Know"

TOAD:	*He'll never know*
FROG:	*He will not ever suspect*
TOAD:	*Who raked the yard*
FROG:	*Nor will he ever detect*
FROG AND TOAD:	*He will come home*
TOAD:	*He'll scratch his head*
FROG:	*He'll furrow his brow*
TOAD:	*He'll stroke his chin*
FROG AND TOAD:	*And wonder how how*
	Ow, my aching back!
TOAD:	*The work is slow*
FROG:	*Oh what a tedious chore*
TOAD:	*And kind of dull*
FROG:	*Raking is rather a bore*
FROG AND TOAD:	*But despite a little ache*
	I'm gonna rake rake rake rake
	Ache ache ache

There is a dance break, where FROG *and* TOAD *rake the leaves into two neat piles.* FROG *leaps.*

FROG: Leap.

TOAD: No leap.

The dance continues.

FROG AND TOAD:	*He'll wonder what*
	What in the world has occurred

And when he asks
I will not utter a word
He'll wonder how
How could this possibly be
He'll wonder who
He might even think it was me
But if he asks

FROG: Frog

TOAD: Toad

FROG AND TOAD: *Was it you?*
Not me
Well then who?
Who raked up the mess?

TOAD: *I haven't a guess*

FROG: *I haven't even a clue*

FROG AND TOAD: *Hee hee hee hee*
Ha ha
Hoo hoo hoo
I wish I could see him see it
He'll do a double take

FROG: *It's inconceivable*

TOAD: *It's unbelievable*

FROG AND TOAD: *I left the leaves*
The leaves have left
And I never lifted a rake

FROG *and* TOAD *head back to their houses. Two* SQUIRRELS *emerge.*

SQUIRREL 1: Look at this pile of leaves in Toad's yard.

SQUIRREL 2: Look at this pile of leaves in Frog's yard.

SQUIRRELS: Let's mess 'em up.

The SQUIRRELS *ransack the leaves.* FROG *and* TOAD *meet center.*

FROG: Hello, Toad.

TOAD: Hello, Frog.

FROG: How was your walk?

TOAD: Brisk, very brisk. And your stroll?

FROG: Leisurely, very leisurely.

TOAD: Ah well, I'm off to do some chores.

FROG: Really? So am I.

TOAD: OK then, I'll see you soon.

FROG: Yes indeed. Good-bye, Toad.

TOAD: So long, Frog.

FROG *(same time as* TOAD*)*: *He'll never know*

Think of how happy he'll be

He'll never know

Almost as happy as me

TOAD *(same time as* FROG*)*: *Think of how happy*

How happy he'll be

Almost as happy

As happy as me

FROG AND TOAD: *He'll never ever ever know*

He'll never ever ever know

He'll never ever ever

FROG *and* TOAD *notice the mess of leaves in their respective yards.*

FROG AND TOAD: *Oh*

I'll rake my leaves tomorrow.

The scene shifts. FROG *is at home. He pours tea.* TOAD *enters.*

TOAD: Hello, Frog. I'm sorry if I am late.

FROG: You're not late.

TOAD: Am I early?

FROG: No, you're right on time. I was just pouring the tea.

TOAD: I never know whether I am late or early. My clock is broken.

FROG: I know, Toad.

TOAD: The weather is terrible.

FROG: It is a dark and stormy night.

TOAD: Yes, it is, Frog.

FROG: It is a very good night for something. Do you know what it is?

TOAD: A cup of tea?

FROG: Well, yes, that, but also for something else.

TOAD: A cookie?

FROG: Well, yes, that, but also for something else.

TOAD: I give up, Frog. What is a dark and stormy night good for?

FROG: Do you give up?

TOAD: I already gave up.

FROG: So you did. Would you like me to tell you?

TOAD: Yes, Frog, tell me.

FROG: All right, I'll tell you. It is a good night for a scary story.

TOAD: Yes, I suppose it is.

FROG: Would you like to hear one?

TOAD: I don't know, Frog.

FROG: Don't you like to be scared?

TOAD: I'm not so sure.

FROG: When I was a very small frog, I went on a picnic with my parents . . .

At center in masks stand YOUNG FROG *with* MOTHER *and* FATHER FROG.

Song: "Shivers"

YOUNG FROG:	*Mother Frog and Father Frog*
	It was a lovely picnic in the wood
FATHER FROG:	*Mother Frog*
MOTHER FROG:	*Yes, Father Frog*
FATHER FROG:	*I have some news*
	It isn't very good
MOTHER FROG:	*What is the news?*
YOUNG FROG:	*What is the news?*

MOTHER FROG AND YOUNG FROG: *Father Frog*

What is the news?

FATHER FROG:	*When we set out on our picnic*
	The sun was on the right

I could tell direction
By the angle of the light

But now it's gotten cloudy
We've traveled pretty far
And I hate to have to tell you
But I don't know where we are

MOTHER FROG: *You mean we're lost?*

FATHER FROG: *Yes, we are lost*

YOUNG FROG: *We are lost?*

FATHER FROG: *Yes, we are lost*

TOAD: *You were lost?*

FROG: *And young Frog*
Yes, we were lost.

TOAD, MOTHER FROG, FATHER FROG, AND YOUNG FROG: *My goodness*

TOAD: *You were*

MOTHER FROG, FATHER FROG, AND YOUNG FROG: *We are*

ALL: *Lost*

MOTHER FROG: *Oh boo hoo hoo hoo*
Hoo hoo hoo
Hoo hoo hoo
Hoo hoo hoo

YOUNG FROG: There, there, Mother. Why are you so upset?

MOTHER FROG: It's nothing, son. Mother's only tired. That's all.

FATHER FROG: Don't you think we should tell him, dear?

YOUNG FROG: Tell me what?

TOAD: Tell him what?

FATHER FROG: What lurks out there.

YOUNG FROG: What lurks out there?

TOAD: What lurks out there?

MOTHER FROG: This is bound to frighten you.

FROG: This is bound to frighten you.

TOAD AND YOUNG FROG: Tell me!

FROG AND FATHER FROG: Very well . . .

FATHER FROG: *There is a frog*

A large and terrible frog

He is terribly large

And largely terrible terrible

MOTHER FROG: *Terrible*

TOAD AND YOUNG FROG: *Terrible?*

FROG: *Terrible!*

FATHER FROG: *Large and terrible frog*

He's mean and awful

And he's awful mean

And his wrinkly skin

Is pasty green

He eats little bunnies

Dipped in dirt

And he likes frog children

For dessert

TOAD AND YOUNG FROG: Oh my.

FATHER FROG: *He is a frog*

A large and terrible frog

He is terribly large

And largely terrible terrible

MOTHER FROG: *Terrible*

TOAD AND YOUNG FROG: *Terrible?*

FROG: *Terrible!*

FATHER FROG: *Large and terrible frog*

Your Mother and I will go off in search of the pathway home.

You stay right here.

FROG: And so off my parents went in search of the pathway home.

TOAD: They left you all alone?

FROG: Yes, and soon it became dark.

TOAD: Did this really happen, Frog?

FROG: Maybe yes and maybe no. Should I stop telling you the story?

TOAD: No, no, no. Tell me. Tell me.

FROG: All right. Well as I said, it was getting dark, and there I was . . .

YOUNG FROG: *I'm a young little frog*

All alone in the night

My parents have left
Which doesn't seem right
I am very afraid
That is how I feel
I don't wish to end up
A meal

I think eating others is rude
And I bet that it hurts being chewed

I have such ambitious
Dreams and wishes
And none of my plans include
Not growing up
Because I wound up
Being food

FROG: And I waited and waited, and it grew darker and darker. And suddenly, I had the feeling I was not alone.

TOAD: Not alone?

FROG: Not alone. And then I looked up, and I saw two great eyes staring right at me!

TOAD AND YOUNG FROG: Ahhhhhh!

YOUNG FROG: Who are you?

LARGE AND TERRIBLE FROG: I am the Large and Terrible Frog.

TOAD AND YOUNG FROG: Ahhhhh!

YOUNG FROG: Are you going to eat me?

LARGE AND TERRIBLE FROG: Not just yet. I have eaten so many frog children already tonight that I have no appetite.

YOUNG FROG: Oh well. It was very nice to have met you, I'll be going now.

LARGE AND TERRIBLE FROG: Not so fast. You must do something for me.

YOUNG FROG: Oh, I'd be only too happy to. What is it?

LARGE AND TERRIBLE FROG: After dinner, I like to have a little exercise so I can work up an appetite for a late snack.

YOUNG FROG: Exercise?

LARGE AND TERRIBLE FROG: Yes, skipping rope. And you shall turn for me. Take hold of that end.

YOUNG FROG: Yes, your large and terribleness.

LARGE AND TERRIBLE FROG: *Skippy skippy skippy skippy*
Every night
Skipping helps to generate an appetite

Tadpole tadpole pollywog
Soon I will be snacking on a little frog
Skippy skippy skippy skippy
Every night
Skipping helps to generate an appetite

Some like muffins
Some like scones
I like the taste of little froggy bones
All right, my appetite has returned. Come to me, little Frog.

YOUNG FROG *stands motionless.*

TOAD: This is terrible.

FROG: Well, he is the large and terrible frog.

TOAD: *What did you do?*

YOUNG FROG: *What shall I do?*

TOAD: *What did you do?*

YOUNG FROG: *What shall I do?*

TOAD AND YOUNG FROG: *Whatever*

TOAD: *Did you?*

YOUNG FROG: *Shall I?*

TOAD AND YOUNG FROG: *Do?*

FROG: *He started coming toward me*
But my hand was on the rope
He was just enormous
But he also was a dope

I ran around in circles
Til I tied him to the tree

LARGE AND TERRIBLE FROG: *You little whippersnapper*
What have you done to me?

FROG: *And then I ran*
And ran and ran
And ran and ran
And ran and ran

MOTHER FROG AND FATHER FROG:
He ran and ran and ran and ran and ran
And ran and ran

YOUNG FROG: *I ran and ran and ran and then*
I found my parents in a glen

MOTHER FROG, FATHER FROG, AND YOUNG FROG:
So then we came upon a path
And we went home and took a bath
A long and hot and steamy

YOUNG FROG: *Absolutely dreamy*

MOTHER FROG, FATHER FROG, AND YOUNG FROG:
Finally out of trouble
Bubble

TOAD: Did this really happen, Frog?

FROG: Maybe yes and maybe no.

MOTHER FROG, FATHER FROG, AND YOUNG FROG: *Bath*

It snows. SNAIL *appears.*

Song: "The Letter" (reprise)

SNAIL: *I'm carrying a letter*
A most important letter
A letter that was written by Frog
But in the snowy frosting running is exhausting
So maybe I'll slow to a jog

I'm the snail with the mail
I'll deliver without fail
In the ice and snow and slush

And though it's getting dusky
I'm pretending I'm a husky
Mush mush mush mush mush mush mush

At the top of a hill, FROG *and* TOAD *are dressed for winter.*

FROG: Toad?

TOAD: Yes, Frog?

FROG: I'm just curious. Did you happen to get any mail today?

TOAD: No, I did not, Frog! I never get any mail, and it makes me unhappy. You know that. So why do you insist on bringing it up all the time?

FROG: I'm sorry, Toad.

TOAD: It's all right.

FROG: I wonder what time it is?

TOAD: I don't know that either, Frog. As I have repeatedly explained to you, my new clock is broken. I need to get a new clock.

FROG: Of course. That slipped my mind. Well, here we are at the top of the hill. Look at that view.

TOAD: The snow is lovely. But it's an awfully long way down.

FROG: It will be easy on my sled.

TOAD: Oh I don't know, Frog. I don't think you should go. It looks scary.

FROG: Don't be silly, Toad. It's not as if I'll be riding all alone.

TOAD: Oh, someone is going with you?

FROG: Yes, of course.

TOAD: Oh, well that makes all the difference.

FROG: Yes, it does.

TOAD: Who is going with you?

FROG: You are.

TOAD: Oh no, Frog.

FROG: Don't be nervous, Toad. I'll be behind you the whole time. It's pleasant sledding down the hill.

TOAD: It's more pleasant sitting in a warm house and eating soup.

FROG: We can do that once we reach the bottom. Come on. Take a risk.

TOAD: Oh very well, Frog. I'll go through with it.

FROG: That's fine. You'll see. It's pleasant sledding down the hill.

FROG and TOAD board the sled.

FROG: Here we go.

They begin down the hill on the sled.

Song: "Down the Hill"

FROG AND TOAD: *Down the hill*
                   We are sliding
                   Down the hill
                   Gently gliding
                   Down the hill

                   What a thrill
                   So exciting

It's a thrill
To be riding
Down the hill

Oh to see the scenery
Such a lovely sight
Don't you love the greenery
Frosted all in white

TOAD: *This is rather pleasant, Frog*

FROG: *I told you*

TOAD: *You were right*

FROG AND TOAD: *It's pleasant sledding down the hill*

FROG: *Now we go*
                            Where it's steeper
                            And the snow
                            Somewhat deeper
                            Down the hill

Toad (Mark Linn-Baker) and Frog (Jay Goede) sled down a hill. Photograph by Rob Levine.

TOAD: Is it safe, Frog?

FROG: Absolutely, Toad.

> *There's a bump*
> *Up ahead there*
> *Which we'll jump*
> *With our sled there*
> *Down the hill*

The sled goes over a bump and takes to the air. FROG *is thrown off the back and into a snowbank.*

TOAD:

> Ahhhhhhhh.
> *My that was inspiring*
> *Riding through the air*
> *Though I must admit to you*
> *It gave me quite a scare*
> *Why are you so quiet, Frog?*
> *Oh you're no longer there*
> *It's pleasant sledding down the . . . (pause)*
> *Frooooooog!*

TOAD *and the sled disappear from view. Three* MOLES *pop their heads out from the snowbank.* MOLE 2 *has a pair of binoculars.*

MOLE 1: Frog, what are you doing here?

FROG: Hello, Moles. I was thrown from the sled. And now Toad is going down the hill alone.

MOLE 1: He'll be fine as long as he doesn't take the path on the left.
(*to* MOLE 2) Which path did he take?

MOLE 2 (*looking through the binoculars*): The path on the left.

MOLES:

> *Down the hill*
> *Going faster*
> *Heading straight*
> *For disaster*
> *Down the hill*

MOLE 1:	*Watch the trees*
MOLE 2:	*Watch the boulders*
MOLES:	*Tuck your knees*
	To your shoulders
	Down the hill

TOAD *comes back into sight. He is terrified.*

TOAD:	Ahhhhhhhhhhh!
	I have never been brave
	I have never known how
	And chances are slim
	I'm gonna start now
	I'm a terrified toad
	On a runaway sled
	Soon I am going to be dead
	I'll be smashed on the side of a rock
	So I doubt I'll be needing that clock
FROG AND MOLES:	*Down the hill*
	Going faster
	Down the hill
	Going faster
	Down the hill
	Going faster
	Down the hill
	Going faster

TOAD *is catapulted into a snowbank downstage. He is momentarily out of view. He then pops his head through the top of the snowbank.* FROG *joins him.*

FROG: Toad, that was magnificent.

TOAD: I'm alive. Thank goodness. I'm alive!

FROG: Of course you are.

TOAD: I'm so happy.

FROG: Wonderful.

TOAD: And angry.

FROG: Why?

TOAD: Frog, you left me all alone.

FROG: I couldn't help it, Toad.

TOAD: Oh yes, you could have. You could have not suggested that we go sledding in the first place and exposing us to such a terrible risk.

FROG: Now, Toad.

TOAD: Don't now Toad me, Frog. I was in absolute peril.

FROG: I'm sorry, Toad. (TOAD *storms off.*) Where are you going?

TOAD: I'm going home to eat some soup. And I will never speak with you again.

FROG: But Toad . . .

TOAD *indicates that his mouth has been sealed.* SNAIL *enters.*

SNAIL: *I'm the snail with the mail*
           I'll deliver without fail . . .
           Toad!!!!

TOAD: Oh hello, Snail.

SNAIL: I have a letter for you.

TOAD: You have?

SNAIL: Yes.

SNAIL *hands the letter to* TOAD.

TOAD: Thank you, Snail.

SNAIL: You're welcome. Well, I gotta run.

TOAD *opens the letter and reads.*

TOAD: Dear Toad. Today when you told me that you were sad because you had never received a letter, it made me sad too. I suppose that is how it is with you and me. I am writing this letter, hoping that it will make you feel happy, knowing all along that unless you are happy I cannot be. Your friend, Frog. *(beat)* Frog?

FROG: Yes, Toad?

TOAD: I am speaking to you again.

FROG: I'm glad, Toad.

TOAD: At home, I have some soup.

FROG: That's nice.

TOAD: If you want, I will warm some up for you.

FROG: Why yes, Toad. That would be very pleasant.

FROG *exits with his sled.* TOAD *is left alone with the letter. After a beat, a snowball comes from the direction of* FROG'S *exit, hitting* TOAD. *A curtain falls, and the lights find* SNAIL *in front of it.*

Song: *"I'm Comin' Out of My Shell"*

SNAIL: *I was always timid*
I guess it was because
I may have been ashamed of who I am
Or what I was

I thought "I'm just a snail"
A lot of shell
A little goo

But all of that has changed
As now the following is true

I got something I do
Something I'm proud of
Because I do it pretty well
Bing bang boom
Give me some room
I'm coming out of my shell

Get out the word
Find me a witness
Blow on a trumpet, ring a bell
Holy smokes
Look at me, folks
I'm coming out of my shell

There were slugs who doubted me
I guess that made me nervous
I never even dared to dream
Of life in civil service
They said I wasn't fast enough
They said, hey, you're too gooey
But then I turned around and told 'em
Phooey
That's all hooey

I was nothing but goo
Under the surface
Then everything began to gel
Holy cow
Look at me now
I'm coming out of my
Yes, I deliver
I'm coming out of my
I'm going postal
I'm coming out of my shell

TOAD *is at* TOAD'S *house. A fire burns in the fireplace.* TOAD *is in the kitchen. He gathers a lantern, a rope, and a frying pan during the following:*

TOAD: It's Christmas Eve. The fire is burning. The hot chocolate is ready. But Frog is late. At least I think he is late. But he must be late. It has been dark for a very long time. Maybe something has happened to him. Maybe something bad. Maybe something terrible. Maybe he is lost in the dark, and he cannot find his way, and he is cold and shivering. Or maybe, he has fallen into a deep hole, and he cannot get out, and he is cold and shivering. Or maybe, he is being chased by a wolf, and he's running as fast as he can, and well, he wouldn't be cold and shivering, because when you run, it warms you up, but that is not the point. The point is that Frog may be in terrible danger. I must do something. I must help my friend. I must get a lamp and a rope and a frying pan.

TOAD *steps out into the night with a lamp, a rope, and a frying pan.*

TOAD: Frog! Frog! Don't worry, I'll save you! I am prepared for any situation.

Song: "Toad to the Rescue"

TOAD: If you are . . .
                 Lost in the dark
                 You are lost in the dark
                 And your fingers
                 Are starting to freeze

                 I have a light
                 That will cut through the night
                 So you won't bump your
                 Head on the trees

                 Or if you are . . .

                 Deep in a hole
                 You are stuck in a hole
                 And no one can hear
                 As you shout

I'll bring a rope
A thick piece of rope
And use it
To help pull you ooouuuuut

I am not afraid
Well I am but
I'll be brave

Frog Frog Frog Frog Frog
You are the one
I'm going to save

If there's a . . .
Wolf at your heels
Giant wolf at your heels
And you're running as fast as you can

I'll stop the wolf
I'll in fact bop the wolf
On the head with a big frying paaaaaan

I am not afraid
Well I am but
I'll be brave

Frog Frog Frog Frog Frog

FROG: Hello, Toad.

TOAD: *You are the one*
. . . Frog! You're here! You're not lost in the woods.

FROG: No.

TOAD: You're not stuck at the bottom of a hole?

FROG: No.

TOAD: You're not being chased by a wolf?

FROG: No.

TOAD *(now miffed)*: Well, where have you been?

FROG: I'm sorry to be late, Toad. I was wrapping your gift.

TOAD: Oh. For me?

FROG: Yes.

TOAD: I can open it?

FROG: Of course.

TOAD *tears into the gift.*

TOAD: It's a clock!

FROG: Yes, and it keeps very good time.

TOAD: I needed a clock.

FROG: I know, Toad.

TOAD: Your present isn't here yet.

FROG: That's all right, Toad.

TOAD: It was supposed to have been delivered this afternoon.

FROG: It's being delivered?

TOAD: Yes.

FROG: By whom?

TOAD: Snail. He should be here any minute.

FROG: Maybe we'd better sit down.

TOAD: I'll put the clock on the mantle. This is lovely wrapping paper, Frog.

FROG: Thank you, Toad. This is a very nice fire.

TOAD: It's warm.

FROG: This is a very peaceful Christmas Eve.

TOAD: It didn't start out that way.

FROG: I'm sorry I was late.

TOAD: I was very worried you know.

FROG: I know you were.

TOAD: I was very worried . . .

Song: "Merry Almost Christmas"

TOAD:	*Felt as though there'd be no Christmas*
	Even though it's Christmas Eve
	No it wouldn't feel like Christmas
	Not without you I believe
	Christmas wouldn't come without you
	Only winter's cold I fear
	But it really feels like Christmas
	Now that you are here
	Sure it's cold but we've
	Hot chocolate
	And a fire burning away
FROG:	*By the fire*
	See the clock lit
FROG AND TOAD:	*Now it's almost Christmas day*
	Merry almost Christmas
	Happy that you're here
	Merry almost Christmas
	Happy almost new year
	Christmas feels like Christmas
	Now that you are here
	Merry almost Christmas
	Happy almost New Year
FROG:	*I could not imagine Christmas*
	Couldn't do it if I tried
	No I can't imagine Christmas
	Not without you at my side
	I'll be with you ev'ry Christmas
	We both know that's understood
	Many many nights like this one
	If we're lucky knock on wood
TOAD:	*Sure it's cold but we've hot chocolate*
	And a fire burning away

FROG AND TOAD: *By the fire*
                                See the clock lit
                                Now it's almost
                                Christmas day

MOLES: *Merry almost Christmas*
                                Happy that you're here

ALL: *Merry almost Christmas*
                                Happy almost New Year

                                Christmas feels like Christmas
                                Now that we are here
                                Merry almost Christmas
                                Happy almost New Year

FROG: It's midnight.

TOAD: Merry Christmas, Frog.

FROG: Merry Christmas, Toad.

MOLES: *Happy almost New Year*

FROG *and* TOAD *are asleep in their respective beds. Three* BIRDS *enter.*

Song: "Finale"

THREE BIRDS: *We flew south for the winter*
                                South for the winter
                                Just like at the op'ning of the show
                                Tra la la la la
                                Tra la la la la la
                                And then of course the problem with the
                                Snow

                                But . . .
                                The winter now is over
                                The snow has all been snowed
                                Spring is here
                                Which starts a year
                                With Frog and Toad

MAN BIRD: Well, here we are again, folks. You know, through the years some things change, and that's good. And some things don't change, and that's good too.

LADY BIRDS: Chirp, chirpitty-chirp.

MAN BIRD: One thing that will never change: Frog and Toad will always be good friends.

FROG *hops up from his bed in full dress.*

FROG:
I'd like to sing a little ode
About my good friend Toad
Toad with whom I frequently take tea
He's not so good at sports
And of course he's got those warts
But Toad has been a lovely friend to me

Toad, I feel, is vastly underrated
And furthermore, I think, misunderstood
And in conclusion I will add
He is the finest friend
Of all the critters in the neighborhood

TOAD *pops up from his bed.*

TOAD:
I love a lively dialogue
With my good friend Frog
Chatting over cozy cups of tea
He knows just the thing to say
That will brighten up my day
Oh Frog has been a lovely friend to me

Frog is very kindly in his nature
Magnanimous whenever playing host
Of all the creatures in my sphere of influence
I'm fondest of the frog the most

TOAD: Hello, Frog.

FROG: Hello, Toad. Are you hibernating?

TOAD: Why yes, I am. And you?

FROG: Oh yes, most definitely. And I have had many, many dreams.

TOAD: Well, so have I.

FROG: Have they been pleasant dreams?

TOAD: Some have been pleasant, and some have been not so pleasant. But you have been in every one of them.

FROG: Funny, you have been in all of my dreams too.

TOAD: I had one not so pleasant dream, where we went swimming.

FROG: Really? So did I. And I had a dream that you made the most wonderful cookies.

TOAD: Really? So did I. And I dreamed that we went down a hill on a sled.

FROG: Really? So did I.

TOAD: This is uncanny.

FROG: Remarkable. Well, I'm getting ready to wake up, so you better get back to your own dream. I'll see you when you wake up.

TOAD: Yes, I'd better get back to hibernating. Spring is nearly here.

FROG: Oh, I think it's just around the corner. Birds?

THREE BIRDS: *The sun is out*
The sky is clear
We came back
Spring must be here
So let's begin another year

ALL: *A year with Frog and Toad*
A year with Frog and Toad!

Blackout.

THE END

ELISSA ADAMS is director of new play development at Children's
Theatre Company. She has overseen the commissioning and
development of more than twenty new plays at CTC since 1998,
including *Esperanza Rising, Brooklyn Bridge, A Very Old Man with
Enormous Wings, Reeling, Five Fingers of Funk, Korczak's Children,*
and *Anon(ymous)*. She received a McKnight Foundation Theater
Artist Fellowship, is a frequent guest dramaturge at the Sundance
Theatre Lab, and has served on numerous panels for Theatre
Communications Group.

LIZ DUFFY ADAMS is a New Dramatists alumna and has received a
Women of Achievement Award, Lillian Hellman Award, New York
Foundation for the Arts Fellowship, Will Glickman Award, and
MacDowell Colony residencies. Her play *Or* premiered off-Broadway
at Women's Project and has been produced numerous times, includ-
ing at the Magic Theatre and Seattle Repertory Theatre. Other plays
include *Dog Act; Wet, or Isabella the Pirate Queen Enters the Horse
Latitudes; The Listener; The Reckless Ruthless Brutal Charge of It or, The
Train Play;* and *One Big Lie*. Publications include *Poodle with Guitar
and Dark Glasses* in Applause's *Best American Short Plays 2000–2001;
Or* in Smith and Kraus's "Best Plays of 2010"; and several plays in

acting editions by Playscripts, Inc., and Dramatists Play Service. She was the 2012–13 Briggs-Copeland Visiting Lecturer in Playwriting at Harvard University.

LUDWIG BEMELMANS (1896–1963) was born in the Austrian Tirol and came to the United States in 1914. Although best known for his children's books, he also wrote fiction and nonfiction for adults on subjects he knew best: hotels, traveling, and Hollywood. He was a frequent contributor to magazines, including *The New Yorker, Town and Country,* and *Holiday.* He was also a painter, and his art was displayed in exhibitions around the world.

PETER BROSIUS has been artistic director of Children's Theatre Company since 1997. Under his leadership, CTC established Threshold, a new play laboratory that has allowed CTC to create world premiere productions with the leading playwrights in America. He directed the world premieres of *Bert and Ernie, Goodnight!; Iqbal; Iron Ring; Madeline and the Gypsies; Average Family; The Lost Boys of Sudan; Anon(ymous); Reeling; The Monkey King; Hansel and Gretel; The Snow Queen;* and *Mississippi Panorama,* all commissioned and workshopped in Threshold. He is the recipient of numerous awards, including Theatre Communications Group's Alan Schneider Directors' Award and honors from the Los Angeles Drama Critics Circle and Dramalogue.

LISA D'AMOUR is a playwright and interdisciplinary artist. She is half of the Obie Award–winning performance duo PearlDamour, whose work has been presented by HERE Arts Center, PS122, the Whitney Museum of Art, the Walker Art Center, and the FuseBox Festival. Her plays have been commissioned and produced by theatres across the country. *Detroit* was a finalist for the 2011 Pulitzer Prize in Drama and the 2011 Susan Smith Blackburn Prize. She is the recipient of the 2008 Alpert Award in the Arts in theatre, the 2011 Steinberg Playwright Award, and the 2013 Doris Duke Performing Artist Award.

MICHAEL KOERNER is a composer, music director, and musician who lives in Minneapolis. Since 1983, he has composed and has been the musical director for more than twenty productions at the Children's Theatre Company. During his twenty-five-year association with Theatre de la Jeune Lune in Minneapolis, he composed the music and musical directed twenty-five productions, including *Cyrano, Yang Zen Froggs, The Hunchback of Notre Dame, The Kitchen,* and *Circus.*

BARRY KORNHAUSER recently joined the staff of Millersville University to spearhead the school's new family arts collaborative. Previously he served as the playwright-in-residence and as the director of theatre for young audiences at the National Historic Landmark Fulton Theatre in Lancaster, Pennsylvania. His plays have been commissioned and produced by the Tony Award–winning theatres the Alliance, La Jolla Playhouse, and the Shakespeare Theatre, and have been invited to festivals such as One Theatre World, New York University's Provincetown Playhouse New Plays for Young Audiences, the International Quest Fest, San Diego Theatre of the World, the Bonderman, the Playground, and the Kennedy Center's New Visions/New Voices. He received the American Alliance for Theatre and Education (AATE) Charlotte Chorpenning Cup, honoring "a body of distinguished work by a nationally known writer of outstanding plays for children." Other accolades include the Twin Cities' Ivey Award for Playwriting (for *Reeling*, commissioned and produced by CTC), the Helen Hayes Outstanding Play Award *(Cyrano)*, the Bonderman Prize *(Worlds Apart)*, and two AATE Distinguished Play Awards *(This Is Not a Pipe Dream* and *Balloonacy)*.

ARNOLD LOBEL (1922–1987) wrote or illustrated more than seventy books for children. To his illustrating credit are a Caldecott Medal book, *Fables,* and two Caldecott Honor Books, his own *Frog and Toad Are Friends* and *Hildilid's Night* by Cheli Durán Ryan. As an author he received a Newbery Honor Book award for *Frog and Toad Together.* He collaborated with his wife, Anita, a distinguished children's book author and artist, on *How the Rooster Saved the Day,* chosen by *School Library Journal* as one of the Best Books of the Year in 1977. They collaborated on three more books, *A Treeful of Pigs,* a 1979 American Library Association Notable Book; *On Market Street,* a 1982 Caldecott Honor Book; and *The Rose in My Garden,* a 1984 Boston Globe/Horn Book Honor Book.

ELLEN MADDOW is a founding member of the New York–based Talking Band and has written text and music for many of its works, including *The Peripherals* (an indie rock musical), *Panic! Euphoria! Blackout, Flip Side* (published in *Plays and Playwrights 2010*), *Delicious Rivers, Painted Snake in a Painted Chair* (for which she received an Obie Award), and five pieces about the avant-garde housewife Betty Suffer. She wrote music for Talking Band's productions of *The Walk across America for Mother Earth* (by Taylor Mac), *Star Messengers,*

Radnevsky's Real Magic, Belize, and *The Parrot* (by Paul Zimet). She is the recipient of the Frederick Loewe Award in Musical Theatre, a McKnight Playwriting Fellowship, NEA/TCG Theatre Residency Program for Playwrights, Meet the Composer grants, ASCAP Special Awards, and a New York Theatre.com People of the Year Award. She was a member of the Open Theatre and is an alumnus of New Dramatists.

ROBERT REALE is a New York composer. His musicals include Broadway productions of *A Year with Frog and Toad* (Tony nomination) and off-Broadway productions of *Once Around the City* (Second Stage) and *Quark Victory* (Williamstown Theatre Festival). His music for plays includes Richard Dresser's *Rounding Third* (directed by John Rando), *Diva* (Williamstown Theatre Festival), and *Salvation's Moon*. Music for films includes *Ten-13, Passing Over, Wigstock, Dealers among Dealers,* and *The Victim,* and for television, *PrimeTime, 20/20, Inside Edition, Out There* (theme), *Invent This* (theme), *Mugshots, Crime Stories, The System, The Mailman and the Pirhana, Case Closed,* and *The Royals: Dynasty or Disaster?* As a composer and record producer he has worked with Julie Andrews, Mel Tormé, Sid Caesar, and Imogene Coca.

WILLIE REALE is a freelance writer. He received two Tony nominations for his book and lyrics to *A Year with Frog and Toad*. In 1981, he founded the 52nd Street Project, an organization that brings inner-city children together with professional theatre artists, and was its artistic director for eighteen years. The programs of the 52nd Street Project are documented through a series of publications, *The Kid Theater Kit*; for the kit he wrote "52 Pick Up," the Project's how-to manual, as well as plays and song lyrics, including two full-length musicals, all of which are available through Dramatists Play Service. He was awarded a MacArthur grant in recognition of his ingenuity in creating theatre and theatre education programs for young people.

SXIP SHIREY is a composer and performer in New York City. His music is surprising and made by deep, sexy beats played on industrial flutes, bullhorn harmonicas, regurgitated music box, triple extended pennywhistles, miniature handbell choir, obnoxiophone, glass bowls with red marbles, human beat box, and a clutch of curious objects. He has played exploding circus organ for the pyrotechnic clowns of the Daredevil Opera Company at the Sydney Opera House and the Kennedy Center, industrial flutes for acrobats on mechanical jumping boots at the New Victory Theater on Broadway, tamponophone with the Bindlestiff Family Cirkus at Bonnaroo Music and Arts

Festival, hillbilly music for gypsies in Transylvania, and gypsy music for hillbillies in West Virginia with the Luminescent Orchestrii.

JEANINE TESORI is one of the most prolific and honored female theatrical composers. In 2015 she won the Tony Award for Best Original Score for *Fun Home* (shared with Lisa Kron; they were the first female writing team to win that award). She has written four Tony-nominated scores for Broadway: *Twelfth Night* at Lincoln Center, *Thoroughly Modern Millie* (lyrics by Dick Scanlan), *Caroline, or Change* (lyrics by Tony Kushner), and *Shrek the Musical* (lyrics by David Lindsay-Abaire). Her first off-Broadway musical, *Violet,* written with Brian Crawley, received the New York Drama Critics Circle Award in 1997. She has been the recipient of many honors, including Drama Desk and Obie awards, and was cited by ASCAP as the first woman composer to have "two new musicals running concurrently on Broadway." She composed the music for the New York Shakespeare Festival's production of Brecht's *Mother Courage,* as translated by Tony Kushner, starring Meryl Streep and Kevin Kline. She has written songs for the films *Shrek the Third, Nights in Rodanthe, Winds of Change, Show Business, Wrestling with Angels, Every Day, Mulan II,* and *The Emperor's New Groove 2: Kronk's New Groove.*

CHILDREN'S THEATRE COMPANY (CTC), located in Minneapolis, Minnesota, is widely recognized as the leading theatre for young people and families in North America. Winner of the 2003 Tony® Award for regional theatre, CTC has received numerous honors, including awards from The Joyce Foundation and The Wallace Foundation. It participates in the National Endowment for the Arts New Play Development Program, the Shakespeare for a New Generation program, the EmcArts Innovation Lab funded by the Doris Duke Charitable Foundation, and the New Voices/New Visions 2010 series presented by the John F. Kennedy Center for the Performing Arts. CTC serves more than 250,000 people annually through performances, new play development, theatre arts training, and community and education programs. For more information about Children's Theatre Company, visit www.childrenstheatre.org.